MURDER ON THE OCEANIC

By Edward Marston

THE RAILWAY DETECTIVE SERIES
The Railway Detective • The Excursion Train
The Railway Viaduct • The Iron Horse
Murder on the Brighton Express • The Silver Locomotive Mystery
Railway to the Grave • Blood on the Line
The Stationmaster's Farewell • Peril on the Royal Train
A Ticket to Oblivion • Timetable of Death
Signal for Vengeance • The Circus Train Conspiracy
A Christmas Railway Mystery • Points of Danger
Fear on the Phantom Special • Slaughter in the Sapperton Tunnel
Tragedy on the Branch Line
Inspector Colbeck's Casebook

THE HOME FRONT DETECTIVE SERIES
A Bespoke Murder • Instrument of Slaughter
Five Dead Canaries • Deeds of Darkness
Dance of Death • The Enemy Within
Under Attack • The Unseen Hand • Orders to Kill

THE BOW STREET RIVALS SERIES
Shadow of the Hangman • Steps to the Gallows
Date with the Executioner • Fugitive from the Grave
Rage of the Assassin

THE CAPTAIN RAWSON SERIES
Soldier of Fortune • Drums of War • Fire and Sword
Under Siege • A Very Murdering Battle

THE DOMESDAY SERIES

The Wolves of Savernake • The Ravens of Blackwater
The Dragons of Archenfield • The Lions of the North
The Serpents of Harbledown • The Stallions of Woodstock
The Hawks of Delamere • The Wildcats of Exeter
The Foxes of Warwick • The Owls of Gloucester
The Elephants of Norwich

THE RESTORATION SERIES

The King's Evil • The Amorous Nightingale • The Repentant Rake
The Frost Fair • The Parliament House • The Painted Lady

THE BRACEWELL MYSTERIES

The Queen's Head • The Merry Devils
The Trip to Jerusalem • The Nine Giants
The Mad Courtesan • The Silent Woman
The Roaring Boy • The Laughing Hangman
The Fair Maid of Bohemia • The Wanton Angel
The Devil's Apprentice • The Bawdy Basket
The Vagabond Clown • The Counterfeit Crank
The Malevolent Comedy • The Princess of Denmark

THE OCEAN LINER MYSTERIES

Murder on the Lusitania • Murder on the Mauretania
Murder on the Minnesota • Murder on the Caronia
Murder on the Marmora • Murder on the Salsette
Murder on the Oceanic • Murder on the Celtic

PRAISE FOR EDWARD MARSTON

'A master storyteller'
Daily Mail

'Packed with characters Dickens would have been
proud of. Wonderful [and] well-written'
Time Out

'Once again Marston has created a credible
atmosphere within an intriguing story'
Sunday Telegraph

'Filled with period detail, the pace is steady and
the plot is thick with suspects, solutions and clues.
Marston has a real knack for blending detail,
character and story with great skill'
Historical Novels Review

'The past is brought to life with brilliant
colours, combined with a perfect
whodunnit. Who needs more?'
The Guardian

a&b

MURDER ON THE OCEANIC

EDWARD MARSTON

Allison & Busby Limited
11 Wardour Mews
London W1F 8AN
allisonandbusby.com

First published in 2006 under the name Conrad Allen.
This paperback edition published by Allison & Busby in 2022.

A CIP catalogue record for this book is available from
the British Library.

10 9 8 7 6 5 4 3 2 1

ISBN 978-0-7490-2835-0

Typeset in 10.5/15.5 pt Adobe Garamond Pro by
Typo•glyphix, Burton-on-Trent, DE14 3HE

FSC
www.fsc.org
MIX
Paper from
responsible sources
FSC® C171272

Printed and bound by
CPI Group (UK) Ltd, Croydon, CR0 4YY

ONE

March 1910

'What sort of weather have we got today?'

'It's raining.'

'How do you know?' she asked. 'You haven't looked yet.'

'It always rains in Liverpool.'

'This is Southampton.'

'It makes no difference,' he joked, crossing to the window. 'Choose any port in England and you can guarantee rain on the day you sail.' He pulled back the curtains and early morning sunlight flooded in. 'There you are. What did I tell you?' Genevieve sat up in bed. 'It's a beautiful day, George.'

'Then we must still be in New York.'

'Stop teasing!'

'Well, it's completely out of character for Liverpool.'

'We're in Southampton.'

George Porter Dillman knew exactly where they were but he could not resist some gentle taunting about the vagaries of British weather. It was a bone of contention between him and his wife. Having been born in England, Genevieve loved its climate. Dillman, by contrast, was an American who usually managed to be on the other side of the Atlantic during unsettled weather. His first visit to England had coincided with days of high winds and torrential rain. It was an indelible memory. They were staying at the South Western Hotel, the best in the city and the place where wealthy and important passengers tended to spend the night before departure. George and Genevieve were far from wealthy but, since they were working as detectives aboard the *Oceanic*, they did feel that they had some importance. Posing as passengers, their job was to solve any crimes that occurred aboard and, in their experience, there was no such thing as a trouble-free voyage. Whichever shipping line they worked for, they invariably encountered major problems.

'I daresay that it will be no different with the White Star Line,' he said, slipping on his dressing gown. 'We'll have the usual share of villains aboard.'

'How many passengers?'

'Around seventeen hundred.'

'We could never police them all.'

'Our job is to work largely in first class,' he reminded her. 'That's where the richest pickings are and where we're likely to have the biggest headaches.'

'I feel sorry for the passengers in steerage.'

'So do I. Conditions are far from ideal.'

'I wasn't thinking about their accommodation on board,' she said. 'They're such easy targets before we set sail. Because they're strangers in the city, they're pounced on by all sorts of cheats, liars, and confidence tricksters.'

'Yes,' he agreed, 'the worst are the ones who claim to be official money changers and tell people that they must convert their pound sterling into dollars before they go aboard. They either give their customers an appallingly low rate of exchange or somehow inveigle them into taking a voucher that can be redeemed on the ship.'

'By the time they discover the voucher is worthless, it's too late.'

He nodded. 'There are so many sharks around the docks.'

'We can only catch the ones who sail with us.'

'More should be done to protect emigrants before they leave,' he said, seriously. 'They have little enough to lose. Most of them are only quitting their native country because they're poor and unemployed. And the dreadful thing is,' he added, 'that, after sailing three thousand miles, some of them will be turned back at Ellis Island.'

'I thought that America encouraged immigration.'

'Only if it can pick and choose who it lets in.'

Genevieve smiled. 'Do you think that *I'd* be let in?'

'You're married to me, so you'll be especially welcome.'

'Even though you're only an occasional husband?'

'What do you mean?' he asked, bridling slightly.

'Well, as soon as we step aboard the *Oceanic*, we split up. I go back to being Genevieve Masefield, spinster of this parish, and you are tall, handsome, debonair, unattached George Porter Dillman.'

'It works better that way.'

'I wonder.'

'Genevieve, we must put our duties first.'

'I'd just like to cross the Atlantic one day as your wife.'

'You will, darling.'

He gave her a reassuring kiss. They had met on the maiden voyage of the *Lusitania* and, because Genevieve had been so instrumental in helping Dillman to solve a murder, he had persuaded her to join him as a detective in the pay of the Cunard Line. They proved to be a very effective team and their work drew them ever closer together. It was while they were working for the P&O line that their romance really blossomed and Dillman proposed to her while they were sailing at night on the *Marmora* down the Suez Canal. The ship's captain had performed the marriage ceremony on the following day.

'I'm married on land and widowed at sea,' she complained.

'I love you wherever we are.'

'Really?' She raised a sceptical eyebrow. 'I think that you only disown me on board so that you can flirt with the ladies.'

'There's not much time for flirtation,' he said with a dry laugh. 'Besides, what about you and your admirers? The moment you take off your wedding ring, they come buzzing like wasps around a pot of jam. And that's all to the good,' he went on. 'We each build up a wide circle of acquaintances, far more than if we operated as a couple.'

'As long as you don't forget that I am really Mrs Dillman.'

'Would I ever?'

He smiled fondly then looked at his watch on the bedside table.

'Breakfast should be here before too long,' he noted. 'Will you have a bath before it comes?'

'No, thank you, George.' She stifled a yawn. 'I haven't even woken up properly yet.' She stretched her arms. 'This does make a change from Liverpool. Why did the White Star Line move away from there?'

'For sound commercial reasons,' he explained. 'Southampton

has obvious advantages as a transatlantic terminal port. It's deeper and its double high tides save long and costly delays for ships outside the harbor. Also, of course, it's nearer to London than Liverpool and, more to the point, closer to France. That means we can call in at Cherbourg and pick up European emigrants and American millionaires who've been sampling the delights of Paris.'

'Americans are always so disgustingly rich,' she protested. 'An optical illusion, Genevieve. We have plenty of poor people, believe me. You only get to see the prosperous ones in first class.'

'The more money they have, the more arrogant they get.' 'That applies to people from any nation.'

'Americans are the worst.'

'I dispute that.'

'They act as if they own half the world.'

'In some cases, they do. It's such a massive country with lots of opportunity for people to make their fortunes if they're prepared to work hard enough. Well,' he observed, 'there's no better example of that than one of the passengers we'll be taking back to New York – Mr Morgan.'

'I've never heard of him.'

'Everyone has heard of J. P. Morgan.'

'Ah,' said Genevieve, 'now that name does sound familiar.'

'It ought to. He's the most powerful banker on the planet. John Pierpont Morgan is a financier, steel magnate, and railway baron. He also created a huge shipping syndicate to dominate Atlantic trade. It includes the White Star Line. Be very nice to Mr Morgan when he comes aboard,' he warned. 'Indirectly, he employs us.'

'What kind of a man is he, George?'

'Oh, he's just like me.'

'In what way?'

Dillman grinned. 'He's unique.'

When it was built in 1899, the *Oceanic* was the largest vessel in the world though this claim to fame was obliterated two years later by a German ship. The arrival of Cunard's twin giants in 1907 – the *Lusitania* and *Mauretania* – removed any pretensions that the *Oceanic* might have to superior size or, for that matter, to outstanding speed. It remained one of White Star's flagships, offering extreme luxury and a placid ride to those who could afford to travel first or second class. The one thousand passengers in steerage endured a more spartan crossing.

Manny Ellway was not allowed to savour any of the luxuries either. As a bedroom steward in first class, he was aware of all the extravagance that had been showered on the wealthier people aboard but he was in no position to enjoy it. While his charges would be occupying splendid staterooms, Ellway would be sharing a small cabin with three other stewards. One of them was an old friend of his, Sidney Browne.

'Hello, Sid. Good to see you again.'

'What're you doin' 'ere, Manny?' asked Browne. 'I thought you was sailin' on the *Adriatic*.'

'So did I until Tuesday. I got switched to the *Oceanic* at the last moment.' Ellway beamed. 'My luck is in at last.'

'I wouldn't call it luck. Not on this ship.'

'What do you mean?'

'It's jinxed.'

'Rubbish!'

'It is, Manny. Two years after it was built, it ran down the British coaster *Kincora*, in fog. The coaster sank immediately. Seven dead.'

'Thanks for trying to cheer me up, Sid.'

'I'm only reminding you of the truth,' said Browne, lugubriously. 'The Oceanic's 'ad one or two other scrapes as well. And in 1905, there was a mutiny aboard. Thirty-three stokers were later convicted.'

'I know all that.'

'This ship is cursed.'

Ellway chuckled. 'You always were a miserable devil.'

They were in the little cabin that had been assigned to them and two other stewards. Browne had chosen a top bunk but Ellway opted for a lower one. He was unpacking his case and putting his clothes into a wooden locker. A big, red-faced man in his forties, Sidney Browne was an eternal pessimist, the sort of person who embarked on every voyage fearing the worst, and who felt robbed when it arrived at its destination without incident. Manny Ellway, on the other hand, was a genial character of thirty, a thin, sharp featured man with a neat moustache beneath a hooked nose, and short black hair that was bisected by a centre parting. Nothing ever seemed to depress him. After fifteen years, Ellway had lost none of his enthusiasm for life at sea.

Browne, however, was filled with remorse and resentment.

'I 'ate this job,' he confided. 'I 'ate the work, 'ate the passengers, and 'ate the bloomin' sea. I should've been a boot maker like my father.'

'Then why aren't you, Sid?'

'I lost my way as a young lad.'

'You could always take up the trade now.'

'At my age?' said Browne with a hollow laugh. 'No bleedin' 'ope of that, Manny. Instead of makin' boots, I 'ave to carry on lickin' 'em.'

'Working for White Star gives us lots of privileges.'

'I never noticed any.'

'For a start, we get to see something of the big wide world.'

'Yes – through the port'ole of a tiny cabin like this.'

'We'll have time ashore in New York.'

'Terrible place. Full of drunks. Can't stand it.'

'Yet you always head for the nearest pub when we land.'

'Well, I've got to do somethin' to occupy my time. That's the other thing I loathes about this game, Manny. Too much 'angin' about.'

'There's no pleasing you, is there?' said Ellway with another chuckle. 'You've got a good job with a decent wage and you get to meet lots of interesting people. Think of all the men back in Southampton who're still out of work. They'd give their eyeteeth to be where you are.'

'More fool them!'

'Count your blessings, Sidney.'

'I would, if I 'ad any.'

'You're sharing a cabin with me. Isn't that a blessing?'

'No.'

'Why not?'

'You snore.' Ellway cackled. 'Yes, and that's the other thing I don't like. You never stop laughin'.' He moved away. 'I'm off.'

'Bon voyage, Sid!'

'Same to you,' came the sour rejoinder.

Browne went out and Ellway was left to put a dozen collars into his locker. He liked Sidney Browne. In spite of his melancholy, the other steward was a good friend, loyal and generous towards a chosen few, if openly hostile to others. Browne was also very conscientious and the passengers never saw a hint of his more sombre side. Ellway had at least one good friend in the four-berth cabin. Not that it mattered who teamed up with him on this occasion. It was a voyage that was set completely apart from the many others he had undertaken. His colleagues were simply crossing the Atlantic as a job of work. For Manny Ellway, it was far more than that. As he stowed away the last of his clothing, he gave a secret smile.

Fate had been kind to him. He would seize his opportunity.

Noise and hats. It was always the same. Whenever a ship set sail, Genevieve Masefield was struck by the combination of noise and hats. The tumult was deafening. Every passenger aboard seemed to be at the rail, waving to the crowd of friends and well-wishers below, and shouting their farewells over the sound of the *Oceanic*'s siren and the whirr of its huge twin propellers as they churned up the water. Dockyard clamour added to the cacophony. Iron-shod wagons rattled over cobbles. Electric cranes gave off their distinctive whine. Steam tugs and lighters contributed their shrill wails. Thunderous boat trains arrived and left. Beyond the docks, a city of well over a hundred thousand souls generated its own pandemonium. And above it all was the ceaseless cry of the gulls as they wheeled and dived around the vessel.

Though she had heard it many times before, Genevieve was always taken aback by the sheer volume of noise. Then there were the hats. As she stood at the rail on the promenade deck, she looked down at a rippling sea of them. For the most part, the men wore cloth caps, homburgs, boaters, and bowlers, though top hats were on display as well. It was left to the women at the quayside to explore the full range of headgear. There were hats with wide brims and low crowns, straw hats with flowers or bows, toques, bonnets, snoods, and enormous creations festooned with ostrich plumes or coloured ribbons. Among the poorer sort, headscarves were worn. The *Oceanic* pulled slowly away from the landing stage. Genevieve waved until the cheering faded and the array of hats gradually began to diminish in size.

The young woman standing beside her turned an inquiring face.

'Have you been to New York before, Miss Masefield?'

'Yes,' replied Genevieve. 'As a matter of fact, I have.'

'Is it really as wonderful as they say?'

'It's a very lively city, I can tell you that much.'

'I shall want you to tell me much more than that,' said the other eagerly. 'From the moment we met, I felt certain that we'd be friends.'

Genevieve had fallen into conversation with Blanche Charlbury in the customs shed. Travelling in first class, Blanche was a handsome woman in her twenties with an engaging smile and an exquisite taste in clothes. A picture of elegance herself, Genevieve had to admit that she was outshone on this occasion by the trim Blanche Charlbury. The latter was wearing a smart green, closefitting two-piece suit of a kind that was featured in advertisements in only the most expensive periodicals. Her hat was trimmed with osprey.

'We speak the same language,' said Blanche.

'Do we?'

'Oh yes. You're one of us. I could tell.'

'Thank you.'

Genevieve was grateful to have been accepted at face value and to have befriended someone so quickly. Blanche was going to New York to visit her brother, who had taken up a post in a bank there. She was filled with an almost girlish excitement.

'Dickon assures me that it's the most amazing city in the world.'

'Dickon?'

'My brother. Is it true?'

'In some ways, I suppose that it is.'

'What sorts of ways? No,' said Blanche, dismissing her own question with a wave of her gloved hand, 'tell me everything later when we can sit down in comfort. Oh, we're going to have such a wonderful time, talking to each other! I know it. And are you really travelling alone?'

'Yes, Miss Charlbury.'

'Do call me Blanche – *please*. Formalities always irritate me.'

'Then you must call me Genevieve.'

'Brave Genevieve.'

'There's nothing very brave about crossing the Atlantic.'

'There is if you go unaccompanied. I like to think of myself as having plenty of confidence but I wouldn't have considered this trip if Mark hadn't volunteered to come with me.'

'Mark?'

'My fiancé.'

'Oh,' said Genevieve with mild surprise. 'I didn't see him earlier.'

'Mark is joining the ship at Cherbourg. He's been in Paris.'

'That must have been nice for him.'

'Not really,' said Blanche. 'He was working there. Mark is in the diplomatic service.' She suppressed a giggle. 'Which makes it all the more astonishing that he chose me – for I'm the most undiplomatic creature in the universe.'

'I'm sure that's not true.'

'Mark calls it an attraction of opposites.'

'He's very fortunate to have someone like you, Blanche, and I'll make a point of telling him that.'

'Thank you. A man needs to be reminded of such things regularly.'

'When are you going to get married?'

'This summer.'

'How lovely!'

'I can't wait, Genevieve. It's been such a long engagement.'

'Why was that?'

'Mark kept getting sent here, there, and everywhere so we had to delay things. But he assures me that he won't postpone it again and I intend to hold him to that.'

'How did you meet him in the first place?'

'Dickon was up at Oxford with him. They were in the same dining club. I was introduced to Mark during Eights Week and that was how it all started. We've known each other for seven years now.'

'Long enough to get well acquainted.'

'Yes,' said Blanche, happily. 'I know all his virtues and Mark has discovered all my vices. But they don't seem to have frightened him off. In fact, he says he loves me for my fallibility.'

'He might have phrased that in a more romantic way.'

'He's a diplomat, Genevieve. They don't believe in romance.'

'But you do, surely?'

'Having a doting husband is all the romance that I need. I long for the moment when he slips on the ring and I become Mrs Bossingham.'

'Is that his name – Mark Bossingham?'

'Mark Lindsay Reynolds Bossingham.'

'I look forward to meeting him.'

Genevieve was about to add a comment when she became aware that she was being watched. People had started to drift off to their cabins and spaces appeared on deck. Ten yards away, leaning nonchalantly against a bulkhead, was a tall, slim, angular figure. When Genevieve turned to look at him, she saw a well-dressed man in his thirties with striking good looks and a faint air of decadence. He gave her a dazzling smile and lifted his top hat to her before sauntering off.

Genevieve was annoyed. 'That man was staring at us.'

'No,' said Blanche with a sigh, 'he was staring at *you*. Johnny knows full well that I'm spoken for and, in any case, you're much more beautiful than I. Johnny picked you out at once but that's typical of him. He's a ladies' man in every sense.'

'You know him?'

'Very well. Everyone in my set knows the Honourable Jonathan Killick – though there's nothing particularly honourable about Johnny, I'm afraid. He's a complete rake but a very charming one at that. Watch out.'

'Why?'

'You've obviously caught his eye and that means only one thing.'

'Does it?'

'Yes, Genevieve. Like it or not, you're going to see a lot more of Johnny during this voyage so you may well need me as a bodyguard.'

'I can take care of myself, thank you,' said Genevieve politely.

'Lots of women believe that until they meet Johnny Killick. I was one of them but he almost got through my defences. He can be so amusing when he chooses to be. You'll soon find that out.'

'I'll just have to keep out of his way.'

'That's easier said than done. He's like a shadow. Once he's chosen his target, he'll follow you wherever you go.'

Genevieve was alarmed. She could see trouble ahead.

TWO

'Well,' he asked, sitting back in his chair, 'what do you think of her?'

'She's a fine ship,' replied Dillman. 'No question of that.' 'The *Oceanic* was the pride of the fleet in her day.'

'Her day is not over yet, by a long chalk.'

'I'm glad that you approve.'

'I do, Lester. I've been on bigger, faster, and sleeker vessels but none that felt so wonderfully stable. She glides over the waves.'

'Reserve your judgement until we reach the North Atlantic,' advised Hembrow, 'then you'll see her at her best.'

While the captain was in total charge of the ship, the person to whom George Dillman and Genevieve Masefield were directly answerable was the purser. They could not have found a more helpful and affable colleague than Lester Hembrow, a solid man of middle height with the unmistakable look of a seafarer. The son of a Canadian fisherman, Hembrow had learnt to sail a boat from an early age but he had higher ambitions than simply taking over from his father. He traded life as a deep-sea fisherman for the more secure and structured existence offered by the major shipping companies. Like Dillman, he had started with the Cunard Line but, while still in his thirties, had earned his appointment as a purser with the White Star Line. Hembrow was inordinately proud of the *Oceanic*.

'I just love her,' he admitted. 'She's a beauty!'

'Genevieve and I were certainly impressed when we had our first tour of her yesterday. Harland & Wolff did their usual excellent job. She's well built and full of character.'

'Just like my wife.'

'I'll have to take your word for that, Lester.'

'See for yourself,' said Hembow, cheerfully indicating a photograph on the wall. 'Kitty is right there.'

They were in the purser's office, a room to which an endless stream of passengers would come and go throughout the voyage. Hembrow sat behind a desk that had been cleared for action. Occupying a chair opposite him, Dillman looked up at the photograph. It was a picture of Hembrow's wife and baby son. Kitty Hembrow looked blissfully happy as she beamed at the camera.

'Are you married, George?' asked the purser.

'No, I prefer to stay single.'

'A roving bachelor, then. Keeping your options open.'

'Not exactly,' said Dillman, careful to conceal his true relationship with Genevieve. 'I just think it would be unfair for someone in my situation to get married when I'd spend so much time apart from my wife.'

'That was the attraction for Kitty. She has all the benefits of being Mrs Hembrow without having me under her feet seven days a week. Besides, absence really does make the heart grow fonder. I always have the warmest of welcomes when we dock in New York. Still,' said Hembrow, opening a drawer to extract some sheets of paper, 'you didn't come to hear me talking about my family. This is what you want – the list of passengers.'

'Thank you.' Dillman took the papers from him. 'Is it complete?'

'No, we'll be taking more people on board in Cherbourg.'

'Including the illustrious J.P Morgan, I hear.'

'He's been on one of his buying expeditions to Paris.'

'I'm surprised he doesn't just buy the whole city and have done with it,' said Dillman with a wry smile. 'He can afford it.' He glanced at the list. 'We'll take a close look at this.'

'There'll be further names to add when we reach Queenstown. Most, of course, will be Irish emigrants, hoping to start a new life in America. Steerage will be filled with O'Rourkes, O'Rileys, and O'Rooneys.'

'They'll liven things up down there.'

'That's my worry.'

There was a sharp knock on the door and it opened two inches. 'Fifteen minutes, sir!' said a man's voice.

'Thank you.' As the door closed again, Lester Hembrow got to his feet. 'We've made good time. Cherbourg already.'

'Do we know how many passengers will board here?'

'Over two hundred and fifty.'

'A sizeable number. By the law of averages, there's bound to be at least one villain among them.'

Hembrow grinned. 'I hope that you're not referring to J.P Morgan.'

'He's been called a lot worse than that in his time.'

'Yes – and I can understand why.'

'You've met him?' asked Dillman.

'Face-to-face. He sailed to Europe on the *Oceanic* and he wasn't entirely happy about his stateroom. I was sent in to placate him.'

'And did you?'

'Not really,' said Hembrow with a shrug. 'When he turned those blazing eyes on me, I felt like a rabbit caught in a snare. Don't you dare upset him, George, or you'll get that famous look of his as well.'

'I've heard about that from my father.'

'Have you?'

'He once had some dealings with Mr Morgan and they did not end altogether happily. My father was given that angry stare,' recalled Dillman. 'He said it was quite terrifying – like looking at the lights of an express train coming towards you.'

'While you're tied to the railway line.'

'Yes, he does tend to ride straight over people.'

'I still have the wheel marks on my chest.'

'Mr Morgan is an interesting man.'

'Very interesting.'

'I hope that I get to meet him.'

'You may live to regret saying that,' warned Hembrow.

Cherbourg was a busy port at the tip of the Normandy peninsula and it had profited from the White Star Line's decision to operate from Southampton. It was not simply a point of departure for European emigrants, it attracted people from the Middle East as well. Among the passengers who huddled in the tenders that brought them out to the *Oceanic* were Egyptians, Syrians, and

Libyans. The sea was fairly calm but it still needed ten members of the crew to stop the gangplank from swaying too much as people clambered aboard. It was early evening, dry but crisp, and the new passengers were wrapped up warmly against the stiff breeze. Up on the promenade deck, in addition to her long winter coat, Genevieve Masefield wore scarf, gloves, and hat. Also in a long coat and fur hat, Blanche Charlbury was at her elbow.

Genevieve was hoping for a first glimpse of J. P. Morgan but her companion had eyes for only one person. Blanche eventually saw him in one of the tenders and she waved energetically. 'There he is!' she cried, pointing a finger. 'There's Mark. There's my fiancé. Wave to him, Genevieve.'

'He doesn't know me from Adam,' said Genevieve.

'Mark! We're up here, Mark! Can you see us?'

But her voice was drowned out by the general hubbub. Unable to pick out Mark Bossingham in a crowded tender, Genevieve was rewarded with a sighting of the ship's most famous – and infamous – passenger. She knew that it must be J. P. Morgan because he was the first person to alight from his craft and the crew treated him with great deference. He was a big man in his early seventies, wearing a frock coat and a top hat. From that angle, Genevieve could see nothing of his face but she could feel that he exuded a sense of authority. J. P. Morgan was a presence.

'Come on, Genevieve,' said Blanche, grabbing her by the hand. 'We must go and find him. I'm dying for Mark to meet you.'

'Perhaps this is not the ideal time.'

'Of course it is.'

'No,' decided Genevieve, gently detaching her hand. 'You go and welcome him on your own. It's only right and proper. I'd feel in the way.'

'But he'll want to be introduced to you.'

'And so he will be, Blanche. But not now – later on, perhaps.'

'I want to show you off.'

'You'll have ample opportunity to do that. Your fiancé will not want me there. This is a reunion, after all.'

'So?'

'There's only room for two people – you and Mark.'

'Oh, there won't be any hugs and kisses, if that's what you're afraid of,' said Blanche blithely. 'Mark is rather shy. He hates any public show of affection.'

'I still think he'd rather see you on your own.'

'Very well.'

'In any case,' said Genevieve, 'I've got to decide what to wear for dinner. I don't know about you but crossing the Channel has given me a real appetite.' She patted her friend's arm. 'I'll see you later.'

'Both of us.'

'Yes – both of you.'

Blanche headed for the nearest staircase and Genevieve was able to make her way back to her cabin. Though she was fond of her new friend, she was not quite sure what to make of her. Blanche Charlbury looked and sounded much younger than she was but her adolescent exuberance might simply be a form of defense. Genevieve suspected that she was more intelligent than she appeared to be. One thing was clear. Her parents must have trusted her to let her travel without a chaperone. In some families, the presence of a fiancé on a voyage might be seen as a danger rather than a source of reassurance. Genevieve surmised that Mark Bossingham was a pillar of respectability, immune to temptation, there as Blanche's protector rather than her future husband and lover.

She remembered her own first voyage. Travelling alone, with every intention of settling in America, Genevieve had been the target for all sorts of unwelcome advances. It was only because she met George Dillman during the crossing that her life was given any direction and she was deeply grateful for that. The irony was that, having at last found the love and protection of a husband, she had to surrender it whenever they worked together on board. To all intents and purposes, she was single and therefore – in the eyes of certain men – available. One such unwanted admirer had already appeared. There would be others.

When she reached her cabin, Genevieve was surprised to see the door slightly ajar. She opened it to find that her stewardess was inside, arranging some flowers in a vase.

'Oh,' said the woman, taking a step backward, 'I'm sorry to disturb you, ma'am. I should have done this earlier.'

'Thank you. They brighten up the cabin nicely.'

'I'll get out of your way, ma'am.'

'No, wait,' said Genevieve, holding up a hand. 'I always like to see who's looking after me. What's your name?'

'Edith, ma'am.'

'You don't need to call me that. Edith, is it?'

'Edith Hurst.'

'And where are you from?'

'Southampton.'

'A seafaring family?'

'No, ma'am – I mean, no, Miss Masefield. My father runs the Belvedere Arms. I was born and brought up there. A lot of our customers are sailors. I used to love listening to their stories.'

'So you ran away to sea?'

Edith nodded and gave a nervous laugh. She was a plump

young woman in her early twenties with a plain, round face that was redeemed by dimpled cheeks and a sweet smile. Her uniform was immaculate, her auburn hair well groomed, her manner polite without being in any way obsequious. Genevieve warmed to her at once.

'You'll soon get used to my routine,' she said.

'I'll do my best.'

'Make the bed while I'm having breakfast and turn down the coverlet during dinner.' She looked around. 'You obviously know how to keep a cabin neat and tidy.'

'Thank you.'

'I'm sure that we'll get on very well.'

'If there's anything you need, just give me a call.'

'I shall, Edith.' Genevieve appraised her. The stewardess had a willingness to be of service and a visible desire for approval. 'Do you like doing this job?'

'Oh, I do. I love every moment of it.'

'Even though you spend the whole voyage working?'

'I'm used to that.'

'How long have you been on the *Oceanic*?'

'Six months.'

'Quite an old hand, then. You know the ropes. Am I right in thinking that dinner on the first night is relatively informal?'

'That depends, Miss Masefield.'

'On what?'

'Whether you're English or American.'

'I don't follow.'

'Well,' said Edith, 'some of the English passengers treat dinner as a formal affair on every occasion.'

'You mean that they enjoy dressing up.'

'That's one reason, I suppose.'

'You don't need to tell me what the others are, Edith. I know only too well. The English do tend to be bound by convention. There are certain men who dress up just to put the cat out.'

'Are there?' said the stewardess, eyes widening until she realised that it was a joke. She laughed. 'Oh, Miss Masefield!'

'I need to change now.'

'Of course.'

'Thank you for the flowers.'

'I'll water them every day.'

'Oh, I think I'd enjoy doing that for myself.'

Edith knew it was her cue to leave. 'Goodbye,' she said. Then she tripped out of the cabin and closed the door behind her.

George Dillman subjected his steward to much more of an interrogation but he did so in such a casual way that Manny Ellway did not even know that he was being pumped for information. 'You've dealt with American passengers before, I take it?'

'Lots of them, Mr Dillman.'

'Then you'll know that we're much more demanding than any other kind. We're brash, bullying, and we always complain like mad.'

'That's not true at all.'

'Oh?'

'I've never had the slightest trouble from most of you.'

'No bad language?' asked Dillman, feigning surprise. 'No threats? No hot tempers? No shoes thrown at you?'

Ellway smiled. 'I think you're pulling my leg, Mr Dillman.'

'Why should I do that?'

'You're just having a bit of fun, aren't you, sir?'

'I'm an American. We have no sense of humour whatsoever.'

'That's not my experience,' said the steward. 'There was a gentleman from Virginia on my last eastbound voyage who told the best jokes I've ever heard. That's what I like about Americans. Most of you seem ready for a good laugh.'

Dillman grinned. 'At least, we have one thing in our favour.'

'Lots of them. You give bigger tips, for a start.'

'Are you dropping a hint, Manny?'

'No, sir. It's strictly forbidden.'

'Not in this cabin.'

Manny Ellway relaxed. He had taken to Dillman at once. For his part, the detective had found his steward a mine of useful detail. Within minutes of meeting him in his cabin, Dillman had discovered the man's name, place of birth, preferred hobbies, and attitude to the affairs of the day. He had also learnt about the running of the ship, its many virtues and minor shortcomings, and who occupied the adjoining cabins. Dillman's real purpose aboard was always concealed from most of those working on it so it was important for him to appear to be just another passenger. Manny Ellway, he felt confident, would have him marked down as a pleasant American who liked to tease.

'How many cabins do you look after?' asked Dillman.

'Enough to keep me out of mischief, sir.'

'Anybody special?'

'They're all special to me, Mr Dillman.'

'Good answer. Now tell me the truth.'

'That is the truth, sir,' said Ellway. He took a step closer. 'Now, if you're asking me whether some people stick out more than others, that's a different matter, isn't it?'

'Is it?'

'Well, we always have our fair share of characters.'

'Odd people?'

'Yes, sir. Like them three who joined us in Cherbourg. They'd stand out in any company. Funny lot, them artists.'

'Artists?'

'That's what he is, sir. Abednego Thomas. He's very well known in England – always in the newspapers.' He sounded a note of disapproval. 'He paints them naked ladies.'

'They're called nudes.'

'I know what I calls them and I'm not sure it's decent. Mr Thomas has been living in France but he's going to have an exhibition of his naked ladies in New York. He's taking two of them with him.'

'Two nude women?'

'No, sir. His wife and his model. They're both very beautiful and years younger than him. You won't miss Abednego Thomas. He's the sort of man who makes sure that he gets noticed.'

'Are you his cabin steward?'

'Yes, sir.'

'Do you mind?'

'I'm not paid to mind. I just do whatever I'm told.'

'Even if it means looking after disreputable English artists?'

'Mr Thomas is *Welsh*,' said Ellway in a tone which suggested that that explained everything. 'One of the newspapers has given him a rude nickname but I couldn't bring myself to repeat it.'

Dillman was glad that Manny Ellway was his steward. The man was efficient, courteous, and experienced. He was talkative without being indiscreet and friendly without making any attempt at ingratiating himself. He would be a valuable pair of eyes and ears for the detective.

'Did you know that J. P. Morgan is aboard?' asked Dillman.

'Yes, sir. We was told about him in Southampton.'

'Why?'

'So that we can all be on our best behaviour. Mr Morgan owns us.'

'That's not strictly true but it certainly wouldn't be in your interest to upset him in any way. I'm told that he has a temper.'

'Very true, sir. He's sailed with us before.'

'Did someone feel the full force of that temper?'

'I'm not allowed to pass on gossip, sir.'

'But it's taught you to treat Mr Morgan with great respect.'

'We do that to all our passengers, Mr Dillman. Company policy.'

'J. P. Morgan is a rather special case, however.'

'I wouldn't disagree with that.'

'Are you his steward?'

'Bless you – no, sir! I'm not senior enough for that.'

'Does that make you disappointed or relieved?'

'Neither,' said Ellway, shrugging his shoulders. 'Never really think about things like that. I'm happy to let Sid do the honours.'

'Sid?'

'Sidney Browne, sir. Been a steward a lot longer than me and what he doesn't know about this job ain't worth knowing. Sid always pretends that he hates the life but he loves it, really. One of our veterans, he is. That's why he got to keep an eye on Mr Morgan.'

'A feather in his cap, then.'

'That's not the way he looks at it.'

'Why not?'

Ellway hesitated. 'I shouldn't be telling you this, sir.'

'I don't think that you can tell me anything about Mr Morgan that I don't already know or suspect,' said Dillman, feeling that

31

he might glean some valuable information. 'My family has had dealings with the gentleman, I fear. We build ocean-going yachts and sailing is one of Mr Morgan's favourite leisure pursuits. My father was invited to show him the design for a new yacht and that's when the trouble started.'

'Didn't he like it, sir?'

'Let's just say that he and my father did not part on the best of terms. Words were exchanged. Whatever you do, don't mention this to your friend. If he drops the name of Dillman in Mr Morgan's presence, he's likely to get a flea in his ear.'

'I wouldn't tell anyone a story like that, sir.'

'I knew that I could trust you.'

'There's things you pass on and things you don't.'

'As long as we both understand that.'

'We do, sir.'

Having won his confidence, Dillman felt able to return to his earlier inquiry. He spoke over his shoulder as he was opening a drawer to take out some cufflinks.

'So why isn't this Sidney Browne proud of the fact that he's been selected to serve the most important passenger aboard?'

'Because he's worried.'

'About what?'

'Them things Mr Morgan has in his stateroom.'

'Items that he bought in Paris?' asked Dillman, turning to face him. 'I know that he collects art treasures from all over Europe. That was the whole purpose of his trip. Mr Morgan donates paintings and objets d'art to various galleries and museums.' He saw the blank look on Ellway's face. 'Oh, I'm sorry. Objets d'art are simply artistic objects.'

'Ah, I'm with you now, sir. Old clocks and fancy statues.'

'Antiques of all kind, Manny – including porcelain. I can't see anything there that's going to disturb your friend.'

'Sid feels *responsible*.'

'Why?'

'Because Mr Morgan insists on keeping some of the stuff with him even though passengers are always advised to store anything valuable in our safe. When Sid tried to tell that to Mr Morgan, he just got this black look so he got out of there quick.'

'What sorts of items are actually in there?'

'Books, china, tapestries, paintings . . .'

'Why does Mr Morgan have them with him?'

'So that he can enjoy them. He bought them so he wants the pleasure of looking at them while we sail across the ocean.'

'They should be kept under proper lock and key.'

'That's why Sid is so scared – in case anything happens to the stuff. He thinks he'll be blamed. According to Sid,' he went on, lowering his voice to a confidential whisper, 'those things are worth a fortune. It's like Aladdin's cave in there, sir. What if the wrong sort of person got to hear that there's a treasure trove just the other side of that door?'

Dillman had already asked and answered that very same question.

THREE

The first-class dining room of the *Oceanic* had all the luxury and elegance that had come to be associated with the White Star Line. It was spacious, sumptuous, and designed with a firm commitment to extravagance. Unlimited amounts of money had been lavished upon it. With its polished woodwork, magnificent drapes, glittering chandeliers, marble columns, potted plants, and dazzling array of damask tablecloths and gleaming silver cutlery, it looked more like part of an exclusive hotel than the dining room on a transatlantic liner. As the guests began to arrive that evening, the orchestra played a medley of light classical music.

Genevieve Masefield delayed her entry until the place was half full, not wishing to stand out and thereby attract too much attention. She was wearing a black evening dress with, apart from silver earrings, only one item of jewellery – a silver scorpion –

pinned to her bodice. She carried a silver purse. Genevieve did not have to look for a familiar face. Blanche Charlbury descended on her at once, towing her fiancé behind her.

'There you are, Genevieve,' she said effusively. 'Do join us at our table. I promised Mark that you would. This is Genevieve, Mark.'

'I gathered that,' said Mark Bossingham, offering his hand to Genevieve. 'It's a pleasure to meet you, Miss Masefield.'

Genevieve shook his hand. 'And to meet you, Mr Bossingham.'

'For goodness' sake,' complained Blanche, clicking her tongue, 'we can't have too much decorum at a time like this. Rules are surely relaxed on board a ship. Call each other Mark and Genevieve. We're all friends here, aren't we?'

Genevieve was happy to accede to the request but she could see that Bossingham had severe reservations. Now in his late twenties, he was relatively short, compact, and immaculately groomed. His face was expressionless, his eyes cold, his hair receding. Genevieve sensed a keen intelligence but her first impression was of a highly conventional Englishman who would, in time, stifle all of his wife's *joie de vivre* and bring her to heel. Mark Bossingham would never have allowed the use of Christian names on so short an acquaintance. In the normal course of events, he and Genevieve would never have crossed each other's path and he did not look as if he was overjoyed with their meeting now.

They moved to the table that they shared with five other people. After a battery of introductions with their dinner companions, they sat down. Genevieve was able to take a closer look at Bossingham, who was directly opposite her. Blanche was at her side, patently anxious that friend and fiancé would get along well.

'Blanche has told me so much about you,' began Genevieve.

'Really?' said Bossingham.

'I hear that you're in the diplomatic service.'

'That's right.'

'Following in your father's footsteps.'

'I believe in maintaining tradition.'

'And you were at Oxford with Blanche's brother.'

'That seems like an eternity ago now, Miss Masefield.'

'Genevieve,' prompted Blanche.

'Genevieve,' he said, forcing a smile.

'I even know about your taste in music,' continued Genevieve.

'Do you?'

'And what you like to read. Trollope is your favourite author.'

'Well, there's nothing left for you to find out about me, is there? I have no secrets now so you'll find me very dull.' His eyes flicked to his fiancée. 'I'll have to school Blanche to be more reticent about me.'

'I refuse,' she said with a proprietary smile. 'I want to tell the whole world what a wonderful husband I'm going to have.'

She laughed but Bossingham looked uncomfortable. To hide his unease, he reached for the menu and studied the various items on it. Blanche nudged Genevieve and spoke in a whisper. 'Isn't he just marvellous?'

'Yes, yes.'

'Tell the truth.'

'That is the truth, Blanche.'

'I know. And he's all mine.'

Genevieve noticed that Bossingham, though pretending not to hear, winced slightly. He kept his head down. Genevieve felt that she was being quietly disapproved of and she wondered why. Before the conversation could continue, a tall man in a beautifully tailored three-piece suit swooped down on them. Jonathan Killick had the buoyant confidence of a true socialite.

'Blanche,' he said, taking her gloved hand to kiss it.

'Hello, Johnny,' she said.

'Is Mark going to make an honest woman of you at last?' He gave her a sly wink. 'Not before time, I say.'

'Take care,' said Bossingham. 'That remark is in bad taste.'

'I'm the emperor of bad taste.'

'That's not something to be proud of, Killick.'

'I think it is – I revel in it.'

'You don't have to tell us that,' reproached Blanche.

'I mentioned it in passing for Miss Masefield's benefit,' said Killick, turning his attention to Genevieve with a bold gaze. 'May I say how divine you look this evening, Miss Masefield? One can only judge a woman properly in an evening dress and you are quite exceptional.'

'I don't believe that we've been introduced,' said Genevieve calmly.

'Jonathan Killick at your service.'

She ignored his outstretched hand. 'Good evening, Mr Killick.'

'Travelling alone, I see.'

'No,' said Blanche, 'with friends.'

'You and Mark will not want a third person around all the time. I daresay that Miss Masefield will look for companionship elsewhere.'

'Not in your direction, Johnny.'

'Have you been putting down the poison about me?'

'You do that for yourself,' said Bossingham.

Killick laughed. 'Perhaps you're right, old chap.'

'We'd be grateful if you'd allow us to enjoy our meal.'

'How can you bear such pomposity, Blanche?' asked Killick with a hand on her shoulder. 'He's such a cold fish. Marry me instead.'

'Go away, Johnny,' she said.

'My offer holds.'

She moved his hand away. 'I'm engaged to Mark now.'

'You have my condolences.'

'Goodbye, Killick,' said Bossingham pointedly.

'Cheerio – that includes *you*, Miss Masefield.'

'Goodbye,' said Genevieve.

'I won't be far away.'

Killick broadened his smile and looked deep into her eyes before leaving. He chose a vacant chair at a nearby table so that he could keep Genevieve in view. Killick's arrival brought Bossingham to life.

'Insufferable fellow!' he snapped.

'Johnny is Johnny,' said Blanche tolerantly. 'Ignore him.'

'I object to the way he talks to you.'

'Don't take him so seriously, Mark.'

'He's altogether too familiar.'

'He's familiar with everyone.'

'It's got to stop.'

'What is he doing on this voyage?' asked Genevieve.

'Going to a party in New York, I expect,' said Blanche.

Genevieve was taken aback. 'He'd go all that way for a party?'

'Knowing him, it will be a very special one – the kind that goes on for days and days. He has a lot of friends in America. They like the idea of rubbing shoulders with an aristocrat.'

'A *minor* aristocrat,' corrected Bossingham.

'He belongs to the upper class. That's all that matters to them.'

'I think that we should ostracise him.'

'That would be too harsh on Johnny.'

'Killick is a complete menace.'

'Humour him, Mark. It's the only way.'

'I still find it difficult to believe that he'd go three thousand miles for a social event,' said Genevieve. 'That means he'll spend the best part of two weeks alone on the ship.'

'Except that he won't be alone,' Blanche pointed out.

'No?'

'No,' added Bossingham, 'he'll soon find some poor, unsuspecting young woman to batten on to. The fellow is quite unprincipled. Killick is a born predator.'

'It's true,' said Blanche. 'Johnny is always on the lookout.' Genevieve glanced in the direction of the man about whom they were talking and saw that Killick was staring intently at her. She was disturbed. It was less a gaze of admiration than the cool, objective appraisal of a potential target. Genevieve had the unsettling sensation that he had just marked her out as his next prey.

'Four days out of New York, in 'eavy gales, 'igh seas and snow, she loses a piece of 'er bulwarks and two port'oles was smashed.'

'Who cares?'

'I do, Manny. I told you the *Oceanic* was cursed. She took on lots of water in that incident. Next year – August 1905 – fire damaged woodwork in a third-class compartment as she lay at Liverpool.'

'It was soon put out,' said Manny Ellway, 'and it didn't stop her from sailing almost immediately for New York.'

'It was a sign,' insisted Sidney Browne.

'You and your blinking signs!'

'There was another one in June 1907. Someone set fire to cargo in 'er 'old while she was docked at Pier 48, New York. All the beddin' and fittin's in some of the women's quarters was ruined.

Took 'em two 'ours to bring the blaze under control. Thousands of pounds' worth of damage was done. The *Oceanic*'s departure was 'eld up for days.'

'Bad luck, that's all, Sid.'

'This ship's 'ad nothin' but bad luck.'

Browne had really hit his stride, detailing the various problems that the ship had encountered in her decade afloat. The two men were alone in their cabin, smartening themselves up before going back on duty. Peering into the mirror above the washbasin, Ellway was using a pair of brushes on his hair.

'It goes on and on, Manny,' resumed Browne gloomily. 'As recent as last September, the *Oceanic* 'ad another fire in 'er 'old. If that's not clear proof that she's doomed, I don't know what is.'

'It was a small fire and they soon put it out.'

'What about the one in New York?'

'That was arson,' said Ellway. 'They reckon the man who lit it was in league with some of them dockworkers who was on strike. Pure accident that he chose this ship. Could've been any vessel.'

'Oh no. It just 'ad to be the *Oceanic*. She attracts trouble.'

'Then why does Mr Morgan decide to sail on her?'

'What do you mean?'

'Well, he's rich enough to travel on any ship yet he picked this one. That shows he has no qualms about her. He knows that she's one of the safest liners in the world. That's why J.P. Morgan is here.'

'Yes,' said Browne, rolling his eyes, 'and it's the reason I get so jumpy. I 'ave this thing about him, Manny. What do you call it?'

'A premonition?'

'That's the word – premonition.'

Ellway was scornful. 'Signs, premonitions, bad omens – they're all a load of nonsense. Why can't you see something good for once?'

'I got a sixth sense for disaster.'

'Well, that's the difference between you and me, Sid. I always hopes for the best and you always fears the worst.'

'So would you if you was 'is steward.'

'Who?'

'Mr Morgan. Ole J. P. Moneybags. Fair gives me the creeps, 'e does.'

'Why?'

'It's them eyes of 'is. They bores right through you.'

'Then look the other way.'

'I did, Manny, and what did I see? Them paintin's and such like he keeps in there. Worth a king's ransom, they are. Yet 'e just 'as 'em lyin' about like so many newspapers. It's askin' for trouble.'

'I'm sure that he has some kind of security.'

'The door to his stateroom, that's all. A professional thief could pick that lock in a few seconds. That's where my premonition came in.'

Ellway sighed. 'Here we go again!'

'I got this 'orrible feelin' that someone is about to pounce.'

'He's called the chief steward and he'll be pouncing on the pair of us if we don't get out there.' He put his brushes in the locker. 'Come on, Sid. Try to forget J. P. Morgan.'

' 'Ow can I when 'e's about to bring catastrophe down on us?'

'Play your cards right and you may get the biggest tip of your life.'

'If 'e's still alive to give it to me.'

Ellway cackled. 'What do you think's going to happen to him?' he asked. 'Do you fancy that someone's going to do him in?'

'I got this feelin' in the pit of my stomach.'

'So have I – hunger.'

'I'm serious, Manny.'

'Anybody else would be delighted if he got to look after someone like J. P. Morgan but all you can do is moan. What about your other passengers? There must be one you actually like.'

'I like most of 'em.'

'Then enjoy their company instead of waiting for disaster to strike. That's what I do.' He opened the door and they stepped out of the cabin. 'I've got some really interesting people on my list this time. Abednego Thomas, for instance.'

'Who's 'e when 'e's at 'ome?'

'Abednego Thomas. The artist. You must have heard of him. He told me to be sure to knock on the door before I go into his cabin because he may well be painting.'

'Nothing unusual in that, is there? We have lots of artists on our ships. You can see 'em up on deck any day.'

'Mr Thomas would get arrested if he worked in public.'

'Arrested?'

'He paints naked ladies, Sid. What's more, he's brought his model with him. A French lady. She's gorgeous.'

Browne was intrigued. 'And 'e's goin' to paint 'er when she's got nothing at all on? Is that why you 'ave to knock first?'

'Yes.'

'In your place, I'd peep through the key'ole.'

'People are entitled to their privacy.'

'Lord knows what you might see.'

'You just worry about your own passengers.'

'I'd much rather look after Abednego Thomas than J. P. Morgan.'

'Well, don't ask me to swap,' said Ellway, 'because there's no earthly chance of that. I get on with all my passengers, especially that Mr Dillman. He's a real gentleman and he's fond of a laugh as well. Mr Dillman is one of those Americans who's so nice and well mannered that you think he must have been born in England.' He nudged Browne, who had gone off into a reverie. 'You're not listening, are you?'

'I'm still thinkin' about that painter and 'is French model.'

Her name was Dominique Cadine and Dillman had the good fortune to be sharing a table with her and her travelling companions. She was slim, shapely, and gifted with long, silken black hair that was curled up like a snake on top of her head and held in place with a gold slide. Her dark complexion accentuated the brightness of her large, pale blue, inquiring eyes. She spoke good English but it was heavily accented. Dillman put her in her late twenties. The fair-haired Veronica Thomas was ten years older and, in spite of a much bigger frame, had an equally voluptuous quality about her, one that women in the first-class dining room found rather shocking but which the men secretly admired. Dominique wore a crimson dress that advertised her contours and was complemented by the red rose in her hair. Veronica was in a striking blue and green evening dress.

Accompanying the two women was Abednego Thomas, a gaunt man in his late fifties with a long, unkempt beard and grey hair that fell to his shoulders. His eyes glinted in a craggy face. He wore a crumpled brown suit with a large spotted handkerchief exploding out of its top pocket. Thomas gloried in the fact that his life had been marked by a series of scandals.

'Why did you choose to live in France?' asked Dillman.

'They have a more adult society there,' replied Thomas with a quiet smile. 'More adult and more understanding.'

'What my husband is trying to tell you,' put in Veronica, 'is that he's less likely to end up in court in France. It has true artistic tradition. It does not expect a creative genius to be a saint.'

'Just as well, my love,' said Thomas with a chuckle, slipping an arm around her. 'I was never inclined to sainthood. My impulses took me in the opposite direction.'

Dillman was curious. 'Could you not live and work in Wales?'

'I'd be stoned to death. The Welsh are very puritanical.'

'Nobody could say that of you,' remarked Dominique, displaying a row of perfect teeth. 'I think that you must have French blood in your veins, Abednego.'

'French wine, maybe. I've drunk gallons of it.'

Husband, wife, and model shook with laughter. There was a unity about them that Dillman found fascinating. They were three disparate people held together by an invisible bond. While the Welshman spoke with a musical lilt, his wife had a voice that suggested an acquaintance with the higher echelons of British society. A painter in her own right, Veronica Thomas also designed clothes and jewellery. Examples of the latter encircled her neck and wrists. Both hands were bedecked with rings. Golden earrings dangled from her lobes. Dominique, however, wore almost no jewellery. In a room where most women had reached for diamonds or pearls, she was given an added prominence.

Dillman liked all three of them at once and the trio clearly enjoyed his company, all the more so since he accepted them for what they were instead of resenting their Bohemian lifestyle. The same could not be said of the other four people at the table, two elderly English couples who showed a tight-lipped politeness towards them. Grateful that Dillman was ready to talk to the artist – an ordeal they were spared – they conversed among themselves and resolved never to be caught again at the same table as the outrageous Abednego Thomas and his two women.

'Why did you go to England, Mr Dillman?' asked Veronica.

'I was on a scouting expedition,' he replied.

'Were you looking for a wife?'

'Heavens, no!'

'You would find one very easily,' said Dominique with a dazzling smile. 'American men are more handsome than English ones. They have a sense of mystery about them.'

'I don't feel very mysterious, mademoiselle.'

'Please – my name is Dominique.'

'Then you must feel free to call me George.'

'And what were you scouting for, George?' said Thomas, lifting his glass as the waiter came to refill it with Chablis. 'Painting? Antiques? Are you another J. P. Morgan?'

'Far from it,' said Dillman. 'I don't have the money or the time to indulge myself in that way. No, I was looking for commissions. Back in Boston, I work in the family business. We make ocean-going yachts for people with large bank balances and a love of sailing.'

'Do you sail yourself?'

'Of course. I grew up beside the sea.'

'So did I,' said Veronica, 'but I can neither swim, sail, nor bear to look at the waves rolling ceaselessly on. My people were the same. We're all confirmed landlubbers even though we could see Brighton promenade from our front bedrooms.'

'What about the Pavilion?' asked Dominique.

'That was only a few minutes away.'

'I would love to live there.'

'It would grow stale for you within a week, darling,' said Thomas, stroking her hand affectionately. 'It's an absolute monument to bad taste but, then, so is a lot of English architecture.' He kissed his wife on the cheek. 'You are the exception to the rule, my love.'

'I'm not a piece of architecture.'

'A sculpture, then. Worthy of Michelangelo.'

'I would have thought Michelangelo a little too conventional for your taste,' observed Dillman. 'From what you've been saying, you prefer to push out the frontiers of your art instead of being bound by tradition.'

'I admire the best of any era. Michelangelo was the best of his.'

'What about me?' said his wife, fishing for a compliment. 'The very best of your time.'

Dominique smiled. '*Et moi?*'

'*Incroyable, ma chére.*'

As he ran a finger under her chin, there was a gasp of disbelief from the two elderly Englishwomen at the table, affronted less by the artist's frank admiration for his model than by his wife's calm acceptance of it. The dazed onlookers reached for their glasses and took a long drink of wine to restore their composure.

'What are you working on at the moment?' inquired Dillman.

'Dominique,' replied Thomas.

'I am a Roman goddess this time,' said the model.

'Then you must be Venus,' said Dillman, gallantly.

'*Bien entendu.*'

'Do you intend to paint while on board, Abednego?'

'Nothing would stop me,' asserted Thomas with a grand gesture. 'I work out of compulsion, my friend. I'm not one of those lazy artists who sit around waiting for inspiration to strike. I exercise my talent on a daily basis. Work is dignity.'

'I feel the same,' said Veronica. 'Since we've been given such a precious gift, it's our duty to exercise it. I, too, will paint every day.'

'Though in a different style, I suspect,' said Dillman.

'My work is non-figurative, George.'

'I'd be interested to see some of it.'

'Then you shall,' she said. 'Do you hear that, Abednego? We must invite George to our cabin for a drink. He can look at our paintings.'

'Everything but Venus,' stipulated Thomas.

'He won't even let me see that,' said Dominique, 'and I'm his model. I never get to see any of the paintings until they are finished.'

'And you know why, Dominique. I'm a perfectionist.'

'Especially when it comes to your choice of women,' said Veronica.

Thomas guffawed. 'I couldn't have put it better myself.'

It was an excellent meal and Dillman was delighted to share it with the eccentric trio. He exchanged a few niceties with the others at the table but they preferred to dine in a state of semi-detachment. The more he talked to Abednego Thomas, the more impressed he became by his open disdain for etiquette. Everyone else adhered to strict social rules but the artist might have been having a picnic on the banks of the river Seine. He, his wife, and Dominique were refreshing dinner companions.

Much as he would have liked to, Dillman could not linger over the meal. He was still on duty and dinner was an ideal time for him to take the measure of the first-class passengers. Even while he was talking to his new friends, he was keeping one eye on other tables. Genevieve, he could see, was engrossed with friends of her own. Lester Hembrow, in his best uniform, was standing near the door with the headwaiter. Dillman recognised a number of people he had seen boarding the ship but there was no sign of J. P. Morgan. He wanted to find out why.

When the meal was over, he excused himself from the table. Dominique was sorry to lose him but it was Veronica who got to her feet and planted a warm kiss on each of his cheeks. Dillman crossed to the door and took the purser aside.

'Mr Morgan is dining in his cabin, I presume.'

'Yes, George.'

'Did you know that he's keeping valuable items in his stateroom?'

'No,' said Hembrow, shaking his head, 'but it doesn't surprise me one bit. J. P. Morgan is a law unto himself.'

'Someone should remind him of the need for security. As long as those items are in his possession, they're at risk.'

'Try telling him that. I'm not sure that I'd dare do it.'

'Then it will have to be me,' said Dillman purposefully. 'I'll just have to hope he's forgotten the way that he and my father fell out all those years ago.'

'Mr Morgan is the sort of man who remembers *everything*.' Other diners were now starting to disperse and the purser was soon in demand. Dillman strolled away, rehearsing what he was going to say to their most distinguished passenger. When he reached Morgan's stateroom, he took a deep breath before rapping on the door. It was opened at once by a sturdy individual of middle height. He looked Dillman up and down before speaking. His tone was brusque.

'What do you want?'

'I'd like to speak to Mr Morgan, please,' said Dillman.

'That's not possible.'

'It's on a matter of some importance.'

'It will have to wait all the same.'

'Any delay might be fatal.'

'Why?'

'My name is George Dillman and I'm employed as a detective by the White Star Line. I need to discuss security procedures with Mr Morgan.'

'They are already in hand, Mr Dillman.'

'Are they?'

'Yes,' said the other. 'I take responsibility for such matters. My name is Howard Riedel and I'm experienced in every aspect of security. Far more so than you, I suspect.'

Howard Riedel shot him a confrontational glare. He was a bull-necked man in his fifties with close-cropped hair surmounting a low forehead. His face was that of a retired boxer with a good record behind him. He was Morgan's bodyguard and security adviser.

'How long have you been ship's detective?'

'Over four years,' said Dillman.

'What qualifications do you have?'

'I worked for the Pinkerton Detective Agency.'

'No time in a *real* police department?'

'No, Mr Riedel.'

'Well, I spent most of my life in uniform,' boasted Riedel. 'I've seen it all – rape, theft, arson, kidnap, murder. Seen it and solved it. That's why Mr Morgan picked me. He asked for the best cop in the department and he got me. Not some half-trained Pinkerton operative.'

'We were extremely well trained,' retorted Dillman, 'and most of our work consisted in sweeping up the mess left by real policeman like you. We're both on the same level now, Mr Riedel. We're private detectives – so don't try to pull rank on me.'

'Good night, Dillman.'

'At least, tell Mr Morgan that I'm here.'

'Nobody gets to see him unless I say so.'

'Do you taste his food for him as well?' said Dillman levelly.

'You're not wanted here. Make yourself scarce.'

'If you've been a policeman, you know that prevention is better than solving crime. And the best way to prevent theft is to put anything of real value into the purser's safe. That's what I'd advise most strongly.'

'What I'd advise most strongly,' said Riedel, squaring up to him, 'is that you keep well away from here. All the necessary steps have been taken. You're out of your depth. Leave it to a professional.'

'A professional what?'

Riedel thrust out his jaw. 'You asking for trouble?'

'No,' said Dillman, 'but you and Mr Morgan are. As long as you persist in keeping priceless items here, they're in danger.'

'So is the person who tries to steal them. He has to go past me.'

'You can't be on duty twenty-four hours a day.'

'I'm like a Pinkerton agent,' taunted the other. 'I never sleep.'

'Please pass on my warning to Mr Morgan.'

'He doesn't need warnings. He's got me on his payroll.'

'And do you get paid to obstruct people like me?' said Dillman.

'No, I do that for pleasure.'

'I'll be back in the morning, Mr Riedel.'

'You'll get the same answer. We don't need you, Dillman.'

'I'd like to hear that from Mr Morgan's own lips.'

'Then you're a bigger fool than you look,' said Riedel with a sneer. 'You step on his toes and he'll holler so loud that it'll burst your eardrums. Why don't you hang on to your job while you still have one?'

Dillman bristled. 'I didn't ask for your advice.'

'It comes free. Tangle with Mr Morgan and you'll never work for the White Star Line again. Upset me,' warned Riedel, wagging a finger, 'and I'll tell him what a nuisance you're being. Is that plain enough for you or would you like me to write it down in capital letters? Now go off and bother someone else.'

And he slammed the door unceremoniously in Dillman's face.

FOUR

Queenstown was the last port of call before the long voyage across the Atlantic. The principal purpose of the stop was to pick up Irish emigrants and mail. Many passengers already aboard took the opportunity to send letters and notes back to families and friends in England. Some of the crew did the same. It was mid-morning on the following day when the *Oceanic* steamed up St. George's Channel and passed Daunt's Rock Light Vessel. The ship anchored two miles off Roche's Point so that a hundred or more new passengers could be brought out from Queenstown, along with some twelve hundred sacks of mail. None of the newcomers travelled first class. The overwhelming majority of them were sailing into the unknown in steerage.

Lester Hembrow glanced through the porthole in his office as the last tender was being unloaded. He looked back at Genevieve Masefield.

'The Irish invasion is almost complete,' he said with a smile. 'At least this lot will be able to speak English.'

'Yes, the ones who joined us at Cherbourg were very cosmopolitan.'

'At the last count, fourteen different languages were being spoken in steerage. We're very happy to carry people of any nationality but we can't possibly have interpreters for them all. There's bound to be some confusion down there at first.'

'Do they fall back on sign language?' asked Genevieve.

'For the most part. We have posters in French, German, and Italian but passengers from the Arab countries have to fend for themselves. And with so many people to feed,' Hembrow went on, 'it's impossible to cater to everyone's preferred diet.'

'Cooking for a thousand passengers must be a nightmare.'

'It's not something that I'd care to do, Genevieve. However, let's leave that problem to the kitchen staff. We have troubles of our own.'

'Already?'

'Two ladies have reported thefts during dinner last night.'

'What sorts of thefts?'

'Diamond earrings, in one case.'

'And the other?'

'A purse, belonging to a Mrs Boyd.'

'Are the two ladies certain that they were stolen?' said Genevieve. 'Things can very easily go astray sometimes through sheer carelessness.'

'There's nothing careless about Mrs Farrant,' he told her. 'She may be in her seventies but she has all her faculties intact. Mrs Farrant is convinced that a thief made off with her earrings.'

'What about Mrs Boyd?'

'She's still wondering if she inadvertently put her purse down somewhere and forgot to pick it up. She's an American lady who admits that she's absentminded at times. Mrs Farrant is English.'

'Then I'll start with her.'

'I've written down the numbers of their respective cabins.'

'Thank you, Lester.'

Genevieve took the slip of paper that was offered. Like Dillman, she found the purser agreeable and cooperative. He knew their reputation and had complete trust in them. She felt that it would be a pleasure to work with him, a crucial factor on a vessel that was certain to keep both her and Dillman extremely busy. Genevieve gazed down at his desk. Before they sailed, it had been completely clear. It was now covered with papers, letters, and documents arranged in neat piles.

'These are requests,' he explained, touching one pile. 'Those are complaints, and the rest are to do with administration. When I took this job on, I had no idea there'd be so much paperwork.'

'There's more to come,' she warned. 'After I've spoken to the two ladies, I'll send you a written report on each to keep you up-to-date. I'll also have a word with George about the thefts.'

'How are you and he settling in?'

'Very well.'

'You looked as if you were enjoying your dinner last night.'

'I was,' she said. 'It was delicious. One of the benefits of being a ship's detective is that you get well fed. You just have to remember that you're still working even though you're in convivial company.'

'Yes, it could be distracting.'

'Not if you keep your wits about you. George taught me that.'

'I had a brief word with him in the dining saloon. He went off to brave the wrath of J. P. Morgan.'

'He never even managed to see him.'

'Oh?'

'George told me about it when we met to compare notes last night. It seems that Mr Morgan has a bodyguard called Howard Riedel. He's a former policeman who thinks he can do a much better job at protecting valuables than people like us.'

'What did he tell George?'

'To mind his own business.'

'Was he as blunt as that?'

'Even more so,' said Genevieve. 'When George mentioned that he'd worked for the Pinkerton agency, Mr Riedel showed open contempt. He regards its operatives as rank amateurs.'

'There's nothing amateur about George Dillman. I've seen his record as a ship's detective – and yours, Genevieve. The pair of you are a match for anyone.' He scratched his head. 'But I'm worried about the fact that nobody's got past Mr Morgan's door yet. Someone needs to point out the folly of keeping all those items in his stateroom.'

'I'll volunteer for that task.'

'You?'

'Yes, Lester,' she said. 'I haven't broken the news to George yet but I may succeed where he failed.'

'How?'

'A card was slipped under my door. It's an invitation to drinks in Mr Morgan's stateroom before dinner this evening. Obviously I won't reveal my true identity but I will take the opportunity to suggest that he locks anything of value away.'

'You'll also be able to see it at firsthand.'

'I'm looking forward to that.'

'George is going to be very jealous.'

'No,' she assured him. 'He's the least envious person I know. He'll be thrilled that I have a chance to see Mr Morgan's collection and get close to the great man. There's only one thing that puzzles me.'

'What's that, Genevieve?'

'Well, J. P. Morgan doesn't have a clue who I am. Why on earth has he invited me to a drinks party this evening?'

Hembrow grinned. 'There's an easy answer to that,' he said, cheerily 'Mr Morgan is a collector of beautiful objects.'

George Porter Dillman had watched with interest as the new passengers embarked and he was still standing at the rail on the promenade deck. The noise of pounding feet made him turn round. He was in time to see Howard Riedel running towards him. Wearing a woollen sweater and a pair of slacks, the man was moving at a steady pace, clearly enjoying the attention that he was attracting. When he stopped beside Dillman, his breathing was in no way laboured.

'Physical fitness,' he said proudly. 'That's the first requisite of a good cop. You have to keep your body in trim. Remember that, Dillman.'

'I don't need to, Mr Riedel. I had my run before breakfast when there were not so many people about. It meant that I could go at a much faster speed than you seem to manage.'

'I exercise every day.'

'You look as if you need to,' said Dillman.

Riedel's eye blazed. 'You making fun of me?'

'I admire any man of your age who can still run.'

'Run, fight, shoot, break up a barroom brawl – I can do *anything*.'

'You can even act as watchdog at Mr Morgan's door.'

'Mr Morgan appreciates my range of skills.'

'Does he ever get any exercise himself?' asked Dillman. 'Apart from counting out his money that is?'

'He takes a constitutional every morning.'

'Do you run in front of him with a red flag?'

'I'm just there to keep undesirables like you away from him.'

'What happens to all those things in his stateroom while you're up on deck? Surely, you don't leave them unprotected.'

'We have our system.'

'And what exactly is it?'

'That's nothing to do with you, Dillman,' said Riedel with a complacent smirk. 'You stick to the easy stuff like helping old ladies to find their missing false teeth. Leave the real policework to me.'

'I'm always ready to learn,' said Dillman.

But he was talking to thin air. Riedel had already spun on his heel and jogged away. Another passenger soon took his place. 'Good morning, George,' said Veronica Thomas.

'Oh, good morning.'

'Was that dreadful man a friend of yours?'

'Not exactly.'

'He was so ugly and so full of himself. I saw him earlier, trotting around the deck and leering at some of the young women. Who is he?'

'Howard Riedel. He works for J. P. Morgan, I believe. Mr Riedel and I bumped into each other last night.' Dillman chose his words carefully. 'I think it's fair to say that it was not a meeting of true minds.'

Veronica laughed. 'You two are like chalk and cheese.'

'Which one am I?'

'Cheese, of course. Nice enough to eat.'

Her candid admiration, coupled as it was with a broad smile, might have unnerved some men but Dillman accepted the compliment without a flicker. Now that she was separated from the others, he could see how handsome Veronica Thomas really was. The high cheekbones gave her a regal look and there was a glow to her skin that lent it the sheen of marble. On a cold morning, she was wrapped up in a long coat with a fur collar. A purple cockade was attached to the side of her hat.

'I was watching those Irish people coming aboard,' she said. 'They're so courageous, aren't they?'

'Courageous?'

'Selling everything to start up again in a new country. It means they'll spend the rest of their lives in exile.'

'You live in exile,' he reminded her.

'Hardly! France is my spiritual home.'

'How long have you been there?'

'Twelve years.'

'Is that how long you've been married?'

'Oh no,' she said. 'Abednego had worked his way through two other wives before I came along – two wives of his own, that is, and a number of wives belonging to other men. He simply adores women. My husband is a Welsh mountain goat.'

'Not a dragon?'

'He can breathe fire when he wants to.'

'How did you meet him?'

'In Paris. I knew him by reputation, of course, but I never thought he'd take the slightest interest in me. Until I came along, he favoured exotic French or Italian women – girls like

Dominique who simply bubble with life.' She spread her arms expressively. 'When he had the pick of those ladies, how could such a man even bother to look at a posh Englishwoman named Veronica Hartley-Smythe?'

'Hartley-Smythe? Was that your maiden name?'

'I expected that the hyphen alone would drive him away.'

'Abednego had the wisdom to look beyond your hyphen.'

'That's one way of putting it, George. We met in a bar one night and a week later – even though he was still married to someone else at the time – he was proposing to me.'

'How did your parents take the news?'

'They were horrified,' she said with a grimace. 'It was bad enough for their daughter to declare her insanity by trying to make a living as an artist. To wed someone as notorious as Abednego Thomas was, in their eyes, an assault on everything they held most dear.'

'You were rejecting all their values.'

'Not deliberately. I'd fallen in love, that's all.'

'Did your parents come to accept him as a son-in-law?'

'That was too much to ask of a Hartley-Smythe. They looked on Abednego as a species of satyr – and an ageing one at that. They took the only way out and simply disowned me.'

'So you're an orphan,' said Dillman.

'No, I'm part of an artistic community. They're my family now.'

'It's not the same.'

'When I moved in with Abednego, I lost more than my hyphen. But the gains have completely outweighed the losses.'

'No regrets, then?'

'None whatsoever, George. I discovered the value of true freedom.'

'Most women from your background would be terrified to do that. They need the whole apparatus of class and social etiquette to hold them upright. It was a bold step to break out of all that, Veronica. I take my hat off to you.'

'Thanks.'

'When can I come and look at your work?'

'Why not this evening before dinner?' she suggested. 'We'll have cleaned up by then. Come any earlier and you'll find the pair of us spattered with paint. We're in number twenty-seven.'

'Close to my own cabin,' he said. 'We share the same steward.'

'Manny?'

'Yes, I don't think he's met anyone like you and your husband before. Not to mention Dominique.'

'He doesn't quite know how to take us.'

'Very few people do.'

'You're an exception to the rule, George.'

'It's been a joy to meet the three of you.'

'You might change your mind when you see our paintings.'

Dillman smiled. 'I very much doubt that, Veronica.'

She held his gaze for a long time then she stepped forward for him to give her a farewell kiss her on the cheek. Veronica squeezed his arm.

'I must get back to work,' she said. 'Well see you later.'

'One last thing.'

'Yes?'

'I understand that Abednego has a nickname.'

'Dozens of them.'

'This one is rather scurrilous,' said Dillman, recalling his talk with Manny Ellway. 'My steward was too embarrassed to tell me what it was.'

She laughed aloud. 'Well, I'm not,' she announced. 'Nothing embarrasses me now. His nickname is Abed-We-Go Thomas. I always think it delightfully appropriate.'

'When did you first notice that your purse was missing, Mrs Boyd?'

'When we got back here last night. I think.'

'You only think?'

'No, Miss Masefield. I'm fairly certain. But, then, so is Ethan.'

'Is that your husband?'

'Yes, he believes that I wondered where my purse was when we were up on deck.'

'On deck?' Genevieve consulted her notes. 'You never mentioned going on deck, Mrs Boyd. According to you, when dinner was over, you went to the lounge for an hour then came back here.'

'*After* we'd taken a walk on deck.'

'I see.'

Genevieve added the new detail to her notebook. The interview with Rosalie Boyd was fraught with difficulties. Anxious to get her purse back, she kept changing her story as her memories slowly fell into place. She was a short, slight, dark-haired woman in her late thirties with an exaggerated prettiness that gave her an almost doll-like appearance. Sitting in her cabin, she held her hands in her lap like a well-behaved schoolgirl.

'I never used to be so scatter-brained,' she said, apologetically. 'Ask my husband. When Ethan first met me, I never did things like this.'

'Like what?'

'Mislaying my purse.'

'We don't know that it *was* mislaid, Mrs Boyd.'

'What else could have happened to it?'

'Someone stole it.'

Rosalie was hurt. 'Stole it?' she repeated. 'On a ship like this?'

'Thieves are working on liners all the time, I'm afraid. There are easy pickings for someone with nimble fingers. If your purse had just gone astray, it would have been found and returned by now.'

'Dear me!'

'Because it hasn't been,' said Genevieve, 'we must assume the worst. Let's go back to what you've told me.' She checked her notes. 'You say that you had the purse with you when you left the dining saloon.'

'I think so.'

'What about your husband?'

'Oh, I definitely had him with me.' She gave a brittle laugh. 'I do beg your pardon, Miss Masefield. I see what you mean now. Yes, Ethan will confirm that I had it with me.'

'I may need to speak to him myself.'

'He'd like that. He's always admired English ladies. I think that's why he married me. I come from Boston, you see, and that's about as close to being an Englishwoman as you can get.'

'Is your husband a Bostonian as well?'

'No, he's a New Yorker. There's no comparison.' Rosalie's face clouded. 'I'm worried now. Do you really think that it may have been stolen, Miss Masefield?'

'I'm afraid so,' said Genevieve. 'We certainly have a thief aboard. I've just come from a passenger who reported the theft of a pair of diamond earrings. They were definitely stolen.'

'By whom? One of the crew?'

'It's more likely to have been one of the passengers.'

'That's appalling. Will you be able to catch him?'

'I hope so, Mrs Boyd.'

'And you think the same man could have taken my purse?' 'The same man or the same woman.'

Rosalie shuddered. *A female* thief?'

'There are such things, I promise you.'

'And I thought we'd be perfectly safe on board the *Oceanic*. We had nothing like this when we sailed to Europe. It was a wonderful voyage. This is going to spoil the whole trip.'

'Was there anything of real value in the purse?'

'Not to anyone else,' answered Rosalie. 'I had what any woman would carry. Oh, and a photograph of my stepson. That was very precious to me. Ethan was married once before, you see.' She bit her lip then suddenly brightened. 'When the thief discovers there's no money in there, he might just give the purse back.'

'That's not what usually happens, Mrs Boyd. Thieves tend to take what they want from a purse or a billfold, then toss it into the sea.'

'Gracious!'

'They get rid of the evidence as soon as possible.'

'Ethan will be so upset to hear all this.'

'I'm sorry.'

'Especially when he realizes the photograph of his son has gone.' She wrung her hands. 'Is there no chance that my purse might be recovered?'

'Only a very slim one.' Genevieve flipped over a page in her notebook. 'Perhaps I could take you through it once again,' she said. 'Go back to the moment when you first left this cabin. Whom did you meet in the course of the evening?'

'I've given you all the names.'

'Let me hear them again, please.'

Rosalie Boyd ran her tongue over her upper lip then recounted her movements on the previous evening. She and her husband were just moving to the lounge after dinner when her tale was interrupted. There was a knock on the cabin door. She got up to open it.

'Mrs Boyd?'

'Yes.'

'I have some good news for you.'

Recognizing the voice, Genevieve rose to her feet and went to the door. Lester Hembrow was handing over a purse to Rosalie. 'I believe that this may belong to you, Mrs Boyd.'

'Oh, it does. I'm sure of it.'

'Perhaps you could check the contents.'

Rosalie gave a laugh of gratitude and opened the purse. Genevieve stepped forward so that Hembrow could see her. She was relieved that the purse had been recovered.

'Everything is here,' said a delighted Rosalie. She showed a photograph to Genevieve. 'This is Andrew, my stepson. He's at Harvard.'

'No wonder you're so proud of him.' Genevieve turned to Hembrow. 'Where was the purse found?'

'In the library. It had fallen down behind an armchair.'

'Library? You made no mention of the library, Mrs Boyd.'

'Didn't I? Silly me!' Rosalie gave a wan smile. 'I went in there to get some bedside reading before we came back to the cabin. It was a romance by Ouida. Would you like to see it?'

'No, no,' said Genevieve, putting her notebook away in her reticule. 'I don't think we need to trouble you any further. I'm just glad that everything has ended so happily.'

Rosalie Boyd thanked them profusely then Genevieve and Hembrow left together.

'I hope that every case is solved as easily as that,' said Hembrow. 'Who better than a purser to return a missing purse?'

'The diamond earrings will be more elusive,' Genevieve cautioned. 'I don't think we're likely to find those behind a chair in the library.'

Dressing for dinner was something over which Dillman took great care. Before he had worked for the Pinkerton agency, he had had a short, if erratic, career as an actor. During his time in the profession, he had developed skills that were very useful to a detective. He knew how to look the part. In white tie and tails, he was the epitome of suave elegance. After making a few final adjustments to his appearance in the mirror, he stepped out of his cabin and walked the short distance to the one occupied by Abednego and Veronica Thomas. They gave him a cordial welcome. Abednego pumped his hand then his wife embraced their visitor warmly.

Veronica was wearing another of her own creations, a high-waisted evening gown of red velvet with a broad black sash below the bust. A selection of jewellery was used to artful effect. Abednego was a sworn enemy of smartness. Though he wore formal attire, it was wrinkled, faded, and spectacularly ill-fitting, making him look like a failed conjurer who has just been booed from the stage. Dillman expected him to produce a dove from up his sleeve at any moment. Instead, the artist handed him a glass of champagne.

'We've already started, George. I hope you don't mind.'

'Of course not.'

Abednego raised his glass. 'To friendship!' he toasted.

'Friendship!' said Dillman and Veronica in unison.

After clinking glasses, they sipped their champagne. The cabin bore no resemblance to the one occupied by Dillman even though it was the same size and had identical furniture. The artists had transformed it. Brightly coloured shawls had been thrown over the chairs, paintings of various sizes stood along the walls, and two easels were stored in a corner. There was a strong smell of oil paint.

'Forgive the stink,' said Veronica.

'It's not a stink, my love,' said Abednego, tossing his hair. 'It's the aroma of true art. You are in the melting pot of greatness, George.'

'I'm honoured to be here.'

'Who's your favourite artist?'

Dillman was tactful. 'I don't know that I have a favourite,' he said, not wishing to offend either of them by selecting someone whom they might despise. 'My taste is very catholic. I love Rembrandt and Rubens, Caravaggio as well, and there are some Hieronymus Bosch paintings that I find very arresting.'

'I went through a Bosch period in my youth,' said Thomas.

'What about French artists?' asked Veronica.

'I can't think of any I dislike,' replied Dillman. 'Renoir stands out but, then, so do Delacroix and Courbet. But if you want to know the ugly truth about me, I also have a sneaking fondness for the work of my countryman, Mr James Whistler.'

'A fine artist in his own way,' conceded Veronica.

'But a bully of a man,' said Thomas. 'He always seemed to be looking for a fight. Met him at a party when I was living in London. We got into an argument about Claude Monet. Whistler was so aggressive. He pushed me away. Because I punched him, he threatened to sue me. I've no time for Whistler, alive or dead. Everything he did of any value was stolen from Turner.'

'Abednego!' scolded his wife.

'I'm only being honest.'

'Show some respect to a fellow artist.'

'I'm here to show you *my* respect,' said Dillman, looking at the paintings along the wall. 'What are you going to show me?'

'Only a few examples of our work, George. Most of it is boxed up in the hold, ready for exhibition in New York. Whose paintings would you like to see – mine or Abednego's?'

'Yours, Veronica. Ladies first.'

'Always the gentleman.'

She removed the cloth from one of the paintings and held it up for Dillman to see. He studied it with a mingled surprise and admiration. The one thing he had not expected was a painting of a waterfall, gushing over a precipice with ferocious power. There was an intense drama in the scene, heightened by a threatening sky.

'My parents had prints of Constable everywhere,' she explained. 'All those placid evocations of the English countryside where time stands still. Very restful, of course, but they give no hint of nature at her most exciting. I've tried to counter that.'

'And you've done so very effectively,' said Dillman. 'That waterfall bursts out of the canvas, Veronica. It's remarkable.'

'Thank you.'

'John Constable could certainly not have painted this.'

'Let me show you something else.'

She had two more paintings to offer him. One featured a violent storm in a mountainous region of France while the other depicted the ruinous effects of a flood on a small village. There was an immediacy about both of them that struck Dillman, but he also discerned anger in the paintings. Veronica seemed to be expressing her own rage, using her brush to express some kind of inner turmoil. What Dillman saw on the canvas was quite at variance with the poised and well-spoken woman standing beside him.

'I suspect that you like Turner as well,' he said.

'My mentor – until Abednego came along, that is. Turner's painting of the House of Commons on fire is a masterpiece.'

'All my pictures are masterpieces,' declared Thomas.

'Show one to George.'

'I will.' He picked up a painting that was facing the wall and turned it round for Dillman to see. 'This is from my series of Roman goddesses – Diana the Huntress.'

It was a startling piece of work. Wearing nothing but a pair of sandals, Diana was pursuing a deer through the woodland with a pack of female hunters at her heels, all of them stark naked and carrying bows and arrows. The use of colour was astounding but it was the sense of movement and unadorned feminine beauty that made the painting so striking. Dillman was amazed by the delicacy of the skin tones.

'Did they really hunt in the nude?' he asked.

Thomas gave a wicked cackle. 'She was the goddess of fertility.'

'Do you recognise her?' asked Veronica.

Dillman looked more closely at Diana's face. It had been cleverly disguised but he could see who the model must have been.

'It's Dominique,' he said. 'By the way, where is she?'

'She went to have drinks with J.P. Morgan.'

'Really?' Dillman had been told about the party by Genevieve and was surprised that Dominique was going to it as well. 'Did she have an invitation?'

'No,' said Thomas breezily, 'but that wouldn't stop Dominique. When she heard there was a party in Mr Morgan's stateroom, she invited herself. That's the sort of girl she is – enterprising.' He indicated Diana the Huntress. 'Well, let's be frank, what man in his right mind would dare to turn away someone like this?'

* * *

Since dinner was a formal affair that evening, Genevieve Masefield chose her dress with particular care. She opted for an evening gown of blue velvet trimmed with rosettes. Its low décolletage exposed her shoulders to good advantage and allowed her to wear the opal necklace that her husband had bought her when they were in Australia. Matching earrings enhanced the effect of the necklace. Her hair was swept up so that it curled forward, held in place by some invisible pins. Genevieve's use of cosmetics was frugal but she put a dab of scent in a few strategic places. A stole and a purse completed the outfit.

She paraded around the cabin and looked at herself in the mirror from various angles until she was satisfied. Genevieve was still mystified by her invitation to the party. On what basis had she been selected and how had J. P. Morgan known which cabin she was in? She knew that he was renowned for his love of female company but, since joining the ship at Cherbourg, he had not ventured outside his stateroom. Genevieve could not understand how he even knew of her existence.

Glancing at her watch, she saw that it was time to leave. No sooner had she let herself out of the cabin, however, than she was confronted by the last person she wanted to see. The Honourable Jonathan Killick was standing a few feet away. He looked completely at ease in formal wear and it seemed to reinforce his raffish air. Before she could stop him, he reached out to kiss her hand.

'May I say how charming you look, Miss Masefield?'

'What are you doing here?' she asked, blinking.

'Waiting for you.'

'Me?'

'Who else?'

'How did you know the number of my cabin?'

'I always find out things of real importance to me,' he said with a twinkle in his eye, 'and you most assuredly fall into that category. Five minutes after I first saw you, I knew your name. Blanche Charlbury has filled in some of the other details.' He lifted an eyebrow. 'Has she told you what a dissolute creature I am?'

'You'll have to excuse me,' said Genevieve, trying to move past him, 'but I have an engagement elsewhere.'

He blocked her way. 'I know. I came to escort you there.'

'I'm going to Mr Morgan's stateroom for drinks.'

'So am I, Miss Masefield. He happens to be an acquaintance of mine. When he sent me an invitation, I asked if I could bring someone with me – and who better than you?'

Genevieve gasped. 'This is all *your* doing?'

'Of course.' He offered his arm. 'Shall we go?'

FIVE

Edith Hurst had not taken long to pick out her least favourite passenger. Her name was Hilda Farrant and she treated the stewardess with a mixture of disdain and suspicion. Forthright and sharp-tongued at the best of times, Mrs Farrant had been even more scathing since her diamond earrings had been stolen, criticizing the way that Edith did her work and more or less accusing her of being the thief. The charge had brought a blush to the cheeks of the young stewardess. It was still there later. She felt the need to defend herself to a colleague.

'I'd never steal anything, Mr Browne,' she said.

'I know, Edith.'

'It was wrong of her to look at me like that. Mrs Farrant made me feel as if I'd committed a terrible crime.'

'You're as 'onest as the day is long.'

'Mrs Farrant doesn't think so.'

Edith was doing her rounds to turn down the beds that evening while passengers were away. She met Sidney Browne in a corridor and confided her woes to her senior. Browne listened carefully. He was very sympathetic.

'There's always one,' he told her, knowledgeably. 'No matter 'ow many nice people you 'ave to deal with, there's always one who can be vicious and ungrateful. If somethin' goes missin', we're always the first to get the blame.'

'Nobody's ever turned on me like that before.'

'You'll get used to it.'

'What do you think I should do?'

'Keep out of the old so-and-so's way.'

'Mrs Farrant threatened to complain to the chief steward.' 'Let 'er. We all knows 'ow good you are at your job.'

'Thank you, Mr Browne.'

'Serves 'er right if someone took 'er diamond earrin's. Tell you what, if I knew who the thief was, I'd shake 'is 'and and tell him to steal 'er jewellery box next time.'

She was shocked. 'That's a terrible thing to say!'

'I was only jokin',' he said with a grim chuckle. 'Cheer up, Edith. Don't let that ole battle-axe get you down. You must 'ave some nice passengers on your list as well.'

'They're all nice apart from Mrs Farrant – especially that Genevieve Masefield. You must have seen her. She's so beautiful and gracious. It's a pleasure to look after someone like that. If they were all like Miss Masefield, this voyage would be a delight from start to finish.'

'Well, I can't agree with you there.'

'Why not?'

'I sense trouble in the air. I 'ave this premonition.'

'What about?'

'That rich American who owns the White Star Line.'

'Mr Morgan?'

'Yes,' said Browne, solemnly. 'If you think this Mrs Farrant can put the wind up you, try dealin' with J. P. Morgan. A monster in 'uman form, 'e is. Scared the pants off me with a warning look. It was left to Mr Riedel to put the warning into words.'

'What sort of warning?'

'All I did was to say that anythin' of value was best kept in a safe.'

'And?'

'Mr Riedel told me to shut up and clear off – only 'e used words I couldn't repeat in front of a young lady. Mr Riedel works for Mr Morgan and does 'is dirty work for 'im. The worst of it is, they're 'avin' a party in there at the moment,' he moaned. 'Imagine 'ow much clearin' up I'll 'ave to do afterward. They never thinks of that.'

'No,' she agreed, 'but, when I hear about your problems, I can see that I got off lightly with Mrs Farrant. She may be strict but she keeps the cabin so tidy. There's very little for me to do.'

'Wish I could say the same but there's no chance. They'll make a real mess in that cabin. Still,' he added, philosophically, 'I suppose I shouldn't begrudge Mr Morgan a bit a fun. It won't last.'

'Why not?'

'Because 'e's got a nasty surprise comin' soon, that's why – a real disaster. Don't say I didn't tell you, Edith. I 'ad this premonition, see? So let 'im drink his fill while 'e still can. Time is runnin' out fast.'

* * *

'Do you know what a Book of Hours is, Miss Masefield?' Morgan asked.

'I have a vague idea.'

'Feast your eyes on this one.'

'Thank you, Mr Morgan.'

'It's the most valuable thing in the room.'

Genevieve was intrigued. Disconcerted to learn that she was only there at the request of Jonathan Killick, she was nevertheless grateful that she had accepted the invitation. It gave her an opportunity to mix with some of the most eminent people on board and to meet J. P. Morgan himself. When she had viewed him from a distance as he embarked, the American financier had looked imposing. Close to, he was almost intimidating, a formidable man in his seventies with white, thinning hair, a walrus moustache, and bushy eyebrows above dark, fearsome eyes. But the most prominent feature of his face was a nose so large, purple, and bulbous that it was a gift to cartoonists. Genevieve had to force herself not to stare at it.

'A Book of Hours is an example of devotional literature,' he explained, opening to the first page. 'It's so-called because the main part of it, the Office of the Virgin, is divided into liturgical hours. Do you follow me, Miss Masefield?'

'Very clearly,' she replied.

'This one was commissioned by the Duc d'Aleçon in the early fifteenth century. It's not as famous as *Les Grandes Heures* de Jean Due de Berry but it has great merit in my view.'

'Oh, it does. It's absolutely gorgeous.'

'It took the artist two years to complete.'

'The detail is extraordinary.'

'Note the initials and the line endings,' he said, using a stubby finger to point them out. 'Have you ever seen such calligraphy? And the border work is a delight in itself.'

Genevieve nodded in agreement. On the table in front of her was the most astonishing book she had ever encountered outside a museum. It comprised page after page of exquisitely illuminated manuscript and it took her breath away. What was even more remarkable was that it was J. P. Morgan who was showing it to her. A man best known as a merciless robber baron was displaying quite another side to his character. And though he was customarily laconic in company he was now talking volubly to Genevieve.

'Unfortunately,' he went on, 'the poor Due d'Alengon did not have time to enjoy looking at his Book of Hours.'

'Why not?'

'He was killed at the battle of Agincourt.'

'One of England's great victories.'

'Are you familiar with Shakespeare's *Henry V*?'

'We read it when I was at school,' said Genevieve.

'In the scene where they list the French casualties, you'll find the Due d'Alengon's name mentioned.'

It was another revelation for Genevieve. She had discovered that Morgan was an educated man who spoke French and who had a wide knowledge of European culture. Displayed around the room were other items he had bought on his trip – assorted paintings, some bronze statuettes, Dutch porcelain, jewellery fashioned by German masters, and three French Empire clocks in perfect working order. While drinking their champagne, the twenty or so guests were able to admire the purchases at leisure. Genevieve had soon detached herself from Jonathan Killick and he was paying his attentions to some of the many young women there. One them eased herself forward.

Dominique Cadine was wearing a turquoise evening dress that spilt off her shoulders and clung to her body before spreading out into a bell-like shape around her ankles. Hanging loose, her hair trailed down her back and shimmered in the light.

'I came to thank you for inviting me, Mr Morgan,' she purred.

He stared at her. 'And you are?'

'Dominique Cadine.'

'*Enchanté, mademoiselle.*'

'*Merci beaucoup, monsieur.*'

Dominique introduced herself to Genevieve, who realised how accurate Dillman's description of the model had been. Even in repose, there was an unquenchable vitality about her. The strange thing was that Morgan did not seem to respond to it. When the newcomer tried to initiate conversation, it was Genevieve who replied. Morgan lapsed back into a watchful silence and gave the occasional grunt. Dominique soon drifted away to look at the paintings.

'What an interesting young lady!' Genevieve remarked.

'Yes,' said Morgan. 'So quintessentially French.'

'Is that good or bad?'

'Good, Miss Masefield. Very good.'

'I noticed her last night at dinner.'

'So did every man in the room, I daresay. Do you speak French?'

'To some degree.'

'In my study back home,' he said, 'I have a motto written in blue Provencal script on white enamel. *Pense moult. Parle peu. Écris rien.* Do you know what it stands for?'

'I believe so,' replied Genevieve, translating for him. 'Think a lot. Speak little. Write nothing.'

'It's sage advice.'

'Why must you write nothing?'

'It commits you and it puts you at the risk of indiscretions.'

'Only if something of yours falls into the wrong hands.'

'I believe in safety,' he told her. *Écris rien.*

Genevieve seized her cue. 'If you believe in safety,' she asked with a gesture that took in the whole room, 'why have you got these treasures here? Shouldn't they be locked securely away?'

'They are,' said Howard Riedel, materializing at her elbow. 'They're under my protection.'

Morgan introduced him to Genevieve and she understood why the man had not endeared himself to Dillman. Even in evening wear, Riedel looked like a New York policeman on patrol. She noticed a bulge under his coat and wondered if he was carrying a firearm.

'This room is a real temptation for any thief,' said Genevieve.

'Not as long as I'm here,' insisted Riedel.

'What happens when your back is turned?'

'It never is.'

'Do you stay here all the time?'

'I have a cabin right next door.'

'Then what is to stop someone coming in here at night?'

'Nobody would be suicidal enough to steal from me,' said Morgan, crisply. 'They would not only have to reckon with Howard. They'd never stand a chance of getting any of these items off the ship in New York. There's nowhere to hide on the *Oceanic* and nowhere to run. We'd soon hunt down the thief. Look through the porthole, Miss Masefield,' he advised. 'This vessel is surrounded by thousands of miles of ocean and that's the best security of all.'

* * *

Abednego Thomas's reputation did not frighten everyone away. When he chose a table for six in the dining room that evening, the two empty seats were immediately taken. Declaring themselves to be admirers of his work, Vane and Florence Stiller explained that they had seen some of his paintings in a London gallery. The sisters hailed from Chicago and worked as journalists on the same society magazine. They were alert, talkative, well-informed, middle-aged ladies whose interest in Thomas and his paintings stopped only just short of adulation.

'But would you hang one of my pictures on your wall?' he asked, sounding a note of challenge.

'Without hesitation,' said Florence, the older of the sisters. 'If we could afford to buy one, that is. You've grown too expensive, Mr Thomas.'

'That's my tragedy, ladies. I paint for the masses but it's only the elite who have the money to buy me. But I can warmly recommend my wife's work,' he continued, holding Veronica's hand. 'She is the best artist to come out of England since Joseph Mallord William Turner. Indeed, when I first saw her paintings, I thought that Turner had come back to life in the shape of an adorable woman. Buy her now before the prices shoot up out of reach.'

The women made pleasant inquiries about Veronica's work but it was clear that their real curiosity was reserved for her husband. Vane Stiller was thin and angular while her sister was short and stout. There was little physical resemblance between them, but their voices were almost interchangeable. Dillman was happy to let them monopolise the Welshman and his wife. It left him free to talk to Dominique Cadine.

'I hear that you met Mr Morgan this evening,' he began.

'That's right, George. I went for drinks in his cabin.'

'Alone – and without an invitation?'

Dominique giggled. 'I usually find that people let me into a party,' she said. 'And I wanted to meet the famous J. P. Morgan.'

'Did you enjoy the experience?'

'Not really. He had very little to say to me. His face is so ugly. If he has so much money, why does he not pay a doctor to do something about his nose? It is like a big tomato.'

'Who else was at the party?'

'Lots of people. One of them was not very nice.'

'Oh?'

'His name was Riedel and he kept watching us as if we were going to steal something. I felt him breathing down my neck all the time.'

'Perhaps he just took an interest in you.'

'Someone else did that, George. This Englishman, he wanted to know all about me. His name was Jonathan but he told me to call him Johnny.'

'The Honourable Jonathan Killick?' said Dillman, who had heard Genevieve speak of him. 'I'm told he's very attentive to women.'

She laughed. 'He was, George. He is a roué. He followed me around wherever I went. Johnny tried to impress me by saying he was an aristocrat. Me – a Frenchwoman,' she said, tapping her chest. 'I told him that we send our aristocrats to the guillotine.'

'Did that dampen his ardour?'

'No, he will come back.'

'How do you know that, Dominique?'

'Men like him always do.'

'You've obviously met his type before.'

'Many, many times,' she said wearily. 'The person I felt sorry for was his girlfriend.'

'Girlfriend?'

'Yes,' she replied. 'Johnny arrived with this lovely English lady but he forgot about her when he saw me. You do not take someone to a party like that and then walk away from them.'

'Who was this young lady?'

'The one with Mr Morgan.'

Dominique pointed to a table in the corner where J. P. Morgan was dining with his entourage. When each new course arrived, he and his guests were always the first to be served. Morgan was at one end of the table and Howard Riedel at the other. Of the ten people seated there, six were women and Morgan had taken care to place the two youngest and most attractive ladies on either side of him.

'Which one, Dominique?' he asked.

'On the right. Next to Mr Morgan.'

Dillman gaped. '*That* was Johnny's girlfriend?'

'Well, she came to the party on his arm.'

He could not have been more astonished. It was someone who had earlier expressed a profound dislike of the Honourable Jonathan Killick. The woman he was looking at was Genevieve Masefield.

Blanche Charlbury was also keeping the table under close surveillance. Turning to her fiancé, she pouted resentfully.

'It's not fair,' she protested. 'Mr Morgan has stolen her away.'

'Miss Masefield doesn't have to dine with us every evening.'

'Yes, she does. Genevieve is *mine*.'

'Don't be so possessive.'

'She's a friend, Mark. I want to spend time with her.'

'I thought that the object of this voyage was to spend time with me,' said Bossingham, peevishly. 'I didn't anticipate that I'd have to share you with an interloper.'

'Genevieve is not an interloper.'

'She's beginning to feel like one, Blanche.'

They were sharing a table with six other people and, after exchanging pleasantries with them, they were left largely to their own devices. That suited Mark Bossingham. He was never relaxed with strangers and wanted the opportunity to control his fiancée's behaviour in public. He had warned her to be less impulsive and was relieved when he saw that Genevieve would not join them that evening. The problem was that Blanche kept staring at Morgan and his guests.

'Johnny is to blame for this,' she decided.

'How do you know?'

'He told me that he'd somehow get Genevieve to dine with J. P. Morgan this evening. I didn't believe him because he's always so full of idle boasts. But against all the odds, he's done it.'

'I told you not to speak to Killick.'

'That's easier said than done.'

'You know how much I detest the man.'

'Only because I went to a ball with him once.'

'Please,' he said with suppressed anger. 'That's something I wish to remain firmly in the past.'

'I can't pretend that it never happened, Mark.'

'You must. You've started a new chapter of your life now.'

'A new and better life,' she said, touching his arm. He gave a rare smile. She leant over to him. 'Shall I let you into a secret?'

'If you wish.'

'When we're alone like this – travelling together at last – I feel that I'm married to you already. Do you feel that?'

'Frankly, no.'

'Mark!'

'We must observe the proprieties.'

'Proprieties!' she echoed.

'They are important.'

'You know, there are times when I think that Johnny was right. You can sound very pompous.'

'I'll thank you to keep Killick's name out of the conversation.'

'See? You're doing it again?'

'Blanche!' he said in annoyance. 'For heaven's sake.'

Their neighbours at the table drew them into the general discussion and it was ten minutes before they were able to talk to each other again. Blanche's gaze went straight back to Genevieve Masefield.

'Oh, I do envy her – getting to hobnob with Mr Morgan.'

'Perhaps you should ask yourself how she came to do it.'

'I told you – it was with Johnny's help. He's at the table as well.'

'That's beside the point.'

'Is it?'

'Yes, Blanche.' He spooned some of the dessert into his mouth and swallowed it before speaking again. 'Listen, I know that you've been taken in by Miss Masefield. . . .'

'Genevieve,' she corrected. 'Her name is Genevieve.'

'I prefer to remain on more formal terms with her.'

'And I wasn't taken in. I *like* Genevieve.'

'That's because she's very plausible and you're rather naive.'

'Mark!' she exclaimed.

'Well, how much do you really know about her?'

'Lots. We talked together all the way to Cherbourg.'

'And I daresay that you did most of the talking,' he said, 'and told her things about us that I would have preferred to remain confidential. I suspect that she gave away very little about herself.'

'That's not true at all. Genevieve was very open with me.'

'Why is she sailing to America?'

'To visit friends in New York.'

'What sorts of friends?'

'Family friends, that's all.'

'Did she give you their names,' he pressed, 'tell you where they lived, or what they did? Did you get any details from her?'

'No,' she admitted, 'but it's not the first time she's crossed the Atlantic. At one point, she told me, she even considered emigrating.'

'Why?'

'Because she thought America exciting and full of opportunities.'

He was cynical. 'I'm sure that it is for a woman like her.'

'A woman like what?'

'Oh, come off it, Blanche,' he said irritably. 'Stand back and look at her properly for a moment. Why is Miss Masefield travelling alone?'

'Because she's single.'

'And how many other young, attractive, unattached women are on this ship without a companion or a chaperone? Precious few, I think. It's no accident that Killick headed straight for her.'

'Johnny always pursues beautiful women.'

'Beautiful, *available* women.'

'Genevieve is not available in the sense you mean,' she said hotly, 'and it's ungentlemanly of you even to suggest it. She doesn't like Johnny. You saw how cool she was towards him when he introduced himself at dinner last night.'

'Then why is she sitting at the same table as him?'

'She's there as Mr Morgan's guest.'

'Only because Killick arranged it somehow. He always did have such infernally good connections. Look at her,' he went on, drawing her attention to the table in the corner. 'She's completely at ease.'

'That's because Genevieve is so sophisticated.'

'I can think of another word for it.'

'Mark – why are you being so beastly?'

'I'm only trying to protect you.'

'From what? Enjoying the friendship of nice women?'

'No,' he stressed. 'From being too ready to accept people into your circle when you know so little about them. You're too trusting, Blanche, too uncritical and accommodating.'

She was wounded. 'You've never spoken like this to me before,' she said, tears forming in her eyes. 'I don't mean to upset you, Mark, I really don't. I know I can be unguarded at times, but you used to find that rather appealing when we first met. I want to be a good wife to you. I can learn to be better, I promise you.'

'Let's not talk about that now,' he said, unwilling to discuss their relationship in public and sorry that he had hurt her. 'I shouldn't have criticised you like that, Blanche. Your faults – such as they are – pale into insignificance beside your many virtues.' She gave a brave smile. 'Why don't we forget this conversation and simply enjoy the sorbet?'

'So you're not cross with me anymore?'

'How could I be? You're very special to me.'

'I hate it when we have an argument.'

'Then let's put it all behind us.'

Blanche nodded then took a handkerchief from her purse and dabbed at her eyes. She picked up her glass and took a sip of wine.

'Can't I speak to Genevieve again?' she asked meekly.

'Nobody is stopping you.'

'I had no idea you disapproved of her so much.'

'It's not disapproval. I just have certain reservations.'

'I don't see why.'

'It's quite simple,' he said. 'In my job, I never take people at face value. I always probe beneath the surface. I wonder what they're really thinking behind the bland smile.' He looked across at Genevieve. 'I fancy that there's something about Miss Masefield that isn't quite right.'

'I never noticed it.'

'You wouldn't, you dear thing.'

'What exactly is wrong with her?'

'I think that she's too good to be true.'

Hilda Fanant also had doubts about Genevieve Masefield but they were of a very different kind. When she saw Genevieve leaving the dining room, she got up and followed her out, anxious to comer her.

'Excuse me,' said Mrs Fanant. 'I'd like a word with you.'

Genevieve turned to her. 'Yes, of course.'

'Have you recovered those earrings of mine yet?'

'No, Mrs Fanant. Unfortunately, I haven't.'

'Then why aren't you out looking for them?'

'I've made inquiries throughout the day.'

'What sorts of inquiries?'

'I've spoken to all the people whose names you gave me, and I went back to the cloakroom where the earrings were stolen. I'm slowly building up a more complete picture. I'll track down the thief, Mrs Farrant.'

'How can you do that if you spend your time carousing with your friends? I watched you in there this evening. You were enjoying a party.'

'I have to eat,' said Genevieve reasonably.

'Not when you have important work to do.'

Hilda Farrant was a tall, pug-faced, full-bodied woman in her sixties with a fondness for having her own way. The widow of a wealthy entrepreneur, she had ruled the roost over a house that had eight servants, and she was used to instant obedience. In the eyes of the older woman, Genevieve was no more than a menial at her command and was treated accordingly.

'Have you spoken to the girl?' she demanded.

'What girl?'

'That lazy stewardess. I still think she may be involved.'

'I refuse to believe that,' said Genevieve firmly. 'Edith Hurst is a dedicated young woman. She's responsible for my cabin as well and I have nothing but praise for her.'

'Then she is giving you a better level of service than I get.'

'I beg leave to doubt that.'

'She's the obvious culprit,' argued Mrs Farrant. 'She has access to my cabin and knew that I possessed those earrings.'

'Everyone who saw you wearing them knew that you possessed them. From what you tell me, they were very eyecatching.'

'Pendant earrings, encrusted with diamonds, set in platinum.'

'The thief would have taken note of that.'

'They were a present from my late husband on our last anniversary together. Not that we knew it was the last one at the time, of course,' she said, bitterly. 'That being the case, Miss Masefield, you can understand why they have enormous sentimental value for me.'

'Naturally.'

'Then please find them.'

'I'll make every effort to do so, Mrs Farrant.'

'When you're not wining, dining, and making merry.' Genevieve bit back a reply. There was no point in telling Hilda Farrant that she had deliberately left the table early so that she was not distracted any longer from her duties. Rosalie Boyd had been frustrating to deal with but – as a supposed victim of theft – she was far more amenable than the angry old woman who now confronted Genevieve. Nothing short of the immediate return of her property would appease Mrs Farrant. Even then she would show no gratitude. She would simply complain that it had taken too long. Genevieve went on the attack.

'You must accept some responsibility,' she said politely.

Mrs Farrant glared. 'Surely you're not blaming me?'

'You did leave the earrings unattended in the cloakroom.'

'Only for a very short time.'

'It was the work of a second for someone to take them from your purse,' Genevieve pointed out. 'It was an opportunist crime committed by someone who followed you into the cloakroom. I'm afraid that we're dealing with a professional thief here.'

'One never expects a woman to do such a dreadful thing,' said Mrs Farrant indignantly. 'Especially in first class.'

'That's exactly the place where someone is likely to operate.'

'Then why didn't she steal my purse as well?'

'Because you would have raised the alarm immediately,' said Genevieve, 'and she wished to buy a few precious seconds to escape. As it was, she could count on you washing your hands and drying them before you went to put your earrings back on.'

'There's no need to discuss my movements in the cloakroom.'

'The thief was relying on them, Mrs Farrant. The other reason that she left the purse is that it would be difficult to smuggle out. The earrings could be hidden in a pocket or the palm of her hand. In fact—'

'I don't wish to know *how* it was done,' said the other, cutting Genevieve off. 'I just want her arrested as soon as possible so that I can have my property back. Now – what assurances can you give me?'

'I'm fairly certain that your earrings will be found.'

'Only *fairly* certain?'

'I've never failed to recover stolen jewellery yet, Mrs Farrant.'

'Well, this had better not be the first time that you do,' said the older woman, spitefully. 'Or I shall take up the matter with the captain.'

'There's no need for him to be involved in this.'

'Oh yes, there is, Miss Masefield. I abhor incompetence.'

'I've followed all the usual procedures.'

'Without any visible sign of progress. I suggest that you search harder,' warned Mrs Farrant. 'If those earrings are not found soon, you will be looking for a new job.'

She waddled off towards a companionway and left Genevieve smarting with exasperation. Part of her felt that the woman deserved to lose her earrings but she knew, in her heart, that that was an emotional reaction. Whatever was taken – and from whomever it was stolen – it was her job as a ship's detective to solve the crime and recover the missing items. As she went off to her cabin, she reminded herself that Hilda Farrant was one of the passengers who, indirectly, helped to pay her wages. The older woman had to be treated with respect and swiftly reunited with her beloved earrings.

It was a long walk to her cabin but she was so preoccupied that she seemed to reach it in a split-second. She was still reviewing the uncomfortable conversation with Hilda Farrant when she came round a corner and saw someone lounging against the wall outside her cabin. The sight brought her to an abrupt halt.

'You didn't think that you could escape me *that* easily, did you?'

The Honourable Jonathan Killick flashed his brightest smile.

George Porter Dillman was still engaged in a watching role, using his friendship with Abednego Thomas, his wife, and his model as a convenient camouflage. Having chosen a seat from which he could keep the whole room under casual observation, he took note of social groupings that had been formed, and of the comings and goings of various individuals. It was the second evening afloat and patterns were being established that would continue all the way to New York.

The first person to leave his table was Dominique Cadine, pleading a headache and needing to take some tablets that were in her cabin. She promised to return soon. Veronica adjourned to the cloakroom, leaving her husband to the tender mercies of Vane and Florence Stiller, whose interest in the artist was inexhaustible. He basked in their admiration and flirted with both of them.

'Have you any objection to appearing in the magazine?' asked Vane, hopefully. 'I feel that we have enough material for a dozen articles about the artistic life.'

'I would appear *anywhere* with you, dear lady,' he said.

'Oh, Mr Thomas!'

'And the same goes for your sister.' He beamed at Florence. 'You are both equally captivating.'

'Thank you,' said Florence with a laugh of delight. 'Would you consent to being photographed with us?'

'I would insist on it.'

'It will make such a difference to the article.'

'Yes,' said Vane. 'Our readers would love to see a picture of you.'

'Clothed or in the nude?'

The sisters laughed in unison. Dillman suspected that they would dine out for many months on stories of how they met and interviewed one of the most notorious reprobates in the art world. It was time for the detective to excuse himself so that he could patrol the corridors. Dillman rose from his seat.

'Are you leaving us already?' said Thomas.

'Yes, I promised to meet someone, Abednego.'

'Who is the lucky lady?'

'That would be telling,' said Dillman, discreetly. He looked down at Vane and Florence Stiller. 'It was a pleasure meeting you both.'

They bade him farewell then switched their attention straight back to Thomas, hoping for more vicarious thrills as he talked about the artistic life of Paris. Dillman, meanwhile, slipped out of the room and began his rounds. Most of the passengers had gone to the lounge so the corridors were relatively deserted and it was some time before he actually saw anyone else. When he did, it was not a passenger at all. It was a steward and he was behaving strangely, peering through the keyhole of a cabin. The man straightened up quickly as Dillman approached and gave him a nervous smile.

'Good evening, sir,' he said.

'Hello, Manny. Forgotten your master key?'

'Oh, I'm not responsible for these cabins, sir. They're on Sid's list.'

'Would that be Sidney Browne, by any chance?'

'Yes,' said Ellway in surprise. 'How did you know his name?'

'Because you mentioned it once before.'

'What a memory!'

'He's looking after Mr Morgan's stateroom, isn't he?'

'That's right, sir – at the other end of the corridor. Sid was in there earlier on, cleaning up after a drinks party.'

'Alone?'

'Oh no,' said Ellway, 'there was this man who stood over him and told him to hurry up. I don't think Sid's allowed in there on his own with all that valuable stuff hanging about. Riedel,' he remembered, pursing his lips. 'He was the man who kept an eye on Sid – a Mr Riedel.'

Dillman gave no indication that he had met the fellow himself. What interested him was why Ellway, who had always seemed so honest and straightforward, had been peering into a cabin. The steward seemed to read his mind. He gave a shrug.

'It's unoccupied, sir,' he explained. 'I just wanted to see what it was like, that's all.'

'Sidney Browne must have a master key to it, surely.'

'Yes, sir, but I wouldn't dare to ask him for it. Sid's a stickler for the rules. He'd never let his own mother into a cabin where she was not entitled to be. I respect that.'

'Yet you couldn't resist a peep.'

'My first time on the *Oceanic*. I suppose I'm just curious.'

'What did you see in there?'

'Nothing in particular.'

'You won't be moving in, then?'

'Fat chance of that!'

'I'll leave you to it,' said Dillman, manufacturing a yawn. 'Sea air is so soporific. I think I'll turn in.'

'Good night, sir.'

'Good night, Manny.'

When Dillman continued on his way, he was both puzzled and disappointed. He could not understand why Ellway had deliberately lied to him. The steward went down in his estimation.

It took Genevieve Masefield a long time to get rid of him. Jonathan Killick was like a limpet, clinging to her by means of conversational tricks and using all his charm in an attempt to win her round.

'I took you to meet J.P. Morgan, didn't I?' he said.

'Yes,' she accepted, 'and I was grateful. Though if you'd asked me beforehand to go with you, I'd most certainly have refused.'

'Why? Do you think I have cloven feet and a forked tail?'

'Good night.'

'I'm sure that you'll learn to like me in time.'

'What I'd like at this moment is some privacy.'

'Then why don't you invite me into your cabin?'

'I think you'd better go, Mr Killick,' she said sharply.

'I told you. I'm Johnny to my friends.'

'Well, I'm not sure that I wish to be included among them.'

'At least call me Johnny.'

'No thank you.'

'J. P. Morgan has no objection to my friendship.'

'Then why don't you go and pester him instead?'

'I'm sorry,' he said, changing his tack and gesturing an apology. 'I had no idea that my affection was so misplaced. Do please forgive me.' He backed away. 'We'll have to start afresh in the morning. Good night.'

As soon as he had gone, Genevieve let herself into her cabin and locked the door, relieved that she had finally escaped him. Jonathan Killick had conceded defeat on this occasion but his withdrawal was only tactical. She knew that he would stalk her again. Putting her purse and stole aside, she sat in front of the mirror and began to remove the pins from her hair. When she heard a quiet tap on the cabin door, she tensed involuntarily, fearing that Killick was back. Then she recognised the signal that Dillman always gave when he came to see her.

Genevieve rushed to let him in then flung herself into his arms. Dillman kissed her. 'That's the kind of welcome I like,' he said.

'I'm so pleased to see you, George.'

'I thought you'd cast me aside for an English aristocrat.'

'That man is incorrigible.'

'Yet you let him take you to a party in Mr Morgan's stateroom.'

'I was tricked.'

They sat down and Genevieve explained how she had been invited and what had transpired when she got there. She had enjoyed Morgan's company and been given a privileged look at the various items that had been bought during the visit to Paris. Dillman was interested to hear her good opinion of Morgan and how cultured the man was. He was not at all surprised to learn that she had found Howard Riedel both offensive and overbearing. It was something on which they could both agree.

'What was the most valuable item?' asked Dillman.

'The Book of Hours. That's Mr Morgan's pride and joy.'

'It also appealed to his commercial sense, Genevieve.'

'In what way?'

'The Revenue Act of 1897 imposed a twenty percent tariff on imported works of art,' he told her. 'It's the reason that Mr Morgan leaves most of his paintings with galleries and museums in England so that he can escape paying import duty.'

'And the Book of Hours?'

'No charge on that – books are exempt.'

'He paid hundreds of thousands of dollars for it.'

'Then you can appreciate why he employs Howard Riedel to look after it. I found the man obnoxious but he's an effective guard dog. Nobody would venture anywhere near that book while Riedel is about.'

The first item to be placed in the bag was the Book of Hours. The man worked swiftly, choosing the other items he wanted and wrapping them with care before stowing them away in his bag. When he had finished, he switched off the light, stepped over the dead body of Howard Riedel, and let himself out. It was all done in a matter of minutes.

SIX

'When was the body discovered?' asked George Dillman.

'Shortly after midnight.'

'By whom?'

'Mr Morgan.'

'Was he on his own?'

'Yes,' said Lester Hembrow.

'Where is he now?'

'I've put him in Mr Riedel's cabin for the time being.'

'What was the cause of death?'

'Someone cut his throat.'

'Have you called the doctor?'

'He's examining the body now.'

'Let's get over there.'

Dillman was on the point of undressing when the summons

came. The urgency of the knock on his door told him that something serious had happened and the look on the face of the normally unperturbed Lester Hembrow confirmed it. The purser was ashen, his eyes staring, his forehead lined with concern. As they set off down the corridor, there was a tremble in his voice.

'Of all the people for this to happen to,' he said with a sigh. 'Riedel is an unlikely victim, I grant you.'

'I didn't mean that, George. The one person on this ship we've gone out of our way to treat like royalty is J. P. Morgan and his right-hand man gets murdered under our noses. It couldn't be any worse.'

'Yes, it could.'

'How?'

'Mr Morgan might have been the victim.'

'You're right,' said Hembrow after a moment's consideration.

'That would have been a copper-bottomed calamity. The repercussions would have been unthinkable. We'd be on the front pages of every newspaper in the world.'

'How has Mr Morgan taken it?'

'He's icily calm.'

'Where had he been until midnight?'

'In the lounge with friends.'

When they got to the scene of the crime, Hembrow used a master key to open the door and they stepped into the stateroom. It was divided into three sections – a bedroom, a bathroom, and a large area where passengers could relax in comfort or dine in private. Howard Riedel was lying on his back beside the table, an ugly gash across his throat, his wing collar, white tie, and dress shirt soaked with blood. Dr. Francis Garfield was kneeling beside him. He looked up at the newcomers. The purser introduced

Dillman, who exchanged a nod with the doctor.

'Throat slit from ear to ear,' noted Dillman, crouching down.

'That's right,' replied Garfield.

'Then his killer must have been a strong man.'

'Not necessarily.'

'Mr Riedel kept himself fit. I saw evidence of that myself.' He glanced around. 'He would have put up a fight against any assailant yet there are no signs of a tussle.'

'I know.'

'Then how was he overpowered?'

'I think he was drugged, Mr Dillman.'

'Drugged?'

'He might even have been asleep when he was murdered.'

The doctor got to his feet. He was a slim, wiry man in his forties with horn-rimmed eyeglasses. He spoke with a strong West Country accent. While Dillman carried out his own inspection of the corpse, Hembrow watched him. Garfield ran a worried hand over his bald pate.

'You don't expect this kind of thing on the White Star Line,' he said anxiously. 'I've had deaths before but always from natural causes. A murder introduces all sorts of complications.' Hembrow gave a nod. 'I shudder to think what they are.'

'I'm not really qualified to perform an autopsy.'

'I don't think you'll need to, Dr. Garfield,' said Dillman, getting up to stand beside him. 'I think your initial diagnosis may be correct. Mr Riedel was not the sort of man to be taken unawares. If he put up no resistance, he must have been drugged. There's a smell of whiskey on him,' he added. 'Is there a bottle in here anywhere?'

'No,' said Hembrow, looking around the room.

'Then it must be in his cabin.'

'Oh no!'

'You'd better get in there before Mr Morgan takes a sip of it to steady himself.' The purser moved to the door. 'And you might ask him to make a list of everything that was stolen.'

'He's already doing that.'

Hembrow went out and Dillman gazed down at the body. He had disliked Howard Riedel but he was deeply sorry that the man had been murdered. It told him that they were dealing with a ruthless criminal. If Riedel had been drugged, there would have been no need to kill him. The thief could have taken what he wanted while J. P. Morgan's bodyguard slept peacefully on the floor. It was a gratuitous act of violence.

Dillman searched the room for any clues that might have been left behind. He noticed that three of the paintings had been removed from their frames. No murder weapon was found.

'Have you been in this situation before?' asked Garfield.

'Unfortunately, I have.'

'What do we do next?'

'Make sure as few people as possible know about this.'

'We can hardly conceal it, Mr Dillman.'

'We'll have to somehow,' said the detective. 'If word of a murder gets out, it will spread panic throughout the ship. That will be bad for everyone and will only serve to hinder our investigation.' 'News is bound to seep out somehow.'

'Not if we're careful. The first thing we must do is to move the body to a place of safety where it can be kept on ice. Apart from his employer, Mr Riedel had no friends aboard so he's not going to be missed.'

'What about his steward?'

'Leave him to me. I'll find a way of hiding the truth from him.'

'Is there anything I can do to help?'

'Look for a place where we can keep the body.'

'He obviously can't stay here,' said Garfield. 'Nor can Mr Morgan, for that matter. You can't expect any passenger to sleep in a cabin where a murder has taken place.'

'I wonder.'

'What do you mean?'

'J.P. Morgan is a remarkable man,' said Dillman. 'Don't underestimate him. A lot of business rivals made that mistake and they paid a heavy price.'

When he searched the adjoining cabin, the purser could see no sign of a bottle of whiskey or of any other spirits. J.P. Morgan had clearly drunk nothing since he had been in the room. He was seated at a small table, smoking a cigar and making notes on a piece of headed stationery. He looked tired but composed.

'I wonder if I might ask you a question,' said Hembrow.

'I guess you'll be asking quite a lot.'

'No, sir. I'll leave that to the ship's detective. He's far more experienced at this kind of thing.'

'You mean, he's used to finding murder victims aboard ships?'

'Not exactly, Mr Morgan, but this is not the first unnatural death he's had to deal with. What I wanted to know was this – was Mr Riedel a drinking man?'

'Show me a policeman who isn't.'

'Good point.'

'Howard spent most of his working life with the New York Police Department. It's a tough job. You need something to keep you going.'

Hembrow looked round. 'I don't see any alcohol.'

'He usually kept a bottle of whiskey at hand.'

'It's not here now. Did he drink much over dinner?'

'No,' said Morgan. 'He wasn't partial to wine and he didn't touch the champagne when we had a party before dinner in my stateroom. What he did like was a glass or two of malt whiskey last thing at night. Nothing wrong in that. Why do you ask?'

'The doctor thinks he may have been drugged.'

Morgan blinked. 'Someone spiked his whiskey?'

'Or some other drink.'

'They knocked the poor man out then killed him?'

'It's a strong possibility,' said Hembrow. 'It also looks as if someone deliberately took the bottle away. There's a glass beside the washbasin that smells of whiskey but that's all.'

'How did anyone get in here to do such a thing?'

'That's what we'll have to find out, Mr Morgan.'

'I want answers and I want them quick.'

'Of course.'

'I've not only lost the services of a good man,' said Morgan, eyes blazing with anger, 'I've also had some highly valuable items stolen from my quarters – items that are quite irreplaceable. What sort of a ship are you running here, Mr Hembrow?'

'I'm deeply sorry that this has happened.'

'So you should be.'

'I'm as upset as you are.'

'I very much doubt that.'

'We'll do our utmost to retrieve everything you've lost.' Morgan was sardonic. 'Does that include Howard Riedel?' There was a tap on the door and the purser opened it to admit Dillman. He was introduced as the ship's detective to Morgan but the latter offered no handshake. Hembrow explained that he had been unable to find any whiskey in the cabin.

'The killer was a tidy man,' said Dillman. 'After he committed his crime, he cleaned up carefully and left us no obvious clues.'

'Has the doctor finished in there?'

'Yes. I impressed upon him the need to keep this as secret as we possibly can. If a murder becomes common report, everyone will spend the rest of the voyage looking nervously over their shoulders.' He glanced at the financier. 'And I daresay that Mr Morgan would prefer it if we kept the facts hidden for the time being.'

'Yes,' agreed Morgan. 'There are journalists aboard. If this leaks out, they'll be after me like a pack of hounds. I'm all in favour of publicity but not this kind.'

'The body needs to be moved,' said Dillman. 'Dr. Garfield knows a place where we can store it safely but he'll need a hand to get it there.'

'I'll take care of that,' volunteered Hembrow.

'The chief steward will need to be informed – the captain, too, of course – but that's as far as it goes. We'll invent a cover story to explain Mr Riedel's absence to his steward.'

'Thank you, George. I'll go and help the doctor.'

The purser went out and Dillman was able to look at J. P. Morgan properly for the first time. In spite of his age, and the fact that he was seated, he was a commanding presence in a small cabin. Wreathed in pungent cigar smoke, he glowered at the detective.

'You've done this before, I hear.'

'Yes, Mr Morgan.'

'Did you catch the killer?'

'Eventually, sir – in every case.'

Morgan was curious. 'There's been more than one murder?' 'I had similar problems when I worked for Cunard and for P&O.'

'In other words, murder follows you around.'

'I happened to be in the wrong place at the wrong time.'

'So did Howard Riedel.'

Dillman took out a notebook and pencil then sat on a chair. He checked the brief details he had already jotted down then looked across at Morgan, who stubbed out his cigar in the ashtray. The older man took out a large white handkerchief and blew his nose. It looked more inflamed than ever.

'I need to go over Mr Riedel's movements this evening,' said Dillman, pencil poised. 'I gather that you had a champagne reception in your stateroom before dinner.'

'True.'

'At which, presumably, Mr Riedel was present.'

'True.'

'I'll need the names of all your guests, Mr Morgan.'

'Why?'

'Because one of those people may be involved in some way,' reasoned Dillman. 'My understanding is that you had a collection of art treasures on display. A thief would have had a perfect opportunity to see what there was and exactly where it was kept.'

'There were no thieves there, Mr Dillman.'

'Nevertheless, I would like that list, please.'

There was a long pause. 'You'll get it,' said Morgan.

'When the party was over,' resumed Dillman, 'you and some of your guests came into the first-class dining room. I saw you take a table in the comer. Mr Riedel was not with you at that point.'

'No,' said Morgan gruffly. 'Howard stayed behind to supervise the steward who came in to clear away all the glasses and so on.

The man was never allowed in there on his own. Howard knew how long it had taken me to track down some of those items, and how dear to my heart they were. He sat over them like a mother hen.'

'Is that why he kept leaving the table during the meal?'

'You're very observant, Mr Dillman.'

'Every half an hour, he got up and went out. I timed him.'

'He slipped back to check that the collection was safe and that everything was in order. Howard was a creature of habit.'

'Former policemen often are. It may have been his downfall.'

'Why?'

'Because the killer might have been aware of his routine as well. Mr Riedel made regular visits to your stateroom throughout the evening and then, at ten o'clock, he quit your table for good.'

'He went to stand guard over my collection until I got back myself.'

'Would he have come in here first?'

'Certainly. Howard never missed his glass of whiskey.'

'Someone else realised that.'

'I don't see how,' said Morgan, getting to his feet. 'We've only been on the ship for two days. Last night, I dined in my cabin. How could anybody have known Howard's routine when he didn't go through it until this evening? It's impossible.'

'On this voyage, perhaps,' said Dillman, 'but not on the one to Europe. Were you travelling with anything of value on that occasion?'

'I was, as it happens.'

'Now we're getting somewhere.'

'A few paintings that I was going to loan to a French gallery.'

'And you kept them in your cabin?'

'Of course. Great art is there to be seen.'

'I suspect that you and Mr Riedel were also seen,' said Dillman, 'and your routine studied carefully. The killer then bided his time until you sailed back to New York.'

'You think someone would go to all that trouble?'

'If the stakes were high enough and they clearly are.'

'It doesn't make sense, Mr Dillman,' said Morgan, weighing up the evidence. 'The paintings I took to Paris were very valuable. Why didn't the thief make any attempt to steal those?'

'Because he knew he'd have a far bigger haul when you'd been on your buying expedition. In any case, I don't think his chief interest is in paintings. There were seven altogether in your stateroom and he only took three of them.'

'Leaving the frames behind.'

'It's so much easier to smuggle a canvas out on its own.'

'None of my property will leave this ship,' asserted Morgan, bunching his fists. 'I'll have the luggage of every first-class passenger searched before they're allowed to disembark.'

'That would be a lengthy and disruptive exercise, Mr Morgan, and there's no guarantee that it would work.'

'It's bound to work, man!'

'Not if the killer has a confederate in second class to whom he's passed on his loot. It could be taken ashore with impunity then.'

'We search every second-class passenger as well.'

'There are nearly three hundred of them,' Dillman pointed out, 'and over four hundred in first class. It would take ages, cause great upset, and be a complete waste of time.'

'How do you know that?'

'Because a man who's capable of stealing your property will surely have worked out in advance how to get it off the vessel. This is no random crime, Mr Morgan. It was carefully planned over a period of time.'

'Are you telling me that well *never* catch the villain?'

'Not at all,' replied Dillman. 'Time is on our side and we know he's still on board. We'll find him by a process of elimination.'

'We?'

'I have a partner who'll help me with the investigation. By sheer coincidence, she was invited to drinks in your stateroom and joined you for dinner afterward.'

'A *female* detective?' Morgan was not impressed.

'An extremely good one, sir. We've solved many crimes together, including murders. I worked for the Pinkerton agency for some time and their female operatives were highly efficient. That's why I had no qualms whatsoever in choosing to work with a woman. I've complete confidence in Miss Masefield.' Morgan goggled. 'Miss Genevieve Masefield?'

'You showed her your Book of Hours.'

'I'd never have guessed that she was a detective.'

'That proves how clever she is at disguising her identity. We move unseen around the ship, gathering intelligence as we go. Anonymity is our major weapon.'

'Yes,' said Morgan, flopping into his seat. 'I can see that now.'

He needed a few minutes to collect his thoughts. Dillman waited patiently, making some notes as he did so. At length, Morgan snatched up the sheet of stationery and handed it over to him.

'This is a list of the items stolen,' he said.

'Thank you, sir.' Dillman studied it. 'You've given me their market value as well. That's very helpful. What I'm interested in, however, is the items that were *not* taken. Those paintings, for instance.'

'Renaissance masterpieces. They're so well known that they would be difficult to dispose of – unless the thief knew a private collector with more money than integrity.'

'What about the three that were taken?'

'French paintings. Minor works by major artists.'

'Worth less than the ones that were left behind?'

'Substantially less. The thief is no connoisseur.'

'He spurned your Dutch porcelain as well,' observed Dillman. 'I don't wish to be impertinent, sir, but none of this would have happened if your collection had been kept in one of our safes.'

'Don't you think I realize that?' said Morgan sorrowfully. 'Because of me, Howard Riedel lost his life. He died trying to protect my property. That will prey on my conscience for a long time. I want his killer brought to justice, Mr Dillman.' He gnashed his teeth. 'And I also want everything that was stolen returned to me in good condition.'

'Naturally.' Dillman closed his notebook. 'There is one immediate decision to be made, however.'

'What's that?'

'Where you'll spend the night, sir. This place is hardly convenient but there's an empty cabin at the end of the corridor. I'll ask the purser to open it up and you could move in there temporarily.'

'Why can't I go back to my own bed?'

'Do you want to?'

'Howard's body is being moved, isn't it?' said Morgan 'And he had the decency to bleed onto a red carpet so it doesn't show. I know that most people would run a mile at the thought of sleeping next door to a room where someone was murdered but I'm not so easily spooked.'

'You have strong nerves, Mr Morgan.'

'Essential in business.'

'And in my line,' said Dillman, crossing to the door. 'Let me check to see if they've cleared up in there then you can go back in – though I would recommend that you let me lock the remaining items of your collection away in the safe.'

'In the morning. I need them close to me tonight.'

'As you wish. We've gone as far we can now but I'll have to ask you some more questions tomorrow.'

'Let me ask one of my own, Mr Dillman. Your voice tells me that you hail from Boston. Am I right?'

'I was born and brought up there.'

'It's a city I know very well,' said Morgan. 'Are you, by any chance, related to an Alexander Dillman?'

'He was my father, sir. Built the best yachts in Massachusetts.'

'Yes, some years ago he tried to sell one of them to me but I didn't like the design one bit. I commissioned an Irish-born engineer, John Beavor-Webb, to build *Corsair II* instead. She was a beautiful steam yacht, over two hundred and forty feet in length and weighing five hundred and sixty tons. A joy to sail. Eight years later, the same designer built *Corsair III* for me.'

'I remember reading about the specifications,' recalled Dillman. 'She was over three hundred feet in length this time, stronger and faster but with the same gleaming black steel hull. She had a gilt clipper bow and a curved sheer, raked stack.' Morgan was stunned. 'How did you know all that?'

'My father always kept details of his rivals' work.'

'Did he ever build the yacht that he offered to me?'

'Oh yes, sir.'

'If I remember aright, she was called *Medusa*.'

'A fine vessel. I sailed on her myself.'

'Did she fulfil your expectations?'

'Not really.'

'I thought she wouldn't.'

'No,' said Dillman, enjoying the chance to praise his father's expertise. '*Medusa* only came second in the America's Cup.'

At a time when Genevieve Masefield needed to be on her own, she was assailed by company from all sides. Dillman had visited her cabin at the crack of dawn to tell her about the crimes that had been committed and to gather any relevant information that she could offer. Shaken by news of the death of Howard Riedel and shocked by the theft of precious items that she had actually been shown, Genevieve wanted to have breakfast alone so that she could devote all her attention to the startling developments. Instead, she was intercepted in a corridor by Edith Hurst, stopped by Hilda Farrant, who fired another broadside at her, and detained by a woman who had admired her evening gown and who asked where she had bought it.

When she finally reached the dining room, Genevieve was waylaid again. This time it was by a man in his early forties with long black hair that curled around his ears and was liberally salted with grey.

'Excuse me,' he said. 'May I speak to you a moment?'

'Yes, of course.'

'It's Miss Masefield, isn't it? My wife pointed you out to me. My name is Ethan Boyd. You spoke with Rosalie yesterday.'

'Ah, yes – the stolen purse.'

'The missing purse,' he corrected. 'I just wanted to apologise on my wife's behalf. She does tend to leave things in the oddest

108

places and then forget where they are. Rosalie is so sorry for taking up your time.'

'Not at all, Mr Boyd. That's what I'm here for.'

'It won't happen again.'

'From my point of view, a false alarm is the best kind. No crime was committed and the purse was returned to your wife.'

'I'll chain it to her wrist from now on.'

Ethan Boyd had a pleasant face and an engaging manner. He was smartly dressed in a dark brown suit. Genevieve had been to New York enough times to recognise a Brooklyn accent, though, in his case, it was much softer on the ear.

'On the trip to Europe,' he explained, 'Rosalie mislaid a pearl necklace and swore that she must have forgotten to bring it with us. When we packed our trunk to leave the ship, we found the necklace caught in the lining.'

'I'm glad that that little scare was also unfounded.'

'There won't be a third, I promise you.'

Boyd thanked her again then stepped aside so that she could enter the dining room. It was early and only a few tables were taken. It allowed Genevieve to choose one that was partly concealed by a potted palm. The waiter took her order then she was able to address her mind to the problems with which she and Dillman had been confronted. She could not believe that a man with whom she had dined less than twelve hours ago was now lying dead, or that J. P. Morgan's magnificent collection had been deprived of so many items. It was a crippling double blow. 'Good morning, Genevieve,' said Blanche Charlbury.

'What?'

'May I join you?'

'Yes, yes,' said Genevieve. 'Please do.'

'Thank you,' said Blanche, sitting beside her. She peered at her friend. 'I say, are you all right?'

'I'm fine. Why?'

'You were miles away when I came in. Something on your mind?'

'Nothing important,' said Genevieve, deciding to make the most of the situation. She contrived a smile. 'It's nice to see you again, Blanche. I'm sorry that I deserted you last night but that friend of yours got me invited to Mr Morgan's table.'

'He told me that he would. Johnny knows *everybody*.' Her eyes widened and she leant forward with her elbows on the table. 'Did he make any improper suggestions?'

'I prefer to draw a veil over that.'

'That means he did – trust Johnny!'

'I didn't realize how resourceful he could be.'

'Resourceful?'

'Cunning would be more accurate.'

'It's one of the reasons Mark hates him so much. There are lots of others.' She looked around to make sure that they were not overheard. 'Look, I hope you don't mind, but I may not be able to see as much of you as I'd like.'

'You want to be with your fiancé. That's perfectly understandable.'

'It's not only that.'

'You don't have to explain,' said Genevieve, grateful to be released from too close a friendship with Blanche. 'I've met lots of other people and I've got plenty of things to keep me amused.'

'You have such a gift for being at home wherever you are.'

'I do like the communal life of an ocean liner, I must admit.' Blanche studied her carefully, trying to align her fiancé's harsher comments about Genevieve with her own perceptions. She could detect none of the qualities that Bossingham had divined in the woman and preferred to rely on her own judgement. Genevieve was aware of her scrutiny.

'Why are you looking at me like that?' she asked.

'No reason.'

'Have I got a spot on my nose or something?'

'No,' said Blanche with a giggle. 'But, talking of noses, how ever did Mr Morgan come to have that purple onion in the middle of his face?'

'It's a condition he suffers from.'

'Is there no cure?'

'I wasn't foolish enough to ask him, Blanche, and I'd suggest that you don't do so either. Mr Morgan doesn't like personal questions.'

'What does he like?'

'Business deals and collecting art treasures.'

Blanche's eyes sparkled mischievously. 'According to Mark, he sometimes comes to Paris for another reason altogether. At least, that's the rumour.'

'Go on.'

'Mark loathes scandal. He refuses to talk about such things as a rule – especially with me – but I managed to get it out of him in the end.'

'Get what out?'

'It seems that Mr Morgan stays at the Hotel Bristol.'

'It's one of the best hotels in Paris.'

'Very close to the Vendome.'

'So?'

'Well,' continued Blanche, gabbling like a breathless schoolgirl, 'while Mr Morgan stays at one hotel, his mistress stays only a few doors away at the Vendome. He has a wife back in America but he takes someone else to Paris.'

'She obviously wasn't with him on this occasion.'

'How could she bear him, Genevieve? He's so repulsive.'

'Mr Morgan is a very cultured man. He speaks French, German, and has the most amazing knowledge of art and antiques.'

'Who wants to talk about art and antiques in the bedroom?'

Blanche gave a sudden laugh then blushed at her own boldness. She became contrite. 'Oh, do forgive me. I didn't mean to be indelicate.'

'I take your point nevertheless.'

'He's *old*, Genevieve. I don't care how rich he is.'

'You're far better off with Mark.'

'Yes,' said Blanche, dreamily. 'I wouldn't change him for the world. I know that he's reserved and conventional and wrapped up in his work, but he has so many good qualities. This is the first time we've been properly alone and I find it so exciting. I just wish that he did as well.'

'I'm sure that he's enjoying every moment, Blanche.'

'He just isn't very good at *showing* it.'

'Englishmen of that breed never are.'

'Things will be different when we're married,' said Blanche with more hope than confidence. 'Mark will be able to relax with me, then, and let me get really close to him.'

'I'm sure.'

'I love him so much.'

'Has he always been so undemonstrative?'

'Yes. I blame his time in the diplomatic service.'

'Why?'

'He has to wear a mask all the time and conceal his thoughts.

It's become second nature to him. The worrying thing is,' she confided, 'that I'm not entirely sure what's behind that mask.'

Lester Hembrow had recovered his habitual smile and good humour. Nobody would have guessed from his appearance that he was coping with a dire emergency. When Dillman called at his office that morning, the purser looked calm and in control.

'So far, so good,' he told the detective. 'The body is out of sight and Mr Morgan finally handed over what's left of his art treasures. They're locked up where no thief will be able to get at them.'

'Good. Did you follow my advice with regard to the steward?'

'Yes, we told him that Mr Riedel had been taken ill and was not to be disturbed. He seemed relieved to hear it. I don't think that Riedel was on the friendliest of terms with the fellow.'

'Browne. Sidney Browne.'

'Is that the steward's name?'

'Yes,' said Dillman. 'I feel sorry for any man who had to look after Mr Morgan and his henchman. They could both be very demanding.'

'One of them still is, George.'

'I'm on my way to see him now. I wanted to speak to you first.'

'You've told Genevieve, presumably.'

'The news dazed her. She was at the same table as the two men. She was also at the drinks party beforehand and was able to make some valuable comments about the other guests.'

'You still think one of them may be implicated?'

'It's something I have to consider. However,' Dillman went on, 'that's a matter for speculation. Let's stick to the facts, few and far between as they are. What do we know for certain?'

'That Mr Riedel was killed somewhere between ten o'clock and midnight. Dr. Garfield thought it was earlier rather than later.'

'So do I. The killer would have been afraid that Mr Morgan might return unexpectedly. He'd want to get everything over as quickly as possible. First of all, he drugged Howard Riedel.'

'That would mean he gained access to the man's cabin.'

'There are various ways he could have done that.'

'How could he be sure that Mr Riedel would drink that whiskey?'

'Because he knew him.'

'Knew him?'

'Yes, Lester.'

'You mean that they were acquaintances?'

'My guess is that they'd certainly met before,' said Dillman. 'We have to find a motive for the murder, you see. Why should anyone cut Riedel's throat when he could steal whatever he wanted from that collection and get away with it? There's only one answer.'

'Is there?'

'He *knew* the man. Knew him, studied him, and despised him enough to plot his death. Theft was only secondary. The main reason someone went there last night was to kill a hated enemy.' Dillman inhaled deeply. 'That's our motive, Lester – revenge.'

It was a clear, bright morning and, though the sea was choppy, the *Oceanic* seemed to glide through them without causing any discomfort to its passengers. Hundreds of people took the opportunity for a stroll in the sunshine or playing some of the many deck games that were available. Swathed in thick coats and wearing hats and scarves, some passengers preferred to sit and read. Almost everyone in steerage had come out into the fresh air, glad to escape the cramped conditions in which they were travelling. Their cabins were small, functional, and always shared. In a space the size of J. P. Morgan's stateroom, at least twenty steerage passengers would be sleeping.

Mark Bossingham had also ventured out on deck. Blanche Charlbury had an appointment with the hairdresser after breakfast so he was free to explore the ship alone for a couple of hours. He had not been pleased to find his fiancée at the same table as Genevieve Masefield earlier that morning, and he had gently chided her about it. It annoyed him that Blanche had seemed unrepentant, though she had promised to spend less time with Genevieve in future. Bossingham resolved to keep the two women apart as much as he could because he feared that Genevieve was a bad influence.

It worried him that his future wife still had such youthful impulses and he viewed the trip to New York as a time when he could mould her character into what he considered to be a more appropriate shape. If she were to move in diplomatic circles, Blanche would have to be discreet and circumspect. She had declared herself ready to learn and it was partly on that basis that he had asked for her hand in marriage. Bossingham loved her for her quiet beauty and for what he saw as her many sterling qualities. It was merely a question of easing her more fully into adulthood and he would have the perfect wife.

He was standing at the rail when a companion joined him.

'Good morning,' said Jonathan Killick affably.

'Oh, it's you.'

'What sort of a greeting is that?'

'It's the only one you'll get.'

'I thought you were supposed to be a diplomat.'

'Diplomacy would be wasted on you, Killick.'

'That's true,' said the other with a laugh. 'Where's Blanche?'

'In the hairdressing salon.'

'Let you off the leash, has she?'

'I was never *on* the leash,' said Bossingham with distaste. 'Not in the way that you imply.'

'No, you're too busy trying to keep Blanche tied down.'

'I refuse to discuss our relationship with you.'

'But I'm all in favour of it,' said Killick enthusiastically. 'I think that you're exactly the kind of man that Blanche should marry – safe, respectable, and unthreatening. I just wish that she'd spent a bit more time enjoying herself first.'

'With people like you, I suppose.'

'There *are* no people like me, Bossingham – I'm unique.'

'Uniquely deplorable.'

Killick beamed. 'One has a reputation to maintain.'

'I think that you're a disgrace.'

'Blanche takes a much more generous view of me.'

'She knows you for the libertine that you are.'

'Then why did she agree to come to that ball in Chelsea with me?'

'That was a mistake,' said Bossingham curtly, 'and she realizes that now. You misled her completely. You told her that she'd be going there with a party of eight other people, only to discover, at the last moment, that you were her sole escort.'

'The other eight people dropped out.'

'If they ever existed!'

'Do you question my word?' asked Killick with mock indignation.

'Yes.'

'I resent that.'

'You're a cad.'

Killick was amused. 'Do you know, I haven't been called that since I was caught in a compromising situation with Squiffy Wilson's wife. He said that I was a cad, a bounder, and an utter scoundrel.'

'I'd agree wholeheartedly with that opinion of you.'

'He also threatened to horsewhip me. Would you care to do that?'

It was a direct challenge. Bossingham found him nauseating but he hesitated to offer any physical violence to someone who was bigger, stronger, and – in spite of his dissipated appearance – in better condition than the diplomat. Killick was a talented all-round sportsman who shone at tennis, golf, and polo. Before he was sent down from Oxford, he had also represented the university in the boxing ring.

'I thought not,' said Killick triumphantly. 'You're too scared to back your sneers up with blows. Squiffy Wilson was the same. He called me every name under the sun but he never actually laid a finger on me. You'd have been the same in his position – cowardly.'

'I'd never *be* in his position,' asserted Bossingham.

'Don't you be so sure.'

'No wife of mine would ever behave in that way.'

'That depends how well you treat her, old chap.'

'Some people respect the vows of marriage.'

'I'm quite sure that I would,' said Killick easily, 'if I was ever foolish enough to walk down the aisle. But why tie yourself to one woman when there are so many of them to love?'

'I don't believe that you're capable of love.'

'Then you should ask your fiancée.'

Bossingham tensed. 'What do you mean by that?'

'Talk to Blanche.'

'I've already done so.'

'She obviously hasn't told you everything about us,' said Killick. 'It's true that I only took her out for that magical evening in Chelsea but there was ample evidence of my devotion to her before that. I sent cards, flowers, and all manner of other blandishments.' Bossingham's eyes flared. 'I wonder why Blanche never mentioned any of this to you.'

'You're lying.'

'There's an easy way to prove that – ask your fiancée.'

'This conversation has gone far enough,' said Bossingham, keen to terminate the exchange. 'Good day to you, Killick.'

'Why be so unfriendly? We're fellow travellers on a ship with the most wonderful amenities. Make the most of them. This is my third trip on the *Oceanic* and I always have a whale of a time.'

'One wonders how you can afford it.'

'Strictly speaking, I can't.'

'No,' said Bossingham nastily. 'Everyone knows that you went through your inheritance years ago. You're on the verge of bankruptcy.'

'A gentleman is bound to have a few creditors.'

'You have dozens of them baying at your heels.'

'I always manage to keep just ahead of them.'

'How?' said Bossingham. 'Your family have refused to bail you out again so you have no apparent means of income. It's not as if you've ever had a profession and actually worked for a living.'

'Heaven forbid!'

'You're just a parasite.'

'And proud to be one,' said Killick happily. 'I leave all the toiling to lesser mortals like you. But you're wrong to say that I have no profession at all because I do. A very lucrative one, it is.'

'Cadging money off gullible people?'

'Acquiring it by means of which you would disapprove strongly. Last evening,' he went on, smugly, 'I earned enough to pay for this voyage a thousand times over.'

SEVEN

When he returned to the scene of the crime, Dillman found that J. P. Morgan had been playing solitaire while smoking a large Rosa de Santiago Celestiale. The financier's chair was only yards from where his bodyguard had been murdered but that did not seem to trouble him in the least. Forced to cough by the thick, aromatic fog, Dillman was invited to sit opposite him. He looked down at the cards. Solitaire was Morgan's favourite game and it seemed to define the man. He was disciplined, self-sufficient, and lonely. For all his wealth and success, and in spite of the vast numbers of people employed by corporations he had set up, he seemed to carry an emptiness around with him.

He abandoned his game and looked shrewdly across at Dillman. 'I'm told you have a good record as a ship's detective,' he said. 'I like to think so.'

'Prove it.'

'With your help,' said Dillman, 'I intend to do so.'

'What do you need from me?'

'The names of those who came in here for drinks yesterday.'

'Right here.' Morgan slid a piece of headed stationery across the table to him. 'As you'll see, I've crossed two names off the list.'

'My partner and the Honourable Jonathan Killick.'

'They came together. I can't believe that Miss Masefield would bring a thief and murderer into my circle. Besides, I know the young man socially. I can vouch for him.'

'I'm afraid that I can't,' said Dillman, coolly. 'It might interest you to know that he secured an invitation for Miss Masefield without having the courtesy to mention it to her. She agreed to come here on the false assumption that you had requested her company.'

'Had I been aware of her presence on the ship,' said Morgan with a half smile, 'I might certainly have done that.' His voice hardened. 'If I'd known that she was really a detective, of course, I'd have had second thoughts.'

'The point is that Killick tricked her into letting him escort her.'

'All's fair in love and business.'

'You approve?'

'It's the way of the world, Mr Dillman.'

'I see that you've put a star next to one name,' observed the other, checking the list. 'Dominique Cadine.'

'Correct.'

'Was that because she was not invited?'

'It was, actually. How did you guess?'

'I already knew,' said Dillman. 'The young lady is travelling with Abednego Thomas, the artist, and his wife. Dominique is his model.'

'I admire his taste, though I abhor his paintings.'

'I dined with the three of them last night. Dominique is gregarious. When she heard that there was a party and the opportunity of meeting you, she couldn't resist the temptation to sneak in.'

'What was she after – free champagne or a sighting of me?'

'Both, I suspect, Mr Morgan, but you were the main attraction. There's no equivocation about that. Your renown spread to France years ago. As in America, you're seen there as the Napoleon of Wall Street.'

'I'm not sure that I like that nickname.'

'It's meant as a compliment.'

'Napoleon was defeated. He died in exile.'

'But at his peak, he ruled an empire.'

'By force of arms,' said Morgan, drily. 'My empire is based on sound economics. That's why it's grown and grown.'

'Nevertheless, it's had to be defended by force at times – and so have you, sir. Is it true that Mr Riedel possessed a firearm?'

Morgan was non-committal. 'Why do you say that?'

'My partner got the impression that he was carrying a weapon.'

'He was a policeman. Old habits die hard.'

'I think that there was another reason.'

'Howard was employed to protect my art collection.'

'And to guard you, sir,' said Dillman. 'That was his major task. May I ask if you've ever had death threats?'

'That's a private matter.'

'Not where a murder is concerned. It's very relevant. Hasn't it occurred to you that, if you'd been here last night in place of Mr Riedel, then *you* might have been the victim?'

Morgan pulled on his cigar. 'It crossed my mind.'

'Doesn't that worry you?'

'The only thing I'm worried about is catching the killer.'

'It won't be easy,' Dillman told him. 'When I searched the body, there was no weapon on Mr Riedel. It was stolen along with everything else. The man we're after is armed and dangerous. My belief is that he had a personal motive to commit murder. So I must ask you again, Mr Morgan. Have there been any death threats?'

'People in my position always get lunatics sounding off at them.'

'In what way?'

'They scream and shout at me with impotent rage. I'm a rich man, Mr Dillman. I inspire envy. I get all kinds of poison-pen letters.'

'Can you give me a specific example, sir?'

'A while back – one, maybe two years ago – some maniac wrote that he'd eliminate New York's high financiers, trust magnates, and trust builders. All three hats fit me. We were going to "pass out of the world without anyone suspecting foul play." Those were the exact words.'

'What did you do with the letter?'

'I wasn't supposed to see it. My son, Jack, passed it on to the New York police commissioner along with others like it. He tried to keep all that nonsense from bothering me.'

'I'm not sure that it was nonsense,' argued Dillman. 'You're the nearest thing that America has to a central bank. It isn't just the have-nots who resent your power and position. There must be jealous rivals, political opponents, and foreign interests that would profit from your death. The question is – would they take steps to bring it about?'

'I'm a survivor, Mr Dillman. Always have been.'

'But you made lots of enemies along the way.'

'I was never one to court popularity.'

'Some of the press have mounted strong campaigns against you,' said Dillman. 'When I was in New York last month, I saw you on the front cover of *Puck* magazine. You were embracing what looked like the whole financial district. The caption was MILLION-DOLLAR MERGER.'

Morgan grunted. 'I saw that stupid cartoon. Poor likeness of me, I thought. They had me reaching out for some scrawny kid who was putting a dime into a piggy bank. There was dollar sign on my cuff link.' He took a last puff of his cigar then ground it out in the ashtray. 'Don't they realize how many jobs I've created over the years? Can't they see how much stability I brought to volatile markets?'

'All that some people see is a hate figure, Mr Morgan. One of those people was in this cabin last night.'

'Then why didn't he wait until I came back here?'

'I have a theory about that,' said Dillman, reflectively. 'The killer wanted you to *suffer* and there were two ways of doing that. One was to deprive you of the services of Howard Riedel in the most dramatic fashion. The other was to steal something that you cherished deeply. If you'd been the murder victim, you'd have been spared the anguish that someone is so eager to inflict on you.'

'Oh, there's been anguish all right,' admitted Morgan. 'Lots.'

'I've got another hunch.'

'What is it?'

'Mr Riedel was not only killed so that you might be spared. He has an enemy of his own – someone with a grudge that drove him to cut the man's throat. Well,' Dillman reminded him, 'you found the body. That was a vicious attack on a man in no position to defend himself.'

'It brings us back to the crucial question.'

'What's that?'

'How did the villain get in here in the first place?'

'I've thought about that. The lock wasn't forced, which means that he either obtained a master key somehow . . .'

'Or?'

'Mr Riedel unwittingly let him in. And by the way,' Dillman went on, 'I say 'him' because I'm convinced that the murder was the work of a man. That rules out Dominique Cadine, and I've other reasons for removing her name from any list of suspects. It's not inconceivable, however, that the killer's accomplice was a woman.'

'Accomplice?'

'Somebody would have acted as a lookout, sir. A sizeable haul was taken from here. The thief wouldn't have left until he was certain that the coast was clear. We're looking for at least two people.'

'One of whom carries a knife.'

'And a gun.'

Morgan became pensive. He looked down at the cards as if seeking solace. His forehead was corrugated, his jowls heavy, his nose as unsightly as ever. He was a man who had weathered endless crises because he had always been able to buy his way out of them. Money was of no use in the present emergency. He had to rely on George Dillman and Genevieve Masefield.

'Do you know much about business, Mr Dillman?' Morgan asked.

'Only what I learnt from my father.'

'And what was that?'

'That I didn't really belong in such a world, I guess.'

'There are certain cardinal rules.'

'Beat the other guy to the draw?' suggested Dillman.

'That, too, naturally. But the one I was going to cite is even simpler. Markets hate uncertainty. To maintain a healthy flow of capital, you have to impose structure and confidence.'

'Your career has been living proof of that, sir.'

'I've been through the fires of hell,' said Morgan proudly. 'I've seen wars, financial crashes, hostile takeovers, panics, and other disruptions and I was always in a position to help. I restored certainty.'

'You can't do that here, sir.'

'I'm hoping that you can, Mr Dillman. The *Oceanic* is a microcosm of the money market. If the truth of what happened in here ever got out, we'd have mass hysteria on board. Dabble in business just this once and give us some control and direction.' He searched Dillman's eyes. 'Get out there and catch whoever is responsible for all this turbulence.'

Genevieve Masefield greeted the latest news with irritation and dismay.

'Not another one, Lester.'

'Another two, I'm afraid.'

'Both women?'

'One woman, one man this time,' said the purser. 'Miss Florence Stiller, an American journalist, and Oskar Halberg.'

'The couturier?' asked Genevieve.

'You've *heard* of him?'

'Most women have heard of Oskar Halberg. He's one

of America's most notable dress designers. I've drooled over photographs of his creations many times.'

'Only drooled?'

'My income doesn't permit me to do anything else, I'm afraid.'

'Find his billfold for him and he may slip you a few evening gowns by way of thanks,' said Hembrow. 'At some stage of the evening, he was the victim of a pickpocket.'

'Does he know when the billfold was taken?'

'No, Genevieve. He'd drunk rather a lot last night and didn't even notice that it was gone until he went back to his cabin. Halberg joined us at Cherbourg with a clutch of other people in the same business.'

'They'd been to see the latest Paris fashions, probably.'

'You'll find him in cabin number forty. Oddly enough, that's only two doors away from Florence Stiller and her sister. They're in number thirty-eight. Nice ladies.'

'George knows them.'

'Really?'

'They dined at the same table last night,' she said. 'Not that they had much to say to him. They were too busy worshipping at the feet of Abednego Thomas. George spoke well of them.'

'Miss Stiller was relieved of some jewellery.'

'From her cabin?'

'Yes,' replied Hembrow. 'The theft didn't come to light until she took off the necklace she'd been wearing at dinner. Her sister, Vane, travels with very little jewellery so there was nothing of hers left in the cabin to be stolen.'

'I daresay she was upset on her sister's behalf, though.'

'Yes, Genevieve. You'll find them very pleasant to deal with and very contrite. They know that a jewellery box should have been stored in a safe. Florence Stiller, you'll be relieved to hear, is no Mrs Farrant.'

'What about Halberg?'

'He was a little more theatrical.'

'You mean that he huffed and puffed?'

'Well,' said Hembrow, 'he put on a bravura performance but it was all for show. He blamed me for allowing a pickpocket on board the ship. What am I supposed to do – stand at the gangplank and ask everyone about their criminal record before I let them embark?'

'Did you manage to calm him down?'

'Eventually.'

'Then I'll tackle him first.' Genevieve sighed. 'I was hoping to give George a hand instead of taking on two more cases of my own. I know that the victims are upset at the thefts but they can't really compete with a murder and the disappearance of items from a priceless art collection.'

'Could there be a connection, do you think?'

'Between what?'

'All the crimes so far committed.'

'I doubt it, Lester. A woman stole Mrs Farrant's diamond earrings, that much is clear. No man would venture into the ladies' cloakroom. It was a spur of the moment crime,' she said. 'So, I suspect, were the other two thefts. Someone saw a chance and struck.'

'Isn't that what happened in Mr Morgan's stateroom?'

'No, that was calculated. George thinks that it may even have been planned on the voyage to Europe. From the moment he stepped aboard the *Oceanic* again, Howard Riedel was a marked man. And,' said Genevieve, 'his killer knew exactly what he wanted to steal.'

'Over half a million dollars' worth of Mr Morgan's property.'

'That's another reason to separate the crimes. Why would anyone who'd just made off with all that loot bother with petty theft?'

'It's not petty to Oskar Halberg.'

'Nor to Florence Stiller. But you see what I mean?'

'I do, Genevieve.'

'George will have to manage without me for a little while.'

'I'll warn him of that. He's still tied up with Mr Morgan.'

She sighed. 'That's another little treat I have to come.'

'What is?'

'Talking to J. P. Morgan now that he knows who I really am. I can't say that I'm looking forward to that. He'll feel that I deceived him.'

'Solve the crime and he'll forgive you anything.'

'I'm not sure about that, Lester.'

'The same goes for Oskar Halberg and Florence Stiller. When you catch the thief and recover their property, they'll eat out of your hand.'

'What about Hilda Farrant?'

He laughed. 'She's more likely to bite your hand off.'

Hilda Farrant handed the letter over to Ethan Boyd and he read the neat calligraphy. When he had finished, he passed it on to his wife. The three of them were sitting together in the lounge that morning and Mrs Farrant was still simmering with rage.

'What do you think, Mr Boyd?' she asked.

'I think it will make them sit up and blink when they read it. Most people in your situation would *say* that they were going to complain, but not actually get around to doing it. You've taken action,' said Boyd, 'and I admire you for it. Don't you, Rosalie?'

'Well, yes,' said his wife timidly, giving the letter back to the other woman, 'but I did feel that it was too strongly worded.'

'That's what I liked about it.'

'You wouldn't let me write anything like this, Ethan.'

'You wouldn't be capable of it,' he said fondly. 'You're too kind and forgiving. When your purse went astray, I more or less had to make you report the fact to Mr Hembrow.'

'Don't mention that man,' snapped Mrs Farrant.

'Why not?'

'I found him charming,' said Rosalie Boyd.

'Well, he wasn't very charming to me,' said Mrs Farrant. 'He came out with a battery of excuses and even had the gall to suggest that I was partly to blame for leaving my property unguarded. Then he palmed me off on Miss Masefield.' She held up her letter. 'As I emphasize in this, I expect the personal supervision of the purser. How can a young woman like Miss Masefield solve a crime?'

'Rosalie thought her very efficient,' said Boyd.

'Yes,' added his wife. 'She asked some very searching questions. It was obvious that she's done this kind of thing before. I felt such a fool when I discovered that I'd mislaid my purse in the library.'

'The worst of it is that you wasted Miss Masefield's time. She must have many other commitments on board. You took her away from them. She could have been hunting for Mrs Farrant's earrings, for instance.'

'Oh, I do apologise, Mrs Farrant. Don't be too harsh on me.'

'You made an honest mistake,' said the older woman tolerantly. 'The purser, on the other hand, did not. He fobbed me off on a ship's detective who is far too young and inexperienced to do the job properly.'

'I think you should give her the benefit of the doubt,' said Rosalie.

'So do I,' agreed Boyd. 'Never judge by appearances. You can easily be misled. When I managed a bank in Manhattan, we had a problem with embezzlement and hired a Pinkerton agent to find the culprit. They sent an attractive young woman whom nobody would have suspected of being a detective. I pretended to employ her in a secretarial capacity and she solved the crime within a week.'

His wife nodded. 'There's another point, Ethan. The White Star Line wouldn't hire someone who couldn't do the job. It has a reputation to maintain.'

'I think it's been besmirched by the theft of my earrings,' said Mrs Farrant, still obsessively self-centred. 'I made that very point in my opening paragraph. And the letter will go to the managing director of the shipping line, not to anyone on board this ship. Always protest to the person who is in charge.'

'You may yet have to tear that letter up,' said Rosalie. 'Miss Masefield still has days in which to find your stolen property.' She turned to her husband. 'Do you remember those people we met on the *Adriatic*?'

'Oh yes. I do.' Boyd took over the story. 'They were a delightful couple from Chicago – Tom and Elaine Haxton. We got to know them very well. Money and valuables were stolen from their cabin but, by the end of the voyage, they had it all back again.' Mrs Farrant was not persuaded. 'Was the ship's detective female?'

'No, it was a man.'

'I thought so.'

'You're being very unkind to Miss Masefield.'

'She's had well over twenty-four hours to work on the case and she's made absolutely no progress. Frankly, I doubt if she ever will. That's why I've demanded full compensation for the stolen items. I won't settle for a penny less.'

'Were the diamond earrings insured?'

'No, Mr Boyd. I didn't think it necessary.'

'We insured our valuables before coming on board,' he told her. 'It's a facility that's offered by the shipping line. If you didn't follow their advice, you may find that they refuse to pay any compensation.'

'Then I'll sue the company.'

'Oh, you're so brave, Mrs Farrant,' said Rosalie admiringly. 'I'd never have the courage to do anything like that.'

'Rosalie hates confrontation,' explained her husband.

Mrs Farrant snorted. 'I thrive on it.'

'Those earrings must be very special to you.'

'They're a dear memento of my late husband.'

'What would he have done in these circumstances?'

'Herbert?'

'Would he have written a searing letter of complaint?'

'No,' said Mrs Farrant. 'Herbert was a man of action. He would've gone straight to the captain and demanded that my earrings were promptly found even if it involved a search of every cabin on the ship.'

'Supposing that they were still not tracked down?'

'Then he'd have challenged the captain to a duel.'

'What about the purser?' asked Rosalie.

'Oh, he'd have made that dreadful man walk the plank.'

Dillman knew that one of the prime assets of any detective was thinking time. There was no point in taking precipitate action until all the aspects of a case had first been considered. A few hours' reflection could save him days of undirected legwork. Accordingly, he went straight back to his cabin after the interview with J. P. Morgan and wrote down all the attributes that he felt the killer and his accomplice must possess, uncertain, at this stage, whether he was looking for two men or a man and a woman. His first search was through the names of those who had attended the drinks party given by Morgan the previous evening. Having finished that, he began a trawl through the vastly larger list of passengers in first class. Dillman was so deep in thought that he did not at first hear the tap on his door. After a pause, there was a loud banging that brought him out of his meditation.

He opened the door to let the purser him. Hembrow was worried.

'I've just spoken to the captain,' he said.

'And?'

'He wants to know what's going on, George.'

'We're engaged in a murder investigation,' said Dillman. 'That's what's going on. Doesn't he realize that?'

'He's getting edgy. This is a crisis. He needs to be told that we're making definite headway.'

'Then tell him that we are.'

'Is it true?'

'I hope so.'

'So there's no concrete evidence to show him?'

'No, Lester, but I've worked out lots of things in my mind.'

'The captain wants more than your latest theory.'

'In that case,' said Dillman, glancing down at the notes he had made, 'tell him that I've narrowed down the list of suspects to seventy-three people. It's simply a question of eliminating them one by one.'

Hembrow was astonished. 'How did you arrive at that figure?'

'By deciding that the man who killed Howard Riedel would most probably have boarded the ship at Cherbourg.'

'What makes you think that?'

'The element of calculation involved. He knew exactly when and where to strike. To do that, he had to be certain that Riedel and Mr Morgan were actually travelling on the *Oceanic*.'

'Couldn't he have found that out in advance?' asked the purser. 'If he sailed with us to Europe when Mr Morgan was aboard, it wouldn't have been difficult to establish when the great man was due to return.'

'Maybe not,' said Dillman, 'but there was always the element of chance. Mr Morgan might have changed his mind and sailed on a different vessel. He might have headed home sooner or later than planned. That was too big a risk to take. He was followed.'

'All the way from Paris?'

'And in the city itself, probably.'

'Assuming that you're right – and I've still to be convinced – what made you settle on the number seventy-three? We took over two hundred and fifty passengers on board at Cherbourg.' 'The majority were in steerage. I'm discounting them.'

'If you're simply looking at first class, then the number is even lower. It's only forty-six.'

'Forty-one, Lester.'

'How do you make that out?'

'You're including Riedel and Mr Morgan in that and the two people we can clear of a murder charge are Howard Riedel's employer and the victim.'

'True enough.'

'I've also taken Abednego Thomas, his wife, and his model out of the reckoning. I know them well enough to be certain that they'd not be party to a murder. That gets me to seventy-three.'

'It was only forty-one a moment ago.'

'You're forgetting the thirty-two second-class passengers who joined us at Cherbourg. Add those and you get my total. Yes,' he went on as Hembrow was about to protest, 'I know it would have been easier for a first-class passenger to commit this crime and our search must naturally begin there. But the killer might anticipate that and see second class as a safer place to be. It's sensible for us to throw the net wider.'

'Good thinking.'

'I'll be able to cross many of the names off this list very soon. Some of the passengers will be too old or infirm to be suspects. And there'll be other reasons why we can delete people at a glance.'

'So what do I tell the captain?'

'Say that I've got it down to forty. That's a good, round number.'

'Only if your theory is correct.'

'Yes,' confessed Dillman, 'and I'm not infallible. I don't rule out the possibility that the killer shadowed Morgan and Riedel to Cherbourg then met up with an accomplice already aboard. But I have this strong feeling that we must look to France for the real link.'

'Then you'll have to do it on your own, George.'

'Why?'

'Genevieve has her hands full. Two more cases of theft.'

'Who were the victims?'

'A man who had his pocket picked and a woman whose jewellery box was taken from her cabin. Genevieve said that you knew her. One of two sisters – Miss Florence Stiller.'

'We met over dinner, though she had little time for me.'

'I hear that Abednego Thomas hogged their attention.'

'They're real devotees,' said Dillman. 'They want to write an article about him for their magazine. Needless to say, he basked in female adoration all evening.'

'He isn't called Abed-We-Go for nothing.'

'I'm sorry that this had to happen to one of the sisters. It's the sort of thing that sours a voyage.'

'Unless we can retrieve that jewellery box for her.'

'Genevieve will do her damnedest to get it back, along with the billfold and the diamond earrings that were stolen. It will be tricky, I'm afraid. Small items are easy to conceal. That's not the case with the haul from Mr Morgan's cabin, however.'

'No, you'd need a proper hiding place for that.'

'Yes,' said Dillman. 'Wherever can it be?'

Manny Ellway's duties gave him little free time and most of it was spent with the other stewards. While they moaned about their low wages, or made suggestive remarks about certain female passengers, Ellway tended to stay aloof. He had no complaints to make. Indeed, when he was alone, there was always a smile of satisfaction on his lips. Lunch was served early for the stewards that day but he decided to miss it. Instead, making sure that he was unobserved, he flitted along the corridor and went down a companionway until he reached the second-class area of the ship. He made his way swiftly to a storeroom and, having checked once more to see that he was alone, he took out a key and let himself in. His smile soon blossomed into a full grin.

Genevieve Masefield had some trouble tracking Oskar Halberg down. Since he was not in his cabin, she checked all of the public rooms in search of him. Not finding him in any of them, she went out on deck, only to learn that the couturier had just gone back to his cabin before luncheon. Genevieve went there once again. She introduced herself to Halberg but got a cold reception.

'You want to talk to me *now*?' he asked as if she had just made an impossible demand. 'This is very inconvenient, Miss Masefield.'

'We can talk early this afternoon, if you prefer.'

'I do.'

'I just thought that you'd want to give me an account of what happened sooner rather than later. Then I can start to make inquiries.'

'The purser had a full report from me.'

'I'd rather hear it firsthand,' said Genevieve.

'Well, it can't be this minute.'

Having admired his dress designs for so many years, she was disappointed to find that the middle-aged man who created them was short, lean, stooped, and decidedly ugly. He wore a wig of dark wavy hair that would have suited someone twenty years younger but which only looked absurd on him. His suit was flamboyant, though Genevieve could not see it properly as he had only opened the cabin door a few inches. Oskar Halberg was a tetchy little man and she took against him. He, in turn, was not enamoured of her.

'Why did they send me a woman?' he said.

'Because I'm employed as a ship's detective.'

'Could they find no man to do the job?'

'Of course.'

'Then why use you? When I look at a woman, I see a body that needs to be clothed properly so that it can enhance the personality of its owner. You, for instance,' he went on, eyeing her emerald green suit, 'should always wear blue. Green subdues your essence. The right shade of blue would liberate you.'

'I didn't come to discuss my wardrobe, Mr Halberg,' she said. 'I want to hear about the theft of your billfold.'

'Later.'

'Do you want to give me a time?'

'Three o'clock.'

'Here?'

'Yes. I'm a busy man so please be punctual.'

'You can rely on that, sir.'

'And for evening wear,' he advised, 'you would look best in red.'

'I like to choose my own attire, Mr Halberg.'

'That's all too apparent.'

Genevieve bridled at the note of disapproval in his voice and she was tempted to make a barbed comment about the ridiculous wig that he was wearing, but she said nothing. However impolite they might be, she knew that passengers had to be treated with the utmost politeness.

'I came at a bad time,' she said. 'Do accept my apology?'

'Three o'clock,' he declared.

Then he closed the door. Annoyed by his rudeness, Genevieve walked away, wondering why she had upset him so much. Oskar Halberg, meanwhile, adjusted his wig and beamed at the young woman who was seated in the corner of his cabin.

'What was that all about?' she said.

He flicked a dismissive hand. 'Nothing, nothing.'

'Who was that lady?'

'Nobody,' said Halberg. 'That's why I sent her on her way. I only wish to talk to you, my dear.'

Dominique Cadine was pleased to hear it.

The conversation took place on the promenade deck. With luncheon being served soon, most people had left and it was possible for Blanche Charlbury and Mark Bossingham to talk in private at last, their earlier attempts to do so being frustrated by the presence of others.

'Why must we talk out here?' said Blanche, mystified.

'Because there's nowhere else to do it.'

'Yes, there is, Mark. I can think of two highly suitable places.'

'Blanche!'

'Well, we could certainly have privacy in one of our cabins.'

'It would be quite improper for me to come to your cabin.'

'Then I'll come to yours.'

'That's out of the question,' reproved Bossingham, 'and you know it. I'm in a position of trust here. I gave your parents an undertaking that I'd behave like a gentleman towards you.'

She sighed. 'Yes, I can always count on you to do that.'

'We are only engaged, Blanche – not married.'

'Betrothal entitles us to some degree of closeness, doesn't it?'

'We've spent every day together.'

'But always in public.'

'What else are you suggesting?'

Blanche lacked the courage to reply. He looked so stern and righteous that she could not stand up against him, still less even hint at a flagrant breach of decorum. Something had clearly upset him and it was her place to let him air his grievance. She would have to postpone what she hoped would be his transformation into a flesh-and-blood human being until after their wedding.

'What do you wish to discuss?' she said.

'Your relationship with Killick.'

'I've told you everything about that already.'

'Apparently not.'

'What do you mean?'

'I spoke to him this morning,' said Bossingham.

'You usually avoid Johnny like the plague.'

'It was not out of choice, Blanche. But he caught me out here and I couldn't shake the fellow off. He was as disagreeable as ever, especially when he was talking about you.'

'What did he say?'

'He made insinuations.'

'That's nothing new,' she said with a dismissive laugh. 'Johnny is always making insinuations about something or other. Pay no heed to him, Mark. He was only trying to goad you.'

'I'm well aware of that.'

'Then let's put it all aside and go and eat.'

'Not until we've sorted this out,' he said, stopping her with a hand. 'I know that Killick is a compulsive liar and that I probably shouldn't have listened to him, but he touched a raw spot.'

'He can be very cruel at times.'

'Then why did you get involved with him?'

'I wasn't involved,' she replied. 'I've explained that to you. I only ever saw Johnny as a friend – almost like an elder brother.'

'He claims that you had a proper romance.'

'Never!'

'Is it true that he sent you cards and flowers?'

'Yes, but he did that to lots of girls. He's very generous.'

'What did he expect in return for his generosity?'

'I refuse to answer that,' she said, visibly hurt. 'You're the one making insinuations now and I find them quite offensive.'

'I'm sorry, Blanche. I just want to know the truth.'

'It's quite simple. Johnny Killick belongs to my past. You – and only you – belong to my future. That's what makes him so jealous.'

'Jealous?'

'Of course. He envies us. We have something that he could

140

never have. We're in love, Mark. We've made a lasting commitment. Johnny's never done that in his whole life. He has these shallow relationships with a string of women and casts them aside after a few weeks.'

'Is that what he did with you?'

'No,' she retorted. 'I cast *him* aside.'

'So there was a proper relationship?'

'Not really.'

'Are you telling me the truth?'

'Yes!'

'Blanche,' he said, eyes glowing with intensity, 'you can't bring an attachment to an end unless it existed in the first place. You don't cast aside a person whom you describe as a mere friend, a kind of elder brother. Something must have happened between the two of you.'

'What is this?' she cried, lips trembling. 'I thought that we came on this voyage to be together, not to rake over the past. I don't ask you about any of the girls you knew at Oxford. Yet you keep on badgering me about Johnny as if I was a kept woman or something.'

'Perish the thought!'

'How was I to know he'd even be on this ship?'

'You couldn't possibly have done so.'

'I wish that we'd sailed on the *Adriatic* or the *Majestic* now.'

'So do I,' said Bossingham, relenting at the sight of her discomfort.

'I can't seem to do anything right,' she wailed. 'When I make a new friend, you tell me that Genevieve is not a suitable companion for me. When we bump accidentally into Johnny, you get it into your head that I was just another of his fleeting conquests. It's so unjust, Mark.'

'I know and I take it all back.'

'Is this how it's going to be after we're married?'

'No, Blanche.'

'Won't I be allowed to have any friends of my own?'

'Of course you will.'

'But only if they meet with your approval.'

'Look – *please.* Don't get so distressed.'

'You were the one who caused the distress.'

'And I offer my profoundest apologies.'

'It's too late now.'

'Let me make it up to you,' he offered, taking her by the shoulders. 'Come on, darling. Tell me how I can make amends?'

She hesitated. 'Are you serious?' she said at length.

'Ask me anything.'

'Very well – kiss me.'

He blenched. '*Here?*'

'There's hardly anyone about.'

'But this is so public.'

'It's the deck of an ocean liner and that's one of the most romantic places in the world. I want to feel that we're sailing off on our honeymoon, Mark. If I can ask for anything – kiss me.'

'Very well,' he said, steeling himself to give her a peck on the cheek. He stood back from her. 'There you are, Blanche.'

'Yes,' she said sadly. 'Here I am.'

'Where on earth have you been hiding, George?' said Veronica, enfolding him in her arms. 'We were about to send out a search party for you.'

'I missed luncheon. I wasn't feeling hungry.'

'I was hungry for your companionship.'

'I'm flattered to hear that, Veronica.'

'Didn't you want to see me?'

'I'm always happy to do that,' said Dillman gallantly.

He had come looking for them in the lounge but Veronica Thomas was there without either her husband or Dominique Cadine. Leaping up from her seat, she gave him the sort of unrestrained welcome that made tongues click in every part of the room. They sat down together. Ready to enjoy her company, he also wanted to use Veronica as a source of information.

'You joined the ship at Cherbourg, didn't you?' he said.

'That's right. We stayed overnight there.'

'Did you get to meet any of the other passengers?'

'Lots of them,' replied Veronica. 'I made a point of speaking to some of the steerage passengers. They must be really desperate to endure the conditions down there in the hope of finding a better life in America. You hear the most heartrending stories about the horrors they faced in their native countries. We're so *lucky*, George.'

'I know.'

'Abednego identified with them even more than me. He may be successful now but he had almost twenty years of living in abject poverty before his paintings finally began to sell.'

'Did he ever contemplate emigration to America?'

'No – he thinks it's full of philistines.'

'Then why has he agreed to have an exhibition there?'

'Abednego wants to educate them. Also,' she added with a laugh, 'he likes American women.'

'And they certainly like him,' said Dillman, 'if Florence and Vane Stiller are anything to go by. They idolised him.'

'When we went to the lounge after dinner, they were hanging

on every word he said as if it were Holy Writ. It was midnight before the two ladies let us get away.' She stroked his hand. 'I was hoping that you'd come to the lounge with us, George, so that we could talk some more. I'd have enjoyed that.'

'I decided to have an early night.'

'Alone?'

'Alone.'

'What a pity!'

Their eyes locked for a moment and Dillman could read more than a passing interest in her gaze. The admiration between them was mutual but he could not understand why a married woman, travelling with her husband, was so blatant about her feelings for him. He probed for more detail that might help his investigation.

'Did you see anything of J. P. Morgan in Cherbourg?' he said.

'We deliberately kept out of his way.'

'Why was that?'

'My husband doesn't like Mr Morgan.'

'I've got no time for people like that,' said Abednego Thomas, arriving in time to hear the remark. 'Can't stand the man, George.'

'But he's one of the world's great art lovers,' said Dillman.

'Art *buyers*, maybe, and that's not the same thing.'

'I'm told that he's a very cultured man.'

'That's a matter of opinion,' said Thomas, sitting opposite him. 'When I look at a painting, I see its intrinsic skill and beauty. When someone like Morgan looks at one, he sees a financial investment.'

'Be fair. There's more to it than that. J. P. Morgan has presented masterpieces to galleries and museums around the globe. He's made it possible for ordinary people to view the very best of art.'

'Only because he's too mean to pay the import duty on any

paintings he takes back to America. He's no philanthropist. And he knows nothing about the way that artists actually work.'

'J. P. Morgan is my husband's *bête noire*,' explained Veronica. 'He came into a gallery in Paris where some of Abednego's paintings were on display. He made some very cutting remarks about them.'

'He said that my paintings were obscene when all I'm doing is following an honourable tradition of depicting female nudes. Obscene!' said Thomas with passion. 'Morgan is the obscenity. What's more obscene than ruining his competitors by any means he can? Did you know that the man you call an art lover managed to evade the draft during the American Civil War then made a profit by selling defective rifles to the Union army? That was immoral.'

'A lot of people might level that charge against you,' said Dillman.

'Sexual morality doesn't count.'

'It does to them, Abednego.'

'I'm talking about the way we treat our fellow human beings. I show them some respect. All that Morgan does is trample on them. He uses his money to crush any opposition,' he went on, waving a fist, 'and leaves thousands of ruined families in his wake. Worst of all to me, as a painter, is that he tries to pass himself off as a patron of the arts.'

'I can see why you didn't get invited to his drinks party.'

'We wouldn't have gone if we had been, George.'

'Dominique went.'

'That was different,' said Veronica easily. 'She likes parties and she was curious to meet Mr Morgan face-to-face.'

'Even though she knows that Abednego detests him?'

'Even then.'

145

'I've no power to stop her,' said Thomas, 'and I wouldn't be unwise enough to try. Dominique does exactly what she wants.'

'But you employ her,' said Dillman. 'You pay her wages.'

'We have an arrangement.'

'Don't you think that she should have been more loyal to you?'

'Oh, Dominique is very loyal to me. I have no worries on that score. And if she wants to go and meet someone whom I dislike,' said Thomas, 'I don't see it as a betrayal. Dominique Cadine is a free spirit. She's also a very special young lady.'

'Yes,' said Veronica, smiling. 'Very special indeed.'

EIGHT

Since she was not due to meet Oskar Halberg until three o'clock
that afternoon, Genevieve Masefield decided to interview one
of the other victims of theft beforehand. Immediately after
luncheon, therefore, she went to the cabin occupied by Florence
and Vane Stiller. When she knocked on their door, however,
the person who opened it was Edith Hurst. The stewardess was
surprised to see her.

'Oh – Miss Masefield!'

'Hello, Edith.'

'I didn't expect to see you here.'

'I wanted to speak to Miss Stiller.'

'Which one?' asked Edith. 'There are two of them.'

'Miss Florence Stiller. Have you any idea where she might be?'

'Both ladies are in the library.'

'Thank you.' Genevieve remembered something. 'How are you getting on with Mrs Farrant?'

'She's worse than ever.'

'I hope that she's still not accusing you of the crime.'

'No, but I feel guilty nonetheless,' said Edith. 'Whenever I go anywhere near that cabin, I get this prickly sensation all over.'

'It will pass. What are you doing here?'

'Making the beds.'

'This late?'

'I usually do it when they've gone to breakfast but they didn't stir out of their cabin until well after noon. This is the first chance I've had to get in here. It's upset my routine.'

'Then I won't detain you any longer.'

'Goodbye, Miss Masefield.'

'Goodbye – and good luck with Mrs Farrant!'

Genevieve went back down the corridor and up the main staircase. She reached the library in minutes. It was a well-stocked room of medium size with leather sofas and matching armchairs. At one end was a long table with a number of chairs around it. Hundreds of books lined the walls. Florence and Vane Stiller were the only people there. Seated at the table, Florence was writing a letter. Her sister was reading a book. Genevieve introduced herself and saw at once that she would have a more comfortable time than Hilda Farrant had given her. Unlike Mrs Farrant, the two sisters were pleased that a female detective was handling the case. Indeed, she aroused their curiosity.

'How long have you been doing this sort of work?' asked Florence.

'Some years now,' replied Genevieve.

'Do you enjoy it?'

'When I achieve a measure of success.'

'Isn't it dangerous, Miss Masefield?'

'Occasionally.'

'How did you get drawn into this profession in the first place?' said Vane. 'I can scent a story here. I don't suppose that you'd let us feature you in an article, would you?'

'No, Miss Stiller,' said Genevieve firmly. 'Ships' detectives work most effectively if they're invisible. If you put my photograph in your magazine, it would be difficult for me to find employment.'

'Oh dear! We can't have that.'

'In any case, Vane,' said her sister, 'Miss Masefield has come to ask the questions, not to answer them. We must cooperate.'

'I'll do anything to get your jewellery box back, Florence.'

'Perhaps we could start with a description of its contents,' said Genevieve, taking her notebook from her bag. 'Some idea of cost would also be useful.'

'I've already prepared a list.' Florence handed it over to her. 'There's nothing terribly valuable there but I've had some of those items for over thirty years. They're *part* of me.'

'You'll never see Florence without jewellery of some kind,' said Vane, indicating the silver earrings and the cameo brooch that her sister wore. 'With a name like mine, I suppose that I should be vain but I have no fondness for ornaments.'

'It's not a question of vanity. I just like to make the most of myself. Besides,' said Florence, 'some of the things stolen were gifts from gentleman admirers. They have a value well beyond their price.'

'When did you last see the jewellery box?' asked Genevieve.

'Just before we left our cabin – about seven o'clock.'

'And you're certain that you locked the door?'

'Absolutely certain.'

'How long were you away?'

'Let me see,' said Florence, doing some swift mental arithmetic. 'It must have been five hours at least. We got back here around midnight.'

'Yes,' confirmed Vane. 'We had the good fortune to share a table with Abednego Thomas, the artist. What an extraordinary man! Are you familiar with his paintings, Miss Masefield?'

'No – only with his reputation.' The sisters laughed gaily. 'In view of that, you were both extremely daring. Most ladies would be frightened off by Mr Thomas's rather lurid past.'

'He's a man who enjoys life. There's nothing wrong in that.' 'And he's such a wonderful raconteur,' said Florence. 'Though some of his stories are a little too colourful for our readers. Artists are a different species, I always think. While the rest of us obey all those silly, restrictive, social rules, they strike out on their own.'

'What jewellery were you wearing last night?' said Genevieve.

'Everything I'm wearing now.' Florence touched her brooch and earrings then held out both hands. They were covered in rings and there was a gold bracelet around one wrist. 'Oh, and there was a ruby necklace that I've kept in my bag all day. I daren't leave anything else in the cabin now.'

'Lightning doesn't strike twice in the same spot,' said Vane. 'We can't be too careful, even if it is a case of closing the stable door after the horse has bolted.'

'In other words,' said Genevieve, 'you would have been seen as a woman with good taste in jewellery. The thief would have hoped you had more of it in your cabin.'

Florence was upset. 'You mean that I was *watched*?'

'Almost certainly.'

'What a hideous thought! It's alarming enough to know that someone went through our personal belongings. Vane and I felt invaded. It never occurred to me that I'd been singled out.'

'It's the way that thieves work on a ship. They identify targets.'

'How dreadful!' exclaimed Florence, hand to her throat.

'Did you notice anyone paying particular attention to your jewellery in the course of the evening?'

'No, Miss Masefield.'

'To be honest,' said Vane, 'we were far too preoccupied with Abednego Thomas, and he could hardly be the thief. We never let him out of our sight. After dinner, we sat in the lounge for hours with him, his wife, and a Mademoiselle Cadine.'

'There was someone else at our table, Vane.'

'Really, Florence!' scolded her sister. 'You surely can't suspect Mr Dillman. He was the soul of decency. In answer to your question, Miss Masefield, there was nobody who showed undue interest in the jewellery that Florence was wearing.'

'Where was the jewellery box kept?' said Genevieve.

'On top of the wardrobe.'

'It was completely out of sight,' put in Florence. 'I chose it because it was the safest spot in the cabin.'

'And, therefore,' Genevieve told her, 'one of the first places any thief would look. They know every inch of these cabins. It's a matter of seconds for them to check the usual hiding places.'

'You make me feel very naive.'

'You were unfortunate, Miss Stiller, that's all. Ordinarily, your possessions would have been untouched even if you'd left them in full view. Thefts are the exception rather than the rule.'

'Have there been any others on board?'

'Two, as it happens.'

'Jewellery in both cases?'

'No,' said Genevieve. 'A pickpocket relieved one gentleman of his billfold last night. Whether or not he or she is also the thief who visited your cabin, only time will tell.'

'But you will catch him, won't you?' asked Vane.

'I think so.'

'What makes you so confident, Miss Masefield?'

'I believe that the thief made a big mistake in moving so early in the voyage. We still have ample time to hunt him down. If he'd stayed his hand until the final night afloat, he'd have made it much more awkward for us. What I suggest,' Genevieve went on, 'is that you tell nobody else about what happened. It will only spread disquiet.'

'We've not breathed a word – even to Mr Thomas.'

'No,' said Florence. 'What would he think of me if he realised how careless I'd been? Vane and I would not confide in anyone.'

Genevieve was pleased. 'That's very sensible. There is something else you could do to help.'

'What's that?'

'I wonder if you'd rack your brains for me and give me a list of all the people you've met since you've been on the *Oceanic*.'

'But there are dozens, Miss Masefield.'

'The thief may be among them,' said Genevieve. 'He or she is someone who has probably met you and taken the trouble to watch your movements. Put down every name that you can think of, however casual the acquaintance might be.'

'I'll do that,' offered Vane. 'My memory is better.'

'Start with Mr Thomas, then,' said her sister.

'He'd have no reason to steal from us. He's a friend. The same goes for his wife and his model. There's no point in confusing Miss

Masefield by giving more names than we need.' Vane Stiller was businesslike. 'We must put down everyone else instead.'

'Does that include George Dillman?' asked Florence.

'Yes,' said Genevieve with equanimity. 'Put his name at the very top of the list. I'll make a point of sounding him out.'

A biting wind was scouring the deck that afternoon and only the most intrepid passengers in first and second class dared to stay outside for long. It was another matter in steerage. Nothing but the most inclement weather would keep the emigrants indoors. Wearing the warmest clothes they could muster, they huddled on deck and shivered in the cold. Even that was preferable to spending more time than was necessary in their cheerless cabins or in the bare and incommodious public rooms.

Blanche Charlbury did not even think of going out onto the promenade deck. Like most people in first class, she opted for the lounge. She was just lowering herself into a chair when Jonathan Killick appeared out of nowhere to accost her.

'Ah, I've caught you alone at last,' he said, sitting beside her. 'Where's the blighted Bossingham?'

'He's gone to get a book for me from his cabin.'

'If you were engaged to me, you'd have no time for reading.'

'Stop it, Johnny! I won't listen to that kind of talk.'

'Would you prefer me to be high-minded and quote Shakespeare? I know a couple of speeches out of *Julius Caesar*.'

'Don't be silly. I need to speak to you.'

'*Speak. Caesar is turned to hear.*'

'Whatever did you say to Mark? He was really vexed earlier on.'

'That was the object of the exercise.'

'You gave him completely the wrong impression,' she said, reaching out to jab him in the ribs. 'That was so naughty of you.'

'Naughtiness becomes me.'

'You taunted Mark without mercy.'

'I told him the truth, that's all.'

'What truth?'

'That I fell in love with you and that you encouraged me.'

'That's not what happened,' she protested, 'and you know it.' 'All I know is that a heavenly creature called Blanche Charlbury once let me send her cards and flowers and boxes of chocolates for months on end.'

'I couldn't stop you.'

'No,' he said, 'but you could have returned them.'

'That would have been petty. Besides, as you well know, I like flowers and I adore chocolates.'

'What about the cards? Did you keep them?'

'For a time.'

'You'd only have done that if they meant something to you.'

'I was flattered at first,' she confessed, 'but the effect soon wore off. And as soon as Mark came on the scene, I burnt everything you ever sent me. It was time to start afresh.'

'And what about Bossingham? Did he start afresh as well?'

'I don't know what you mean.'

'Come on, Blanche,' he teased. 'Even you can't be that innocent. You surely don't believe that he was a vestal virgin before he took an interest in you. I knew him vaguely at Oxford, remember.'

'Until you were sent down.'

Killick laughed. 'Yes, that was inevitable – but I had the time of my life while I was there. Two terms of complete abandon.'

'You were supposed to be there to study.'

'And that's exactly what I did. I studied female anatomy.'

'Mark got a first in Greats.'

'He didn't keep his nose in books all the time,' said Killick with a knowing grin. 'Nor, for that matter, did your brother. Dickon knew how to celebrate. I helped to carry him back to college after a club dinner on more than one occasion.'

'Dickon was never very good at holding his drink.'

'Nor was Bossingham.'

'Mark is very abstemious.'

'Only since he met you, Blanche. When he was an undergraduate, he knew every pub in the city – especially the ones where you'd find the prettiest girls.'

'You're making this up, Johnny,' she said reprovingly, 'and I don't like it. Mark has told me everything about his four years at Balliol so you don't need you to invent spiteful tales.'

'Did he tell you about Alicia Tremaine?'

'Who?'

'Alicia Tremaine – the pride of Henley. Except that she spent most of her time at Oxford, going from party to party. Does the name ring a bell?'

'No.'

'I thought not. And I bet that Dickon didn't mention her either. It was your brother who passed her on to Bossingham when he'd had his fill of her charms. I saw the two of them at a college ball – Bossingham and Alicia, that is. They drank enough bubbly to float a battleship. And when Alicia was sloshed, she was also very compliant.'

'I don't believe a word of this.'

'It's the gospel truth.'

'Mark is above the kind of thing you're suggesting.'

'Then ask him – here he comes.'

Blanche was relieved to see her fiancé approaching. Though she had pretended to discount it, she was upset by what Killick had told her. It had planted a seed of doubt in her mind and she needed immediate reassurance. Mark Bossingham was not pleased to see the other man.

'What are you doing here?' he asked, inhospitably.

Killick got up. 'I was just leaving.'

'Good.'

'What have you brought for Blanche?'

'Trollope,' said Bossingham, holding up the book. '*The Warden*. I'm taking Blanche's reading in hand.'

'Thank you, Mark,' she said, receiving the book from him. 'I'll enjoy reading this.'

'It's about the only thing you will enjoy on this voyage,' said Killick with a smirk. 'Bossingham will make sure of that.'

'Be quiet, Johnny.'

'My lips are sealed.'

'Goodbye,' said Bossingham pointedly.

Killick laughed in his face, blew a kiss to Blanche then sauntered off. Seething with exasperation, Bossingham sat beside his fiancée and watched the departing figure.

'What did he want?'

'He was only trying to stir up trouble.'

'Trouble?'

'Yes, Mark,' she said. 'You know what he's like. First, he tells you downright lies about me in order to upset you. And now, he makes all sorts of ridiculous claims about you.'

'What sorts of claims?'

'It was about your time as an undergraduate.'

'I hardly knew Killick at Oxford.'

'You were in the same dining club for a couple of terms. Johnny remembers my brother having so much to drink that he had to be carried back to his room – that much I can believe. Dickon was like that. But,' she went on, 'I refuse to believe that you were like that as well.'

'Is that what he told you?'

'Yes – but it's not true, is it?'

'No,' he asserted hotly 'Not at all.'

'And I don't think that she ever existed.'

'Who?'

'Some girl he said you took to a college ball. Johnny even had the nerve to suggest that my brother had passed her on to you.'

'Dickon did no such thing.'

'You'd never behave in the way that Johnny implied.'

'The man is incorrigible.'

'My only worry was that he did seem so sure of his facts.'

Bossingham looked uneasy. 'What was the name he gave you?'

'Alicia Tremaine.'

'Oh, I see.'

'She came from Henley, apparently.'

'Did she?'

'I bet you've never even heard of her, have you?'

'No, Blanche,' he said, shifting uneasily in his seat. 'I don't know anyone of that name and I never did.'

Dillman was coining down the main staircase when he caught sight of Manny Ellway. He was grateful for a chance meeting with his steward. Ever since he had seen the man peering into an empty stateroom not far from J. P. Morgan's, his suspicions had been aroused. Ellway's manner was as open and plausible as ever but the detective no longer placed full trust in him.

'Are you keeping busy, Manny?' he asked.

'No time for slacking in this job, sir, or I'll have the chief steward on my tail. He's a real martinet.'

'How many ships have you worked on?'

'Several,' said the other, 'but this is my favourite.'

'Is that because *I'm* on it?'

Ellway chuckled. 'That's part of the reason.'

'What about Abednego Thomas?'

'Yes, it's a treat to look after him as well, Mr Dillman. Though he does make a mess in his cabin. He's in there painting most of the day with that French lady.'

'I believe that Mrs Thomas has been working in there with them.'

'That's right,' said Ellway. 'She's a very talented woman. As well as painting, she designs jewellery and clothing. She showed me some of her drawings.'

'I'm told that she's going to exhibit her jewellery in New York so it must be of the highest quality. By the way,' said Dillman, casually, 'how is that friend of yours getting on with Mr Morgan?'

'Sid? Not very well, from what I hear.'

'Mr Morgan isn't known for being friendly.'

'He's been very unfriendly to Sid,' said Ellway. 'Still, there's been two improvements. The stateroom was filled with things that Mr Morgan had bought in Paris and Sid wasn't allowed in there without someone standing over him. That really upset him. He'd never touch anyone's property. Anyway, it's all gone now. That's made Sid feel a lot happier.'

'Where has it gone to?'

'Been locked away properly, it seems. High time as well.'

'You said that there were two improvements.'

'Yes. The other one is to do with Mr Riedel.'

'Oh, I met him,' said Dillman. 'He works for Mr Morgan.' 'He used to make Sid's life a misery whenever he went in there. But he's been taken ill so Sid doesn't even get to see him. Dealing with Mr Morgan is bad enough,' said Ellway, 'but this Mr Riedel was even worse. He treated Sid like dirt.'

'There's no need for that. Your friend is doing an important job.'

'Somebody has to look after the cabins.'

'A vital service.'

'Passengers expect their accommodation to be clean and tidy.'

'Talking of cabins,' said Dillman, watching him carefully, 'have you been back to take a second peep at that empty one near Mr Morgan's stateroom?'

'No, no.'

'You wouldn't have seen much through a keyhole, anyway.'

Ellway gave a nervous laugh. 'That's true, sir.'

'But, then, it's a standard design – very similar to some of the cabins that you go into every day.'

'I suppose so.'

'Wouldn't your master key have fitted the door?'

'No, Mr Dillman. It only fits the cabins on the deck where I'm assigned. It's a question of security, you see. It stops people from going into places where they've no right to be.'

'Even stewards?'

'Even us, sir. We're under strict supervision.'

'What about the passengers?'

'There's no way that they could get into someone else's cabin.'

'I'm relieved to hear it.'

'It's the reason we have such a good security record on the White Star Line. There's very little crime on board our ships.'

'None at all, I hope.'

There was a telltale pause and Manny Ellway's eyelids flickered.

'None at all, sir. Especially on the *Oceanic*.'

The first thing that Genevieve Masefield noticed when she went into his cabin was the smell of perfume. She surmised that Oskar Halberg had already had one female guest in there since luncheon. Conscious of the fact that she was somewhat taller than he, Halberg waved her to a chair and remained on his feet. The wig seemed to have moved half an inch forward on his head, giving him a more sinister appearance. He stood back with a hand on his hip.

'I trust that this won't take too much time.'

'I just need a few details, Mr Halberg,' said Genevieve, notepad at the ready. 'The purser has given me the basic facts but I require more than that to work on.'

'My billfold was stolen. What else do you need to know?'

'Where and with whom you spent the evening.'

'I had dinner with friends.'

'Could you give me their names, please?'

He struck a pose. 'You surely don't suspect any of them?'

'I have to look at every possibility.'

'Well, you can exclude my dinner companions,' he said, fussily. 'I've known most of them for years. We're all in the same business and, though we might steal each other's designs, we'd never stoop to lifting someone's billfold from his back pocket.'

'Is that where it was kept, Mr Halberg?'

He slapped his hip. 'Right here.'

'What did you do after dinner?'

'I went for a smoke. I always have a cigar after dinner.'

'Were you on your own?'

'No,' he replied. 'I was part of a circle that included J. P. Morgan. And there's no need to write down *his* name either. Whoever else stole my billfold, it was not him.'

'I assume that you were drinking during this time?'

'Do you have any objection to that?'

'None at all,' said Genevieve with an emollient smile, but alcohol does tend to blur our sensibilities. It means that we lower our guard.'

'You don't expect to need a guard on a ship like the *Oceanic*.'

'Pickpockets take advantage of the fact.'

'Well, I want this man caught and punished.'

'Was there much money in your billfold?'

'That's immaterial,' he said. 'The fact is that I'm a victim of a crime and I'm disgusted that it took place on the White Star Line.'

'I share that disgust.'

'Then why aren't you searching for the man right now?'

'Because I'm not even sure that it was a man,' she explained. 'Two female passengers have also had things stolen and, in one case, the thief was certainly a woman. It's not impossible that she was responsible for all three crimes.'

Halberg was shaken. 'I was robbed by a *woman*!' he gasped.

'I can't say for certain but it's something we must consider. For that reason, I have to ask you a personal question.'

'I have nothing to hide, Miss Masefield.'

'Did you embrace any ladies in the course of the evening?'

'Dozens of them,' he said, airily. 'They expect it of me. I have my own method. Hands on both shoulders, a kiss on each cheek –

that's how I always greet my friends.'

'What about new acquaintances you may have made?'

'I would have given any lady a farewell kiss.'

'Even if she were a complete stranger?'

'Miss Masefield,' he replied with condescension, 'I can see that you are not familiar with the world of fashion. Designers are artists. We're not hidebound by convention. We express our affection freely.'

'That being the case, I'd like a list of all the female passengers with whom you came into contact last night – as well as the men.'

'It will be a long list.'

'I'll be able to eliminate most names on it very quickly.'

'I'm not even sure if I can remember everyone.'

'Take it in stages,' she advised. 'Begin with the people at your table, then we'll move on to the smoking room. Where did you go after that – to the lounge?'

'Yes.'

'With another group of people altogether?'

'Yes.'

'And after that?'

'I had a drink with friends.'

'Where?'

'In their cabin.'

'How many of you were there?'

'That's of no consequence,' he said, evasively. 'The one thing I can guarantee is that my billfold was not taken there. The theft must have occurred in one of the public rooms.'

'Did anyone brush up against you at any point?'

'Only when we were leaving the dining room.'

'Pickpockets love crowds. They have an excuse to touch you.'

'You think that it happened there?'

'It may have done,' said Genevieve, 'but I've no means of knowing yet.' She lifted her pencil. 'The important thing is to stop this pickpocket before he strikes again. Now, Mr Halberg, give me those names, please.'

The lounge was busier than ever when they got there. Unable to find a comer on their own, Florence and Vane Stiller had to ask an American couple if they might join them. They introduced themselves and learnt that they were talking to Ethan and Rosalie Boyd.

'We live in the nation's capital,' said Boyd. 'I run a bank there. I used to work in New York but I wanted something less hectic.'

'If you're involved in banking,' observed Florence, 'then you must know Mr Morgan,'

'Everyone knows J. P. Morgan.'

'He has so much money that he doesn't know what to do with it.'

'I think that he does, Miss Stiller – every last cent of it.'

'Do you regard him as the ogre he's sometimes portrayed?'

'Not at all,' said Boyd, pleasantly. 'I take my hat off to him. Even during a depression, J. P. Morgan somehow knows how to turn a profit. I wish that I had his business acumen.'

'You do have it, Ethan,' said his wife loyally.

'We tried to get an interview with Mr Morgan for our magazine,' said Vane, 'but he refused. He obviously doesn't think much of the *Ladies' Home Journal*.'

Rosalie was interested. 'Do you write for that?'

'Yes, Mrs Boyd. We both do.'

'I have a subscription to your magazine. I love it.'

'I'm so glad. Among other things, I'm the travel correspondent.

Florence writes feature articles of all kinds. She's doing one on Abednego Thomas at the moment.'

'It's a joint venture, really,' said Florence.

'Is he that mad Welsh artist?' asked Boyd.

'He's very controversial, if that's what you mean.'

'He paints female nudes or something.'

'Is that true?' said Rosalie, mildly shocked.

'Very true,' replied Vane. 'And they're strikingly lifelike. He uses them to illustrate the myths of Ancient Rome. Also, of course, he does have a highly irregular private life.'

'Three wives to date,' said Florence with a titter, 'quite apart from other liaisons along the way. The world of art is so liberated.'

'That kind of thing doesn't happen in banking,' said Boyd. 'I'm pleased to hear it,' said Rosalie.

'Three wives? Think of the expense.'

'And the scandal.'

'That's what attracted us to him, Mrs Boyd,' said Vane. 'There's something so untamed and delightfully louche about him. Our readers will adore hearing about Abednego Thomas.'

Boyd was sceptical. 'I would have thought him too raw a subject for a women's magazine.'

'Then you've obviously never read the *Ladies' Home Journal*. It's not solely made up of recipes and knitting patterns. We always respect the intelligence of our readers – well, Mrs Boyd is one of them. We tackle serious subjects in every walk of life, and we're not afraid to launch major campaigns on issues of the day.'

'Stop it, Vane,' reproached her sister. 'You're starting to sound like an advertisement and Mr Boyd already has one of those. His wife has a subscription. What better advertisement could there be than that?'

'I read it from cover to cover,' said Rosalie.

'Look out for our article on Mr Thomas.'

'I shall – and I hope to meet him in person before the voyage is over. He sounds like a fascinating man.'

'I doubt if you'll come across his like in banking circles.'

'That's a relief!' said Boyd with a grin.

All four of them laughed. By the time that tea arrived, they were firm friends. Rosalie talked at length about her stepson, and the sisters explained how they had chosen journalism instead of marriage.

Vane was wistful. 'I'm still not sure if we made the right choice.'

'It's too late now,' Florence pointed out.

'Not necessarily,' said Boyd with a touch of gallantry.

'Thank you, kind sir.'

'A proposal may be even closer than you think.'

'Really?'

'If this artist is so fond of getting married, the chances are that he'll be looking for a fourth wife.' The sisters both simpered. 'His problem is that he'll have a terrible job trying to decide between you.'

'Don't be such a tease, Ethan,' said Rosalie.

'I'm not teasing. They're very eligible ladies.'

'Well, yes. They are.'

'It's never too late, Rosalie. Look at your aunt.'

'Yes, she never married until she was quite old. We thought she'd die an old maid but she spent her sixtieth birthday on her honeymoon in Florida. What's more, her husband was years younger than she was.'

'That story would make a good article in our magazine,' said Vane.

'Do you think that your aunt would speak to us?' asked Florence.

'Oh, I'm sure she would,' said Rosalie.

'Could we have her address?'

'It wouldn't be much use, I'm afraid. Unfortunately, Aunt Hetty died some years ago, but she did say that getting married was the best thing she'd ever done in her life.'

'Abednego Thomas said exactly the same thing,' noted Boyd, wryly. 'On three separate occasions.'

The two sisters went off into peals of well-bred laughter.

J. P. Morgan had no reason to stay in his stateroom. Deprived of his art treasures, and lacking a bodyguard, he could have neither pleasure nor company there. He still had many friends and business associates aboard so he decided to enjoy dinner with them. Apart from anything else, he would be giving the impression that nothing untoward had happened. Those who sat at his table would be totally unaware that a major theft had occurred in his stateroom and that the corpse of Howard Riedel was hidden away somewhere on the ship. Morgan intended to keep them ignorant of the harsh truth.

When he had dressed for dinner, he let himself out of his room and ambled along the corridor. Hearing sounds of rapid footsteps behind him, he turned round. A wild-eyed Abednego Thomas and a sleek Dominique Cadine were hurrying towards him.

'I'm glad we've bumped into each other, Mr Morgan,' said Thomas.

'Do I know you, sir?'

'Well enough to cast aspersions on my paintings.'

'Ah, of course,' said Morgan. 'You're that renegade Welshman who thinks the canvas is a fit place for pornography. And you, mademoiselle,' he added, switching his gaze to Dominique, 'like to force your way into parties to which you are not invited. Artist and model – two of a kind.'

'Watch that evil tongue of yours,' warned Thomas.

'Then go your way.'

'Not until I've spoken my mind.'

'You do have one, then?'

'Sneer all you will, you bloodsucker!'

'Abednego is a wonderful artist,' said Dominique stoutly. 'He has a huge reputation in France.'

'A reputation for what?' asked Morgan. 'Profligacy?'

'Magnificent paintings.'

'I find them squalid and uninspiring.'

'You wouldn't recognise artistic talent in a hundred years,' said Thomas, bitterly. 'You've no idea of the pain and suffering that goes into the making of a genius – because that's what it takes, Mr Morgan. Mine isn't a profession where you can feed off other people like a vulture. You have to go through rites of passage on your own – rejection, poverty, hardship, the contempt of philistines like you.'

'That's enough,' cautioned Dominique.

'Oh no, it isn't.'

'He's not even listening, Abednego.'

'Yes, I am,' said Morgan calmly. 'Let him rant on.'

'I speak on behalf of all artists,' continued Thomas, pointing an accusatory finger. 'You're a monster, sir, a devil in human guise.'

'Simply because I find your work so offensive?'

'It's not offensive,' said Dominique. 'It's beautiful.'

'Let me answer him, darling,' said Thomas. 'This is my fight.

167

And no, Mr Morgan,' he went on, rounding on the other man. 'This is nothing to do with me. I don't care two hoots what you think of my work. Quite frankly, I'd be offended if you *liked* it. My argument is with the way that you plunder works of art in ever-increasing numbers without any real understanding of their true worth.'

'I always pay the going rate.'

'Worth and price are two different things.'

'Not to me, Mr Thomas.'

'You just buy indiscriminately.'

'I can at least disabuse you of that,' said Morgan sternly, 'and I call upon Mademoiselle Cadine to bear me out here. She saw my most recent purchases. They were on display at the party. Tell Mr Thomas the truth,' he invited her. 'I never choose at random. When it comes to art – as with everything else – I employ the greatest care. I can afford the best and so I buy it. Correct, mademoiselle?'

'They were excellent paintings,' she conceded.

'That's not the point,' argued Thomas.

'Yes, it is,' said Morgan. 'I discriminate. I know how to separate the wheat from the chaff, how, for example, to select a Renoir and spurn an Abednego Thomas.'

'You don't even understand what I'm saying, do you?'

'Artists need patrons. That's what I am.'

'No, Mr Morgan. You're a symbol of destruction.'

'By creating one of the finest private collections in existence?'

'By using the American dollar like a sledgehammer to smash your way through the art world,' said Thomas vehemently. 'By treating masterpieces as no more than expensive wallpaper for your mansion.'

'Much of what I buy goes into public galleries.'

'Only so that you can peddle the myth of your benevolence. Every donation you make to a public institution is nothing more than a smokescreen for your financial tyranny. You fool nobody, Mr Morgan.'

'Leave him be, Abednego,' said Dominique.

'Somebody had to tell him.'

'It is – what is the phrase – like water off a duck's back.'

'Very well put,' said Morgan with a glacial smile. 'People have been hurling insults at me for half a century and they've done it with far more venom and eloquence than Mr Thomas can manage. But the odd thing is that I'm still here and still doing what I believe I was put on this earth to do. Save your energy for those atrocious paintings of yours, Thomas. I bid you both good evening.'

J. P. Morgan walked off and left the artist fuming. Thomas was all for charging after him to continue the argument but he was restrained by Dominique Cadine. He glared at the American financier.

'I'll *kill* that bastard one day!' he said. 'I swear it!'

It was a paradox. Having married Genevieve Masefield in order to be close to her, George Dillman continued in a profession that kept them apart of necessity. During their three days on board the *Oceanic*, he had seen very little of his wife, and their conversations had been restricted very largely to the crimes that had occurred on board. When she came to his cabin before dinner that evening, he was reminded why he had fallen in love with her and reached out to hold her for a full minute.

'What have I done to deserve that?' she asked, breaking away.

'Do you object?'

'Quite the opposite.'

'I just wanted you to see how wonderful I think you are.' He stood back to admire her. 'That pink dress looks absolutely gorgeous on you, Genevieve. It's your colour.'

'Don't tell that to Oskar Halberg.'

'Why not?'

'He thinks I should wear a specific shade of blue. It would bring out my full essence – at least, that's what he said. When it comes to an evening gown, he'd prefer me in red.'

'You look marvellous in *anything*.'

'Thank you, George.'

'And out of it.'

'Now, now,' she said with a laugh. 'You know our agreement. Work comes first. How are you getting on?'

'Slowly.'

'Any leads at all?'

'I feel that I'm moving in the right direction. I've been working my way through the list of first- and second-class passengers who joined us at Cherbourg. I've whittled the number of suspects down to twenty-two.'

'Supposing that the killer is not among them?'

'Then the instincts I hoped I'd been sharpening over the years have let me down. Howard Riedel was kept under surveillance – on board this ship and off it. Somebody was able to kill two birds with one stone.'

'Murder a hated enemy and steal a collection of art treasures.'

'Yes, Genevieve,' he said. 'And there was another bonus.'

'Was there?'

'It was a way of infuriating J. P. Morgan.'

'Which upset him most, do you think – the death of his bodyguard or the loss of his property?'

'The latter. Howard Riedel can be replaced. The other items can't. Each and every one of them is unique.'

'Especially that Book of Hours. It was ravishing.'

'Just like you.'

He brushed her lips with a kiss. They had agreed to meet in order to bring each other up to date with the progress of their investigations. Dillman was his usual elegant self while Genevieve was wearing a full-length pink evening gown of chiffon-velours with graceful folds, a pointed Court bodice, and lace revers falling tastefully over the décolletage. Her hair was up, throwing her gold earrings into prominence. There was a pink choker around her neck, supporting a single large ruby.

'How far have you got, Genevieve?' he asked.

'I'm still in the early stages.'

'Two more cases dropped into your lap, I hear.'

'Yes – Florence Stiller and Oskar Halberg. You've already had the pleasure of meeting Miss Stiller, I believe. Spare yourself the trouble of an encounter with Mr Halberg.'

'Why? Will he tell me I'd look fetching in a red evening gown?'

'He's such a tetchy gentleman.'

Genevieve gave him an account of her dealings with the two victims and told him how she was looking closely at the various people whom they had each befriended on board. He was amused to hear that his own name had been at the top of one list. No definite suspect had so far emerged and Genevieve was keeping an open mind.

'My big problem is Mrs Farrant,' she said.

'Is she still ranting and raving?'

'She's gone beyond that stage, George. It appears that she's written a letter of complaint to the managing director of the White

Star Line and she's cited my alleged incompetence as a major cause of her resentment.'

'What a dreadful woman!' he said. 'Have you seen this letter?'

'No, I only got to hear of it through the kindness of Rosalie Boyd.'

'Was she the lady whose purse went astray?'

'That's the one. She and her husband have been apologizing about that incident ever since. When they met Mrs Farrant, she insisted on showing them her malicious letter. I'm worried, George.'

'She'll change her tune when you find her diamond earrings.'

'That's neither here nor there,' she said anxiously. 'What disturbs me is that Hilda Farrant is sounding off in public. I warned her to say nothing about the theft and so did Lester Hembrow, but has that stopped her? Oh no. If we're not careful, she'll tell everyone in first class that I work as a ship's detective.'

'That would be fatal. Shall I have a word with her?'

'No, it's my problem. We don't want to expose your cover as well.'

'What about the others?'

'They've been much more discreet. I stressed the importance of keeping details of the crime secret for the time being. That's why Mrs Boyd warned me.'

'Good for her!'

'As it is,' Genevieve continued, 'rather too many people are aware that I'm not the innocuous passenger that I pretend to be. I'm going to have to dodge one of them this very evening.'

'Who's that?'

'J. P. Morgan. I met him under false pretences.'

'You didn't go to that party in order to spy on him, Genevieve. If you hadn't been tricked by that smooth-talking Englishman, you'd never have been there in the first place.'

'Mr Morgan may not see it that way.'

'Ignore him,' he instructed.

'What if he confronts me?'

'He won't do that,' said Dillman. 'He knows that you're helping me to solve the two crimes that took place in his stateroom and he'll admire you for that – especially if we secure an early arrest. We're working together on this as a team.'

'When I'm not diverted by other things.'

'Yes, I could really do with your full-time assistance, Genevieve.'

'Then you know what you have to do,' she told him. 'Pray that I have a clear run from now on. I certainly don't want to have any other cases to distract me.'

The thief walked the length of the corridor to make sure that it was safe to make a move, then doubled back to the cabin that had been chosen. A key went into the lock, the door opened, and someone else's possessions were soon at the mercy of the intruder. It was a profitable visit.

NINE

'May I say how positively divine you look this evening, Miss Masefield?'

'Thank you,' said Genevieve guardedly.

'Your wardrobe is an endless source of wonder.'

'There's no need to exaggerate.'

'But then,' said Killick, 'it's not really the clothing that makes the difference, I always think. It's the woman inside it.'

Genevieve Masefield had delayed her arrival so that the first class dining room would be fairly full and most of the tables would be taken. In the few days afloat, new acquaintances had developed into friends and firm groups had been formed. Unwilling to sit with Blanche Charlbury again, she looked around for a vacant chair at another table. Before she could see one, however, Jonathan Killick strode across the room to kiss her hand and shower her with compliments.

'I feel very honoured,' he said.

'Why?'

'Because I'm the only man aboard who's had the good fortune to act as your escort twice. I regard that as a blessing.'

'Forgive me if I choose another word for it.'

'A curse?' He gave a disarming smile. 'Am I really that bad?'

'I don't like to be hoodwinked,' she told him.

'You were pleased to be invited to Mr Morgan's party, weren't you?'

'Yes, of course.'

'Then you ought to be grateful to the person who contrived it.'

'Had I known in advance, I might have been.'

'Then again,' he said, 'you might have refused to accompany someone like me and I couldn't take that risk. I had to work in a more mysterious way.'

'A more underhanded way.'

'It amounts to the same thing.'

'Not in my dictionary,' said Genevieve, looking around. 'Now, you'll have to excuse me while I find myself a seat.'

'But one is already waiting for you.'

'I'm sorry but I like to choose my own dinner companions.'

He spread his arms. 'Nobody is forcing you, Miss Masefield.'

'Then perhaps you'd be good enough to leave me alone.'

'Of course,' he said. 'I'll just have to disappoint Mr Morgan and tell him that you refuse to join his table again.'

Genevieve was checked. 'Mr Morgan?'

'That's why I'm here – as his emissary.'

'Is this another of your ruses?' she challenged.

'If you don't believe me, look at his table. It's over in the corner once again. You see? He's beckoning you over.'

Genevieve was startled. Seated at the head of the table, Morgan was smiling in her direction and gesturing her across. The rest of the seats were occupied but the chairs either side of him had been kept empty. He patted one of them to indicate that Genevieve should take it.

'And no,' said Killick in her ear, 'this is not my doing. Mr Morgan specifically asked for you to join his party. His taste for female company of the highest order is quite faultless. Shall we go?'

With grave misgivings, Genevieve walked towards the table and tried to conjure up a smile that would conceal her unease. Morgan got up to pull back a chair for her and she sat down, wondering what his motive was for inviting her there. When the Honourable Jonathan Killick sat opposite her, Morgan looked first at him and then at Genevieve.

'How well do you two know each other?' he asked.

'Not well at all,' said Genevieve, making it clear that Killick had no idea that she was a ship's detective. 'In fact, we're complete strangers.'

'I see.'

'But that could all change,' said Killick with supreme confidence. 'Who knows what we could have become by the end of this voyage?'

Florence and Vane Stiller were indefatigable. Having interviewed their favourite living artist on the previous evening, they had turned their attention to a concert pianist from Belgium who was on his way to play with some of the major American orchestras. Freed from their hero-worship, Abednego Thomas chose a table for six and, since George Dillman was with them once more, there were two free seats. Ethan and Rosalie Boyd asked if they might take them. The newcomers pretended not to know who Thomas was but it was clear from Rosalie's respectful scrutiny of his ravaged countenance that she had heard something about him. Still bruised from his verbal skirmish with J. P. Morgan, the artist was unusually subdued. Then he discovered that Boyd was a banker.

'Are you a friend of Morgan?' he asked belligerently.

'Not exactly,' replied Boyd.

'What do you think of him?'

'Well, you have to admire the man's success.'

'At what cost in human misery was it achieved, though?'

'He does have a ruthless streak. We all know that.'

'You don't have to be ruthless in business,' said Rosalie sweetly. 'Ethan isn't and they made him president of the bank. He got where he is by hard work and knowledge of finance.'

'There was some luck attached to it as well,' admitted Boyd. Dillman liked the couple. They were amiable companions. Ethan Boyd was intrigued to learn that Dominique was the model for all of Thomas's recent paintings and he wanted to know how she had come into the art world. Rosalie, meanwhile, reserved her curiosity for Thomas, amazed at some of the stories he told about his erratic life in Paris. There was a bumbling innocence about her that Dillman found engaging. He had no difficulty in believing that she could have left her purse in the library and forgotten all about it. What touched him was the way that Boyd tolerated his wife's obvious limitations.

Dillman spent most of the first course talking to Veronica Thomas.

'I always associate ocean liners with honeymoons,' she said.

'Oh, I daresay that we have a few newly married couples here.'

'A voyage is always so romantic.'

'Did you spend your honeymoon on a ship in the Atlantic?'

'No, George. It was on a barge in the Seine.'

'That's not a bad substitute,' said Dillman.

'It is if the barge leaks and you don't know how to control it properly.' Veronica smiled at him. 'It's a pity that you weren't with us.'

'Me?'

'An experienced sailor. Abednego was hopeless.'

'Steering a barge is not as easy as it looks.'

'That's what Dominique and I found out.'

Dillman was astonished. 'Dominique was with you at the time?'

'She goes everywhere with us. Abednego wanted it to be a working honeymoon so I took all my materials as well. He took his model.'

'Didn't the barge seem a little crowded at times?'

She laughed. 'Well, it wouldn't have suited everybody.'

'I'm probably one of them, Veronica.'

'We started as we intended to go on.'

'Cruising up the Seine in a leaky barge?'

'Putting our work first all the time. Being an artist is not like any other job,' she said with a note of resignation. 'It's a way of life.'

Dillman had grown fond of Veronica Thomas. She was older and less shapely than Dominique but she had a dignity and intelligence that the Frenchwoman lacked. She had also sacrificed far more to reach her goal. Dominique Cadine had grown up in the artistic community of Paris whereas Veronica had repudiated her background and gone to live in a foreign country. For the model, it had been a natural progression; for the wife, it had been a complete metamorphosis.

'You've acquired one admirer since you've been on board,' he said.

'Have I?'

'Manny Ellway, the steward.'

'Oh,' she said with undisguised disappointment. 'I was hoping that it would be you, George.'

'You can take my admiration for granted.' Veronica's foot touched his leg affectionately under the table. 'Manny was so impressed with those designs you showed him.'

'I may even make some of that jewellery before we get to New York.'

'You have all the necessary equipment?'

'In our cabin. The precious metals are locked away in a safe. They're far too valuable to leave lying around.'

'I agree, Veronica.'

She fondled the gold clasp fastened to one shoulder of her dress.

'This is one my latest pieces,' she said. 'I made it before we left.'

'And I daresay that you designed the dress as well, Veronica. You really are a woman of many parts.'

'Oh, I have all sorts of hidden talents. So do you, I expect.'

'I like to think so.'

'It would be interesting to find out what they are.'

When her foot rubbed against his leg again, it stayed there for much longer and it was accompanied by a meaningful stare. Dillman was confused. Veronica was sitting next to a husband she professed to adore and yet she was flirting unashamedly with the detective. He was not sure how to respond. Ethan Boyd came to his rescue.

'And what line are you in, Mr Dillman?' he asked.

'I work in the family business. We build ocean-going yachts.'

'Really? You should talk to J. P. Morgan.'

'I already have,' said Dillman.

'So have I,' added Thomas, curling his lip. 'I could have punched him in the face for what he's done to the art world.'

'Calm down, Abednego,' soothed Veronica.

'You know how I feel about him, my love.'

'That's why you should think happier thoughts.'

She kissed him on the cheek and whispered something in his ear. He gave a ripe chuckle. His good humour returned. Boyd waited until the artist was talking to Rosalie before he turned to Dillman again.

'You spoke to Mr Morgan?' he said.

'It was on behalf of my father, really,' explained Dillman. 'He was invited to submit the design of a new yacht to Mr Morgan and got an earful of abuse for his pains. Our yacht was called *Medusa*. I had the pleasure of pointing out that it came second in the America's Cup.'

'I guess that put Morgan in his place.'

'He's no authority on yachts, I can tell you.'

'Maybe not, but you can't fault him when it comes to high finance. Nor when it comes to his choice of women either,' he went on, looking in the direction of Morgan's table. 'That lady on his right is an English rose by the name of Genevieve Masefield.' He nudged the detective with his elbow. 'She's beautiful, isn't she? Wouldn't you like to have someone like that sitting next to you?'

Dillman gave a quiet smile. 'I do believe I would.'

Blanche Charlbury and Mark Bossingham were sharing a table with a retired Anglican bishop and his wife, a Dutch engineer with a poor command of English, an ancient lady from Baltimore, desperately hard of hearing, and a young French couple making their first visit to America. Conversation ebbed and flowed but there was little opportunity for Blanche to broach any intimate topics with her fiancé. It was only when three people left the table towards the end of the evening that they were able to talk more freely together.

Bossingham turned a jaundiced eye on the table in the corner. 'Look at him,' he said, enviously. 'How does he do it? Killick has got himself a seat next to Mr Morgan this time.'

'So has Genevieve.'

'It's patently obvious why she's there.'

'Mark!'

'She used her charm on Morgan. I saw her for what she was at the very start. Miss Masefield is nothing but an adventuress.'

'That's a wicked thing to say.'

'Then why is she dining with the richest man on the whole ship?'

'Because he invited her, probably,' said Blanche.

'And why did he do that?'

'You're worse than Johnny with your insinuations.'

'I hate people who dissemble – and that's what she's doing.'

'Well, I like Genevieve, whatever you say.'

There was a long silence while coffee was served. Bossingham was sulking. She did her best to make peace with him. Blanche put a hand on his arm and spoke in a low, coaxing voice.

'Let's not argue,' she said.

'Who's arguing? I merely gave you my opinion.'

'Forget everyone else, Mark. The only people that really matter on this ship are the two of us. If we have each other, we don't need anyone else to make this voyage pleasurable.'

'That's what I said to you when I first joined the ship.'

'And you were so right.'

'I usually am.' Her contrition softened him and he even rose to a smile. 'We just require a little more time to get used to each other, that's all. To find our rhythm as companions.' He looked at her. 'Have you had time to read any of *Warden* yet?'

'I dipped into the first chapter but I couldn't concentrate.'

'Why not?'

'Something kept popping into my mind,' she said, frowning at the memory. 'Something that Dickon told me a long time ago.'

'And what was that?'

'Well, he met this girl at Oxford and I could tell that he was keen on her. He took her punting on the river and played tennis with her and all that sort of thing.'

'That was years ago, Blanche.'

'Yes, but I'd forgotten her name until now.'

'So?'

'It was Ally. He kept saying that Ally was a topping girl.' Bossingham was irritated. 'Do we really have to talk about Dickon's undergraduate friendships?' he asked. 'He knew dozens of girls when he was at Balliol with me. It's the reason he only got a third in Finals. Your brother was easily led astray.'

'Ally was worth it. That's what he told me. Ally was worth getting no degree at all.' She looked him in the eye. 'I think that Ally must have been this Alicia Tremaine.'

'That's highly unlikely.'

'Dickon talked about visiting her people in Henley. It must be her.'

'Possibly,' he conceded with a shrug. 'I wouldn't know.'

'You must have known.'

'Dickon and I didn't live in each other's pockets.'

'But you were best friends. You shared a room for two years. If he went out with someone called Alicia Tremaine, you'd have been the first person to be told about it.'

'Perhaps I was, perhaps I wasn't.'

'Earlier on, you denied that you'd ever heard the name.'

'I'm still not sure that I have.' Blanche fell silent and regarded him with growing distrust. He became defensive. 'Why did you have to bring up the subject? It's pointless to discuss it. To be honest, I've forgotten most of what happened at Oxford. I've outgrown that period of my life.' Her critical gaze unsettled him. 'All right,' he said at length, 'perhaps there was such a girl but I only ever knew her as Ally. Your brother never told me her full name.'

'But you must have known it if he passed her on to you.'

'You make her sound like a baton in a relay race.'

'I was being polite.'

'Blanche!'

'Did you get to meet her people in Henley as well?'

'I refuse to be cross-examined like this,' he blustered.

'Then why didn't you tell me the truth?'

'I did – I always have.'

'No, you haven't, Mark. You reserved the right to grill me about Johnny Killick, but you're not ready to talk about your own past, are you? According to you, Alicia Tremaine never existed. Now that I've proved that she did, you're still trying to pretend that you had nothing whatsoever to do with her.'

'This is absurd,' he said, trying to bring the conversation to an end with a display of petulance. 'It's demeaning to both of us. One moment, you're saying that we don't need anyone else, and the next, you're dredging up something that happened years ago.'

'So it *did* happen?'

'I'm not saying that.'

'Then what are you saying?'

'That this whole topic is unseemly.'

'We're not really talking about Alicia Tremaine.'

'Then what are we talking about?'

'The principle of trust,' she said. 'The commitment we made to be completely honest with each other. I think you're lying to me and there's an easy way to prove it.'

'Don't believe a syllable that Killick says.'

'I won't. I'll turn to a much more reliable witness.'

'Who's that?'

'My brother.'

Bossingham gulped. 'You can't do that, Blanche.'

'Why not?'

'Look, you're getting this totally out of proportion.'

'I don't like the feeling that you're hiding something from me.'

'There's nothing to hide.'

'Then why are you behaving so strangely?'

'Keep your voice down!' he urged, glancing round. 'This is neither the time nor the place for something as personal as this.'

'Then let's adjourn to your cabin.'

He was outraged. 'Have you taken leave of your senses?'

'You wouldn't have shown such scruples with Alicia Tremaine.'

'I hardly knew the woman.'

'So you *did* inherit her from Dickon.'

'No, and I resent that suggestion.'

'Did you take her out?' she pressed. 'Did she go to a college ball with you?' He pursed his lips and breathed heavily through his nose. 'You might as well tell me, Mark. If you don't, then my brother will.'

'It was a fleeting friendship, that's all.'

Blanche was unconvinced. 'Was it?'

'Stop looking at me like that.'

'Then stop giving me a reason to do so.'

He slapped the table. 'This discussion stops here and now!'

'It does,' she said, tossing her napkin aside. 'I'm leaving.'

'You can't do that, Blanche.'

She got up quickly. 'Don't try to stop me.'

'I *forbid* you to go,' he said, peremptorily.

'Good night, Mark.'

After distributing a farewell smile among the other people at the table, she thrust out her chin and walked purposefully towards the exit. Bossingham was about to follow her. Before he could rise from his seat, however, a hand rested on his shoulder.

'What's happened?' asked Jonathan Killick. 'A lovers' tiff?'

'Go away!'

'Has Blanche found you out at last?'

'This is all *your* responsibility, Killick.'

'Well, I do like to spread light and joy wherever I can,' said the other, happily. 'That's probably why I could never get into the diplomatic service like you. I'm too hopelessly indiscreet.'

Genevieve Masefield's fears had proved groundless. Summoned to sit beside J. P. Morgan, she thought that he would somehow express his anger at being deceived by her, without giving away her role on board the *Oceanic*. In fact, he was consistently pleasant, talking about his art collection, revealing the global extent of his social contacts, and most surprising of all, showing a detailed knowledge of the Bible. There was no hint of any grievance against Genevieve. It was only when Jonathan Killick departed that Morgan slowly moved the conversation to a more personal level.

'Do you know much about him?' he asked, indicating the table at which the Welsh artist was seated. 'Abednego Thomas, I mean.'

'Only that he has a reputation for being unorthodox.'

'He's a deviant, Miss Masefield – an abnormality, a purveyor of smut and depravity. Worlds away from his biblical counterpart.'

'Wasn't he one of the men in the fiery furnace?' said Genevieve. 'Shadrach, Meshach, and Abednego. They upset King Nebuchadnezzar by refusing to worship the Babylonian gods.'

'I'm glad to hear that someone else reads the Old Testament,' he said, impressed. 'The Book of Daniel – Chapter Three. Abednego was ready to die for his faith. That Welsh impostor doesn't even have one. I'm much more entitled to that name,' he claimed, bluntly. 'For I've been thrust into the fiery furnace many times. It's been heated to seven times its original fury.'

'By whom?'

'My rivals, my detractors, and most of all, by a hostile press. But my faith has brought me through it, and it will sustain me through this latest visit to the furnace. I think you know what I mean.'

'Yes, Mr Morgan – events in your stateroom.'

'More intense heat.'

'We hope to cool it very soon.'

'Someone wanted to cause me serious injury.'

'They'll be apprehended.'

'Can you offer me any assurances to that effect?'

'Bear with us, Mr Morgan.'

'What exactly have you been doing?'

'Inquiries have been made. The net is closing in.'

'I'd like to be there when it's pulled tight,' he growled.

'We shall see.' Noticing that Killick was about to rejoin them, she sat back and changed the subject. 'How did you acquire your detailed knowledge of the Bible?'

'By reading it, of course.'

'Your memory is phenomenal.'

'Yes,' said Killick, resuming his seat. 'All that I can remember of my Scripture lessons are the juicy bits – Cain killing his brother, David slaying Goliath, Delilah betraying poor old Samson. Oh, and all the begetting that went on in the Holy Land.'

'Read the parable of the sower and his seeds,' advised Morgan.

'Is that about begetting as well?'

'No, Jonathan. It's about the folly of planting seed in soil where it will never grow. Your Scripture teacher faced the same problem when she threw biblical wisdom onto the stony ground of your brain.'

Killick laughed. 'How right you are, Mr Morgan!'

'It's not something to be proud of,' said Genevieve.

'I've learnt to live with my afflictions.'

'You do admit that you have some, then?'

'We all have defects. Don't you agree, Mr Morgan?'

'Yes,' he replied. 'The trick is to use them to your advantage.'

'That's what I always do. But while we're talking about afflictions, Miss Masefield,' he went on, 'have you been looking at the one who belongs to Blanche Charlbury?'

'Are you referring to her fiancé?'

'Mark Bossingham. To marry him would be to commit suicide.'

Morgan was amused. 'Do I take it that you have designs on this young lady yourself?'

'I did,' confessed Killick, 'but, with typical altruism, I was ready to lose her to a better man. Unfortunately, Bossingham is not that person. He'll only crush her spirit and rob her of her delightful spontaneity. I think that Blanche finally realised that.'

'Is that why you went over to him?' asked Genevieve.

'I went to save a damsel in distress.'

'Very chivalrous of you, Jonathan,' said Morgan.

'I was too late, as it happens. I've been keeping an eye on them all evening,' said Killick, 'and I could see that a storm was brewing. They had an argument of some kind then Blanche leapt up from the table and charged off. She's probably weeping her heart out now.'

'Then it's up to her fiancé to console her.'

'Any other person would be aware of that, Mr Morgan, but not this particular one. In order to console her, Bossingham would have to visit her cabin, you see, and that would mean stepping over an invisible line that divides betrothal from marriage.'

'I've met him,' said Genevieve. 'He's a slave to propriety.'

'So, alas, am I,' said Killick with a hand on his heart, 'or I'd be the first to offer my sympathy. Given the circumstances, it looks as if that duty falls to you, Miss Masefield.'

'Me?'

'At this moment in time, you're probably the best friend that Blanche has on this ship. She's in great distress, I can tell.' Genevieve made an instant decision. 'I'll have to go to her.'

By the end of the meal, Abednego Thomas had sufficiently overcome his hatred of bankers to invite Ethan Boyd and his wife to join them in the lounge. The Americans were happy to accept the invitation, untroubled by the fact that most people in first class would treat the artist like a pariah. The Welshman looked across at Dillman.

'You'll come with us as well, George.'

'I'll join you in due course,' said Dillman.

Veronica was dismayed. 'We can't let you run away from us.'

'I'll be back before long.'

'I'll come searching for you, if you don't.'

As they got up to leave the dining room, Dillman made sure that he was at the back of the group so that he could slip away once they were outside. He hoped to catch Genevieve's eye before he left but she seemed to have vanished already. Morgan was hauling himself out of his seat before leading his party towards the door. Jonathan Killick was at his elbow. Dillman was pleased to see that the financier was keeping up appearances so well. Diverting attention away from the crimes that had occurred in his stateroom was of crucial importance.

The first place that Dillman visited was the purser's cabin. Lester Hembrow looked resplendent in his uniform but his face was clouded. He was under severe pressure from the captain to make an arrest.

'I told him that he must be patient,' he said.

'Well get there in time.'

'How many suspects are left on the list?'

'Thirteen.'

'That sounds like an ominous number, George.'

'It's unlucky for the killer,' said Dillman. 'I know that.'

'You started out with seventy-three. Somehow, you've managed to cross sixty names off the list.'

'Most people crossed their own names off, Lester. I only had to look at them to see that they were innocent. When I sat down to dinner, I had fifteen names left but, by chance, two of those people happened to be at the same table as me.'

'Who were they?'

'Ethan and Rosalie Boyd.'

'Yes,' said Hembrow, 'I met her. Mrs Boyd is a nice lady but a trifle featherbrained. She was the one who reported the theft of a purse that had inadvertently been left in the library.'

'It doesn't surprise me. Her husband is the president of a bank in Washington, D.C. Since they own two holiday homes and can afford to spend a month every year in Europe, I don't think that they need to steal anything from J. P. Morgan.' He gave a dry laugh. 'The only thing that Ethan Boyd would like to steal is his autograph – preferably on a cheque.'

'I doubt if Mr Morgan is in the giving vein just now.'

'We'll have to ask Genevieve.'

'Why?'

'She was bidden to his table for the second time running.'

'In view of what happened, I thought she'd want to avoid him.'

'If he's still angry with her,' said Dillman, 'he didn't show it in public. Whenever I glanced across at them, he and Genevieve seemed to be having an amicable conversation. When he sees her in private, however, it might be a little different.'

'There's one sure way to sweeten his disposition.'

'Yes – catch the villain. I'll get back on his trail, Lester.'

'Please do,' said the purser. 'I'll pacify the captain somehow. Any suggestions as to what I might tell him?'

Dillman grinned. 'Tell him to steer due west and that we're bound to sight land eventually.'

He patted Hembrow on the shoulder then let himself out. Dillman began a systematic patrol of the corridors, beginning in second class then working his way back up the first-class quarters. Very few people were about and he saw nothing suspicious. He concluded his tour by checking on the stateroom occupied by J. P. Morgan, trying the door to make certain that it was locked then doing the same with the adjoining cabin. Howard Riedel's belongings were still inside but he himself was lying on a bed of ice in another part of the vessel.

Dillman strolled along the corridor towards the staircase that would take him up to the lounge. On his way, he passed the cabin that he had seen Manny Ellway peering into and he wondered what had aroused the steward's interest. Curiosity made him stop outside the door. He decided to look through the keyhole himself but met with an insurmountable problem. There was a key in the lock on the other side. When he tried the handle, the door would not budge. Dillman was puzzled. How could an empty cabin be locked from the inside?

Genevieve Masefield was on a mission of mercy. She was sorry to hear that Blanche Charlbury had fallen out with her fiancé but it did provide her with a welcome excuse to leave the table. She felt that she had spent enough time in the company of J. P. Morgan and she was more than ready to escape from Jonathan Killick. Though she did not wish to get involved in a closer friendship with Blanche, she was willing to respond to what seemed to be her hour of need. Reaching the cabin, she tapped on the door. There was no reply. She knocked harder.

'Who is it?' asked a tearful voice from inside the cabin.

'It's me – Genevieve.'

'What are you doing here?'

'I just came to see how you were.'

'This is not a good time to talk, Genevieve.'

'Then I'll leave you be. Good night, Blanche.'

'No, wait,' said the other, changing her mind. The door opened. 'Come inside for a moment.'

Genevieve stepped into the cabin and the door was closed firmly behind her. Blanche had obviously been crying. Her eyes were red, her face lined, and her whole body sagged. She was unrecognizable from the confident young woman who had come into the dining room earlier. Genevieve was so moved to see her in such a state that she offered her hands. After squeezing them gratefully, Blanche flung herself into her friend's arms and sobbed loudly. Genevieve held her tight and let her cry her fill. Then she guided Blanche to a chair.

'What happened?' she asked softly.

'We had a terrible argument.'

'You must have done to flee from the dining room like that.'

'When I heard the knock on the door,' said Blanche, 'I thought that it might be Mark. The awful thing is that I didn't know if I wanted it to be him or not. I'm so glad that it's you.'

'Is there anything I can do to help?'

'You could give me some advice, please.'

'Of course.'

'But first, I must be honest with you. When I told you earlier that I wouldn't be able to see quite so much of you, it wasn't only because I wanted to spend more time alone with Mark.'

'I know, Blanche. It was because he disapproves of me.'

'I can't for the life of me see why.'

'He has his reasons, I'm sure,' said Genevieve, 'but I don't think that I was the cause of the argument – or was I?'

'No, no.'

'Then what was it about?'

'Alicia Tremaine. At least, that's how it all started. Johnny Killick made a point of whispering her name in my ear. According to him, my brother knew the girl at Oxford. That much is true – Dickon was madly in love with someone called Ally when he was at Balliol.'

'How does Mark fit into this?'

'Johnny says that my brother passed her on to him.'

'Passed her on?'

'It sounds dreadful, doesn't it? I know that I'd hate the thought that any man had passed me on like a discarded overcoat.'

'I don't quite see what the problem is, Blanche.'

'Mark denied that he'd ever heard of Alicia Tremaine.'

'Perhaps he hadn't. Perhaps Jonathan Killick was lying.'

'No, Genevieve. The girl existed and Mark must have known her because he and Dickon were like brothers. I pressed him and pressed him over dinner. In the end, he admitted that he'd had what he called a fleeting friendship with her.'

'But it was years ago,' argued Genevieve.

'That's not the point. He *lied* to me. Mark quizzed me very closely about any romances that I'd had in the past, but he kept the truth from me about this particular girl.'

'Why did he do that?'

'Why do you think?'

Genevieve's sympathy welled up. Blanche had set such great store by the voyage. Deeply in love with her fiancé, she saw it as a time for bonding with him, for getting to know him properly and for rehearsing, to some degree, the companionship they would share after marriage. All at once, her certainties had been shattered and she was bereft. The worst of it was that Blanche still had days to spend on the *Oceanic*, followed by a long spell in her fiancé's company in New York, then a return voyage to England. It was a bleak prospect.

'What am I to do, Genevieve?' she bleated.

'Take time to think it over. It may look rather different in the morning. It was wrong of Mark to mislead you like that but he does deserve the chance to explain himself.'

'I don't want to hear any excuses.'

'An apology is definitely in order here,' said Genevieve. 'He has to make amends by being more candid about his past. You're going to be his wife, Blanche. There should be no secrets of that kind between you.'

'Supposing that he won't apologise?'

'Then the situation will become more serious.'

'That's what I'm frightened of,' admitted Blanche, biting her lip. 'It's an awful feeling to know that you've been lied to but I hate the idea that I might actually lose Mark. We're engaged.'

'I'm sure that he doesn't want to lose you either.'

'It may come to that.'

There was a fresh burst of tears and Genevieve put an arm around her as she dabbed at her eyes with an already moist handkerchief. Blanche made an effort to pull herself together. She swallowed hard.

'What would you do in my position?' she asked. 'Not that you'd ever be in similar circumstances, of course.'

'As it happens, I have been.'

Blanche was taken aback. 'You were engaged?'

'For a time.'

'When – and to whom?'

'That's irrelevant,' said Genevieve, reluctant to give her too much detail. 'The simple fact is that I had a fiancé whom I loved and trusted until he did something that was quite unforgivable. I had no option but to break the engagement off.'

'You mean that infidelity was involved?' said Blanche, aghast.

'I mean that his behaviour was totally unacceptable. Now, that's not the case here. Mark has been less than honest with you about something that happened during his undergraduate days,' Genevieve went on, 'but I don't feel that that's a good enough reason in itself to make you sever the relationship. That has to be a last resort.'

'I know.'

'Mark has some explaining to do but, by the same token, you must give him the opportunity to do it. It's worth remembering that this whole business blew up because of someone else's mischief-making.'

'Johnny Killick would love to break us up.'

'Then don't give him the pleasure. Close ranks.'

'I want an apology first.'

'From what I've seen of Mark, you can count on getting one.'

'I ought to get one from Johnny as well but there's no chance of that. Well, you've seen him in action. You know the sort of person he is.'

'Quite,' said Genevieve. 'What interests me is how he got to know about this girl in the first place. Over dinner, he was boasting to us that he got sent down from Oxford after four terms.'

'It was amazing that he lasted that long, Genevieve.'

'Did he overlap with Mark and your brother?'

'For a short while,' said Blanche. 'All three were in the same dining club. Needless to say, Johnny disgraced himself regularly there. And he didn't do a scrap of work.'

'Is that why he was kicked out of Oxford?'

'No,' replied Blanche, 'it was for stealing. They caught him taking money from rooms belonging to one of the dons. Johnny was always short of cash. He even tried to pawn some of the college plate and there was a real scandal about that.'

'I'm not surprised.'

'He was lucky that they didn't prosecute.'

'Why didn't they?'

'His father stepped in and poured oil on troubled waters by making a hefty donation to college funds. But Johnny was sent down on the spot.'

'Serves him right.'

'It wasn't the first time, you see.'

'Oh?'

'He was expelled from Harrow for exactly the same thing.'

'Stealing?'

'Yes, Genevieve,' she said. 'Johnny always claims that he only does it in fun but we don't believe him. It's in his character. He finds it daring to take risks and sail close to the wind. Oddly enough, he does have some good qualities as well and that's why I was drawn to him. He can be kind and extraordinarily generous. But there's one thing about Johnny Killick that all his friends know – he's a thief.'

Fond of a smoke at the end of each day, Sidney Browne had sneaked out on deck to enjoy a cigarette and stare up at the stars. In such moments of contemplation, he wondered what impulse had driven him to become a steward on an ocean liner, and he speculated on how much happier his lot might have been if he had followed his father into the boot-making trade. When his cigarette was almost spent, he took one last pull on it then flicked the butt into the sea. It was time to turn in.

Manny Ellway was the only person in their cabin, sitting on his bunk and reading a newspaper. He looked up with a smile. 'Hello, Sid. Had your fag on deck?'

'Yes,' said Browne gloomily. 'Bleedin' cold out there.'

'Don't know how you can afford to smoke. I can't.'

'It's the only pleasure left in life, Manny. What you got there?'

'One of the passengers gave me this.'

'But it must be days out of date.'

'So what? Time stands still on the Atlantic.' He put the paper aside. 'How are you getting on with Mr Morgan now?'

'Very well. 'Aven't set eyes on 'im all day.'

'Is that bodyguard of his still laid up?'

'Yes,' replied Browne, 'and I 'ope it's somethin' serious. Nasty piece of work, 'e was, that Mr 'oward Riedel. I always gets the worst passengers. I'd change my lot for yours straightaway.'

'You wouldn't say that if you met them.'

'Why not?'

'Well,' said Ellway with a chuckle, 'you may have some nasty people but I've certainly got some really weird ones.'

'Such as?'

'That Welsh artist I told you about – Abednego Thomas.'

Browne smirked. 'The one who paints them naked ladies?'

'He doesn't only paint them, Sid.'

'What do you mean?'

'This is between the two of us, mind. I don't usually tell tales about passengers but I know I can trust you. So keep this to yourself. Right?'

'Right.'

'There's funny goings in that cabin and I'm not at all sure it should be allowed.'

'What did you see?' asked Browne, agog.

'It's not so much what I saw, Sid, as what I worked out. Mr and Mrs Thomas are in one cabin, see, and this French young lady, his model, is in the one next door. At least,' said Ellway, 'that's how it was on the first night.'

Browne rubbed his hands. 'This is gettin' interestin', Manny.'

'Mrs Thomas wears this lovely blue nightdress. She made it herself. She designs all her clothes.'

'So?'

'The French lady has this red silk nightdress.'

'If she's used to posin' naked all day, I'm surprised that she wears anythin' at all in bed. You know what these French women are like.'

'I'm beginning to find out,' admitted Ellway. 'When I turned down the beds earlier, they'd changed places. The red silk nightdress was folded up neatly under the pillow in Mr Thomas's cabin while the blue one had moved to the cabin next door.'

'That *is* weird,' said Browne, 'and no mistake. Why should the two ladies want to wear each other's nightdresses?'

'They don't, Sid.'

'Then why did they . . . ?'

Browne stopped as he realised that another interpretation could be placed on the facts. Ellway was still not certain if he should be shocked or amused, but his friend was not hampered by indecision. Putting his head back, Browne emitted a high pitched cackle.

'The lucky devil!' he cried. 'Abednego Thomas is sleepin' with each of them in turn. I tell you what, Manny, I wouldn't mind bein' an artist if that kind of thing is normal.'

'There's nothing normal about them three.'

'So last night, that old goat takes 'is wife to bed.'

'As far as I could judge.'

'And tonight, 'e's got 'is model lined up. Who can blame 'im? I've seen that Mademoiselle Whatsername. She's gorgeous,' said Browne, licking his lips. 'Any man with red blood in his veins would want to spend the night with 'er.'

George Dillman had completed one half of his search earlier that day, eliminating all the names of second-class passengers on his list. Only thirteen suspects were now left and, as he entered the first-class lounge, he knew that the killer was probably there as well. Abednego Thomas was in his element, surrounded by Florence and Vane Stiller, Ethan and Rosalie Boyd, and a few people whom Dillman did not recognise. While the artist was holding court, his wife sat on the edge of the group with a smile of resignation. As soon as she saw Dillman, she leapt up and kissed him on the lips.

'Where have you been, George?' she asked.

'I had to talk to someone.'

'Not a young lady, I hope.'

'No, no, this was a member of the crew.' He looked at Thomas. 'I see that Abednego has collected some new followers. He does have a way of attracting attention, doesn't he?'

'Yes – if not always of the right kind.'

'Artists need to keep their name before the public.'

'The best way to do that is to produce and sell plenty of paintings. At least, that's how I endeavour to spread the word about Veronica Thomas. I'm not so clever at wooing a crowd as Abednego.'

'How is his latest painting coming along?'

'Nearing completion, he says. Give it a day or two.'

'I'd enjoy seeing it unveiled,' he said, 'and I'd be grateful for a second look at your work as well, Veronica. It's very arresting. My only concern is that both you and your husband are so carefree.'

'Carefree?'

'Those paintings in your cabin must be worth a tidy amount. Aren't you worried that somebody might sneak in there and steal them?'

'Hardly,' she replied. 'Look around you, George. My husband may have seven people sitting at his feet but there are well over two hundred others in here who treat him like a leper. Nudes frighten them. And the man who paints them is therefore an object of disgust.' She looked at him quizzically. 'Are you frightened by the sight of nudity George?'

'Not at all.'

'You don't feel embarrassed or threatened in any way?'

'Why should I?'

'You're very enlightened. Most of your fellow Americans seem to be in the grip of high moral principles.'

'The founding fathers were Puritans, remember. That's not something that can easily be shaken off.'

'You've managed to do it.'

'I've had the good fortune to travel a great deal.'

'That was the first thing I noticed about you. You're urbane.'

'Thank you.'

'What was the first thing you noticed about me?'

'How well the three of you got on with each other,' he said. 'You, Abednego, and Dominique. There was this wonderful togetherness about you. Though you're very individual characters, you managed to blend into one.' He saw that she was waiting for a more personal compliment. 'I also noticed how beautiful you look and how elegantly you dress, Veronica. There are ladies in this room who spend hundreds of dollars on every item in their

200

wardrobe but none of them can match you.'

'I appreciate that remark, George.'

'It was honestly made.'

'I'd expect nothing less from you.'

She reached out to squeeze his hand and he gave her a neutral smile by way of reply. When she locked her eyes on his, he had to force himself to look away. He gazed around.

'I don't see Dominique.'

'She went off to see a friend.'

'I didn't know that she had friends aboard.'

'She didn't when we joined the ship,' said Veronica, easily, 'but she's ubiquitous. I've no idea who this new friend is but one thing I can tell you. It will be a man.'

Dominique Cadine tripped along the corridor and tapped on the door of a cabin. It was opened at once and the face of Oskar Halberg emerged.

'You changed your mind, then?' he said, beaming at her.

'Yes.'

'Come on in, Dominique.'

After half an hour with her friend, Genevieve Masefield felt that she had done all that she could for Blanche Charlbury. The younger woman was still upset but she no longer viewed a possible indiscretion by her fiancé as a strong enough reason to revalue the whole of their relationship. As she bade Blanche farewell, Genevieve told herself that she was leaving her in a far better state than she had found her. After checking the time on her watch, she decided to return to her cabin but someone was lying in wait for her. The moment she turned a corner, he stepped out in front of Genevieve.

Mark Bossingham was throbbing with barely contained anger.

'What did you say to Blanche?' he demanded.

'That's between myself and your fiancée.'

'Have you been trying to turn her against me?'

'She needed no help from me on that score,' said Genevieve, levelly. 'You were the one who upset her, Mr Bossingham. Blanche feels that she's been deceived.'

'She's certainly deceived in you.'

'I don't seek your good opinion.'

'That's just as well, Miss Masefield.'

'I went to Blanche as a friend. After what happened over dinner, she was certainly in need of one. She was very grateful.'

'Don't expect any gratitude from me.'

'I'd never dream of it.'

'I regard you as a malign influence on Blanche.'

'That's an insulting remark, Mr Bossingham, and I can see that I was wrong to think you above such things. Stand aside, please.'

'I'll ask you to keep away from us in the future.'

'I'm more than happy to keep away from you,' she said, 'but your fiancée is a different matter. Blanche has the right to choose her friends and I'm pleased to be among them.'

She moved him gently aside with an arm and continued on her way, wishing that she had not urged Blanche to give him the chance to make amends. His behaviour did not merit it. Bossingham had not been in a diplomatic mood with her and his comments rankled. Genevieve was glad to let herself into her cabin and shut out all memory of him. Her attention was soon fixed on something else.

Lying on the table in front of her was a white envelope with her name on it. How it had got into her cabin, she could only guess and the sight of it was slightly unnerving. She needed a moment before she felt able to reach out for it. There was something inside the envelope, something that jingled slightly as it moved. Genevieve was bewildered. When she opened the envelope, out fell an expensive gold bracelet.

There was a message in the envelope, written in a sloping hand.

As a token of my love and admiration – Johnny

TEN

It was over an hour before the numbers in the first-class lounge began to thin out, and before Dillman felt able to break away from his friends. Abednego Thomas gave him a cheery wave and a ribald comment in Welsh. Veronica took the opportunity to kiss the detective on the lips once again. Ethan and Rosalie Boyd had already left and Dominique had not come back to the lounge. Thomas's other acolytes had faded away. Dillman walked out of the room with Florence and Vane Stiller.

'Where *does* he get his energy from?' wondered Vane.

'Abednego has defied time,' said Dillman. 'He has the stamina of someone half his age.'

'He claims that he gets his zest from a wine bottle.'

'He was only joking,' said Florence. 'That surging power of his doesn't come from drink. It's innate. What keeps him so young and active is his creative spirit.'

'Well, I wish that I had some of it.'

'So do I, Vane.'

'When are you going to have a photograph taken with him?' asked Dillman. 'I know that he's looking for an excuse to stand between the pair of you and slip a hand around your waists.' They laughed. 'And who can blame him?' he added, courteously.

'Oh, Mr Dillman! You say the sweetest things.'

'There's a photographer on board, isn't there?'

'Yes,' replied Vane, taking over, 'and he's hoping to accommodate us tomorrow, if the weather is a little kinder. We wanted the photograph taken in his cabin, with his paintings in the background, but Abednego decided against that in the end. The only examples of his work that he would really like to be photographed are all boxed up in the hold.'

'You'll have to go to his exhibition in New York to see them.'

'We can't wait, can we, Florence?'

'No, dear. It's already in our diary.'

They traded farewells with Dillman then went off in the opposite direction. Before going to his own cabin, Dillman first returned to the one he had peered into earlier. Once again, he put his eye to the keyhole but he had more success this time. There was no obstruction. He found himself looking into a dim interior and was able to pick out the shapes of the furniture. The cabin was self-evidently vacant. If someone had been in there earlier, they had gone now and locked the door behind them. Dillman made a mental note to borrow a master key from the purser next morning so that he could look inside.

When he got back to his own cabin, he slipped off his coat and hung it up in the wardrobe. It was Genevieve's turn to call on him that night so that they could exchange any information they had managed to gather. He was looking forward to their brief reunion, needing, after a long and hectic day, to remind himself that he had a lovely wife on the *Oceanic*, as well as a highly competent partner. A knock on the door made him adjust his tie and pull himself to his full height. It sounded as if Genevieve was as punctual as ever for their meeting. He opened the door with a flourish, ready to enfold her in a warm embrace. 'Come in,' he invited.

'Thank you, George,' said Veronica, pleased with her reception.

He was astonished. 'Oh, it's you.'

'Were you expecting someone else?'

'No, no,' he lied, closing the door after she had stepped inside. 'It's just that I'm rather surprised to see you.'

'Pleasantly surprised, I hope.'

'Yes, Veronica.'

'Your cabin is so much tidier than ours,' she said, looking around it with interest. 'Abednego likes to spread.'

'So I noticed.'

'But there are times when artistic squalor gets me down a little.'

'Squalor?'

'Disorder, confusion, jumble. Our cabin is a mess.'

'I liked all that amiable clutter. It lent a distinct atmosphere.'

'That was the smell of the oil paints.' She moved closer. 'Why have you suddenly become so formal? This can't be the first time that you've had a woman visit you in a cabin.'

'No, it's not.'

'Then make me more welcome. Do you have anything to drink in here?'

'I'm afraid not.'

'Press the bell and summon a steward.'

'I think I've had enough alcohol for one day,' he said, holding up a hand. 'So, perhaps, have you, Veronica.'

'The night is still young.'

'Won't your husband be missing you?'

'Oh, I don't think so. He's used to this kind of thing.'

'And what kind of thing is that?'

'George!' she said with mock censure. 'Do you really have to ask?'

Her purpose was all too apparent and it alarmed Dillman. He did not wish to hurt her feelings by too blunt a rejection but he was very conscious of the fact that Genevieve would be there shortly, and her arrival would introduce all sorts of complications into the situation. Dillman needed to get rid of his visitor quickly.

'Veronica,' he began, 'there's been a misunderstanding.'

She came closer. 'Has there?'

'I really think that you should go back to Abednego.'

'That would be against the rules.'

'Rules?'

'Yes,' she said blandly. 'He doesn't mind my coming here, if that's what's troubling you. And we could easily go to the other cabin. Would you prefer to do that?'

'Which other cabin?'

'Dominique's, of course.'

'Won't she need it for herself?'

'I can see that I'll have to explain it more clearly,' she said, slipping her arms familiarly around his neck. 'Abednego and I have a rather unusual marriage. Most of the time, we live in a ménage à trois. That's why Dominique came on our honeymoon on that barge with us. It's something I had to accept from the very start, you see. Abednego believes in free love. He sleeps with all his models. It helps him to paint them with more insight and accuracy.'

'Don't you mind?'

'Not if I'm allowed to roam outside the bounds of matrimony as well. My husband is spending the night with Dominique so I can look elsewhere. And I'm choosing the most handsome man on board.'

'Unfortunately,' he said, detaching her hands, 'I'm not available.'

She was hurt. 'Doesn't the idea appeal to you?'

'I find you very appealing, Veronica.'

'But you have qualms about my being married.'

'It's not *your* situation that troubles me,' he said gently, 'but my own. The truth of it is that I'm already spoken for.'

'Oh dear!'

'I'm terribly sorry if I gave you the wrong idea.'

'No, no, the fault is mine, George.'

'Friendship is all that I can offer you.'

'Then I'll have to settle for that,' she said wistfully. Her eyelids narrowed. 'Just let me ask you one question.'

'What?'

'It's not because you prefer Dominique, is it? You don't have a prior arrangement with her, by any chance? I'm not jealous as a rule but that would be rather wounding. It's one thing to share my husband with Dominique but quite another to be overshadowed by her.'

'Dominique could never overshadow you, Veronica.'

'Do you really mean that?'

'You're one of the most remarkable women I've ever met.'

He said it with such sincerity that she stepped forward to hug him impulsively. Then she gave a laugh and retreated to the door.

'This has been rather embarrassing, hasn't it?'

'Not really.'

'What are we going to say to each other in the light of day?'

'Good morning, I expect.'

'Do we just forget that this ever happened?'

'No,' said Dillman. 'I'm very flattered. You took me unawares, that's all. I just didn't expect anything like this, Veronica.

'I knew that you had an unconventional marriage but I didn't realize the full import of that.' He reached for the door handle. 'Perhaps I should check if there's anybody about.'

'Yes, I don't wish to compromise you.'

He opened the door and saw, to his intense relief, that the corridor was empty. Standing back, he gave Veronica a smile of farewell. She stole one last kiss then stepped swiftly out of the cabin. He closed the door and leant against it. Dillman blamed himself for being so blind. From the very start, Veronica Thomas had shown a keen interest in him and her affection was undisguised. In rubbing his leg under the table during dinner, she had given him a clear signal and, because Dillman had not objected, she had all the encouragement that she needed.

It had been a narrow escape and he wondered how Genevieve would react when he told her about it. He also wondered why she was late. It was very uncharacteristic of her. At that moment, Dillman felt a great need to see his wife. Where could she possibly be?

Trembling with apprehension, Edith Hurst stood in front of her like a schoolgirl who has been summoned to the headmistress's study. When the call came, she had been about to go to bed.

After hurriedly putting on her uniform, she rushed to the cabin. Genevieve let her in then held up the envelope that had contained the bracelet.

'How did this get here?' she asked sternly.

'A gentleman gave it to me.'

'When?'

'Earlier this evening, Miss Masefield. He said that I was to wait until you had gone to dinner then leave it in your cabin.'

'Did he give his name?'

'No.'

'Did you let him in here at any point?'

Edith blushed. 'No, miss. I'd never do that. I'd lose my job if I did. We have very strict rules about that sort of thing.'

'Rightly so,' said Genevieve. 'When the gentleman spoke to you, did he ask to be let in here?'

'Yes, Miss Masefield. He offered me money.'

'What did you do?'

'I refused to take it.'

'Good girl.'

'He said that he was a friend of yours, but that's no reason to let him in here. Yet I did agree to put the envelope on the table,' said Edith. 'I saw no harm in that. He told me that it was a gift for you. Have I done wrong, Miss Masefield?'

'No, you've behaved well.'

'Thank you.'

'So you can stop being so frightened,' said Genevieve, taking pity on the girl. 'You look as if I'm about to accuse you of some heinous crime. You haven't done something terrible, have you?'

'No, no. I just do my duties.'

'Then I've no complaint. But next time this gentleman asks

you to put something in my cabin, tell him that you're not able to do so.'

'Yes, Miss Masefield.'

'And under no circumstances must he be allowed in here.'

'I understand that.'

'How much did he offer you?'

'Five pounds.'

Genevieve was startled. If Jonathan Killick had been prepared to pay that much for access to her cabin, he would have wanted to do far more than merely leave an envelope there. That disturbed her. She looked at the stewardess, who was standing there with her feet together and hands clasped. Five pounds would have been a big temptation to someone on such a low wage.

'Thank you, Edith,' she said. 'Your behaviour was exemplary. I shall make a point of mentioning this to the chief steward.' The girl's face lit up. 'Now off you go and get a good night's sleep.'

'Yes, Miss Masefield – good night.'

Edith Hurst looked as if a weight had been taken from her shoulders.

Visibility was an important part of the purser's job and Lester Hembrow tried to be seen in or near the public rooms as often as possible. The sight of a uniform was always reassuring to passengers and, even though it exposed him to a lot of pointless questions, he did not mind. Smile intact, he suffered fools very gladly. Occasionally, however, some of his encounters were a little more abrasive.

'Ah, there you are, Hembrow.'

'Hello, Mr Morgan.'

'Don't you ever go to sleep, man?'

'Against company policy,' said the purser cheerfully. 'I'm on call throughout the night. That, alas, is when problems often occur.'

Morgan was rueful. 'Yes, I found that out!'

They were standing outside the lounge after most of the passengers had left. Since nobody else was within earshot, J. P. Morgan felt able to raise a private matter. His eyes flashed.

'I expected some results by now,' he complained.

'They'll not be long coming, sir.'

'Be warned, Hembrow. I won't be fobbed off.'

'I appreciate that, sir.'

'Then give me answers instead of excuses.'

'Mr Dillman has been pursuing the investigation with vigour.'

'Why does he have nothing to show for his efforts?'

'But he does,' said Hembrow, earnestly. 'He's worked through a list of possible suspects and narrowed it down to a dozen or so.'

'And how has he done that?'

'Well, he believes that the killer has been on your tail for some time. Mr Dillman feels certain that the man followed you to Paris and, therefore, must have boarded the ship at Cherbourg.'

'What evidence does he have to prove that?'

'No evidence in the acknowledged sense of the word.'

'So how has he reached this conclusion?'

'It's an educated guess, Mr Morgan.'

'I want more than educated guesses,' snarled the financier. 'Good lord, man! We're discussing a murder and a major art theft here. These are dreadful crimes and they won't be solved by guesswork of any kind.'

'Mr Dillman is an experienced detective. So is Miss Masefield.'

'Yes, I dined with the lady this evening. She told me that the net was closing in but I don't see any proof of that.'

'I've told you, sir,' said Hembrow, wishing that he were not being subjected to such a withering stare. 'The list of suspects is extremely short now. George Dillman has worked through the names of all the relevant passengers who embarked at Cherbourg.'

'What if the killer was already aboard?'

'We think that's only a vague possibility.'

'Almost as vague a possibility as an arrest, by the sound of it.'

'Now, that's unfair, sir.'

'Is it?'

'Mr Morgan—'

'Listen to me,' said Morgan, rudely interrupting him. 'My patience is wearing thin, Hembrow. I'm not used to being kept waiting by anybody, least of all by minor employees of the White Star Line. I demand a speedy resolution or heads will begin to roll.'

'These things can't be rushed.'

'Yes, they can – if there's sufficient urgency.'

'Nobody could work with more urgency than George Dillman. I trust his judgement, Mr Morgan. If he's produced a list of suspects, the chances are that the killer is definitely on it.'

'Then do the obvious thing.'

'What's that, sir?'

'Search the cabins of every person on that list.'

'We couldn't possibly do that.'

'Why not?'

'That would be an unwarrantable invasion of privacy.'

'Howard Riedel was murdered in my stateroom,' Morgan reminded him. 'That's what I call an unwarrantable invasion of privacy, and it's a crime that justifies any response. Search the cabins and you're bound to find the items that were stolen.'

'Not necessarily. A professional thief might not keep such a haul in his cabin. He'd have stowed it safely away elsewhere.'

'Then search the whole ship.'

'That's just not feasible, Mr Morgan.'

'Why not?'

'Because the thief would always be one step ahead of us,' said the purser. 'To conduct a search on that scale would involve a large number of people, and that means the passengers would be aware of it. All the thief has to do is to keep moving his loot whenever we get close to it. We're not dealing with an amateur here, sir.'

'I'm beginning to feel that I am.'

'That's unjust, Mr Morgan.'

'Find me the culprit and find him fast.'

'According to Mr Dillman—'

'Leave him to me,' said Morgan, cutting him off again. 'I'll speak to Dillman myself. He obviously doesn't realize who I am and what I expect of people. I'll see George Dillman tomorrow and light a fire under him. I want my property back.'

Genevieve Masefield gave her husband a succinct account of what had happened.

'What am I to do, George?' she asked.

'You don't usually have a problem getting rid of unwanted suitors.'

'Jonathan Killick is very tenacious.'

'So it seems.'

'He keeps popping up like a jack-in-the-box when I least expect him. Blanche warned me that he never gives up.'

'She also told you that he was a thief,' said Dillman, examining the gold bracelet that had been left as a gift. 'Am I holding stolen goods in my hands?'

'It's not impossible.'

'Well, I doubt if this belonged to anyone on the *Oceanic*. Killick is an intelligent man. He wouldn't risk giving you anything that might be recognised by a previous owner.'

'That's assuming I'd wear it.'

'Would you?'

'Only if it was a present from my loving husband.'

He kissed her. 'You always did drop the subtlest of hints.' They were in Dillman's cabin. Genevieve had explained her delay and he had listened intently. Dillman handed the bracelet back to her.

'Something positive has come out of this,' he observed.

'Yes, I discovered that I have an honest and reliable stewardess.'

'I wish that I could say the same.'

'Why?'

'Because the man who looks after me is not so trustworthy.' He told her about how he had found Manny Ellway peering into the empty cabin, and what happened on the two subsequent occasions when he himself had looked through the keyhole. Genevieve agreed that the steward's conduct had been suspicious.

'I can think of only one reason why he was looking at that cabin,' she said.

'Where better to hide stolen property?'

'Exactly, George. Have you been inside yet?'

'I'll get the key from Lester Hembrow first thing tomorrow.'

'Do you really think that this Manny Ellway could be involved in the crime?' she said. 'What other signs have there been?'

'None beyond the fact that he lied to me.'

'Does he look like a potential killer?'

'No,' admitted Dillman, 'but then potential killers don't look like potential killers. That's what makes our job so fiendishly difficult. If you think about the people we've arrested for murder in the past, not one of them has been an obvious suspect.'

'That's true.'

'From what I know of him, I doubt very much if Ellway would cut a man's throat but he could still be an accomplice. Someone helped the killer to get inside that stateroom.'

'Is he Mr Morgan's steward as well?'

'No, Genevieve. That ambiguous pleasure has fallen to a more experienced man called Sidney Browne. According to Ellway, his colleague would never dream of lending his master key to anyone.'

'So how could Ellway have got hold of it?'

'He shares a cabin with Browne. I checked with the chief steward. There are four of them in there, it seems, cheek by jowl. If they're in and out of their cabin all the time, there might well be an opportunity for Ellway to borrow his friend's master key. It would only have been needed for a very short time.'

'What would be his motive?' she said.

'Money, for a start. Stewards are not well paid, even in first class.'

'There would have had to be a very large cash inducement. Ellway was taking a huge risk in becoming an accessory to murder.'

'He may not have realised that murder was involved.'

'I hadn't thought of that.'

'If it was presented to him as a case of theft,' reasoned Dillman, 'he might have been tempted. Never discount envy as a motive. If one of the richest men in the world is travelling in luxury and you're a menial at his beck and call, how would you feel?'

'That there was some kind of social injustice.'

'Perhaps he sought to redress it.'

'Perhaps,' she agreed. 'Are you going to challenge him?'

'No, I'll just keep a close eye on Manny Ellway. I suggest that you do the same with the Honourable Jonathan Killick.'

'How do I stop him keeping a close eye on me?'

'Only you know that, Genevieve.'

'The first thing I'll do is return this gold bracelet,' she decided. 'Blanche made the mistake of holding on to some of the gifts he sent her and it allowed him to make assumptions.'

'I'm afraid that I was guilty of that this evening.'

'Holding on to a gift?'

'No,' confessed Dillman. 'Allowing someone to make assumptions about my feelings towards them. All that you had to contend with was something inside an envelope. I had the lady herself in this very cabin.'

'Really?' she said, eyebrows lifting. 'Tell me more, George.'

It was early when Mark Bossingham arrived for breakfast but Blanche was already there, sitting alone at a table and studying the menu. He took it as a hopeful sign. Hurrying across to her, he forced a smile.

'Good morning, Blanche,' he said.

'Good morning.'

'May I join you?'

'As long as you haven't come to quarrel with me.'

'No,' he said, taking the seat opposite her, 'I'd rather put all that behind us. Neither of us comes out of that business with any credit.'

'Are you blaming me?' asked Blanche.

'Not at all.'

'You were the person who tried to deceive me.'

'That's a matter of opinion.'

'You were, Mark.' There was a long pause. She searched his face for signs of penitence. 'I was hoping that you might write.'

'Write?'

'A letter of some kind, a note of apology.'

'I see.'

'Something to slip under my door so that I could find it this morning. But I waited in vain. You're not a man for expressing your emotions on paper, are you?'

'I'm a diplomat, Blanche. I'm very careful with my choice of words.'

'Well, you didn't choose the right ones last night.'

He was about to reply when the waiter came to take their order. They made hasty decisions about their respective breakfasts. As soon as the man went away again, Bossingham leant forward.

'What did you say to her?'

'Who?'

'Miss Masefield. She went to your cabin last night.'

'How do you know?'

'I accidentally bumped into her,' he said, 'and I can't say that I was altogether pleased. You know my feelings about her.'

'Genevieve came to me as a friend.'

'And I can imagine what she said.'

'Can you?'

'Of course. She tried to turn you against me, Blanche. That kind of woman always revels in other people's setbacks. She must have been delighted when she saw you charging out of here last night.'

'You're quite wrong. She was very sympathetic.'

'To you, perhaps – not towards me.'

'Wrong again, Mark.'

'What do you mean?'

'It was Genevieve who advised me against an irrevocable step,' she said. 'When I went into that cabin last night, I was convinced that it was all over, that you left me no alternative but to break off the engagement.'

'You can't do that!' he exclaimed.

'That's what she told me.'

'It would be a calamity.'

'Genevieve said that you deserved the chance to explain yourself.'

He was stunned. 'Did she?'

'Yes, Mark. She tried to see it from both points of view.'

'That does surprise me.'

'What's more,' said Blanche, 'she's been in the same situation herself. I don't mean that she had the kind of argument that we did. It was much more serious than that. Genevieve was engaged to be married when her fiancé did something that she described as unforgivable.'

'And what was that?'

'I don't know and, even if I did, I wouldn't tell you. Everything was said in confidence between us. What it amounted to was this: Genevieve advised me not to let a small disagreement look like an enormous one.'

'That was good advice. I endorse it.'

'Then perhaps you'll be courteous enough to give me what I want.'

'And what's that?'

'An apology for misleading me.'

'But I don't believe that I did that.'

'Stop quibbling, Mark.'

'I want my actions to be viewed in the proper light.'

'That's the other thing I feel entitled to ask of you.'

'Other thing?'

'Yes,' she said, taking the initiative and dictating terms. 'I want a full explanation. I demand to know who Alicia Tremaine was and what part she played in your time at Oxford. I'd also like to know why you pretended that you'd never even heard her name.' She raised a palm to silence his protest. 'I'm over twenty one, Mark. I'm not going to have an attack of the vapours if you tell me that you fell head over heels in love with this girl. I'd just like to know the truth. Is that too much to ask?'

'No,' he said, loosening his collar. 'I suppose that it isn't.'

George Dillman got down on knees and tapped the wooden panels hard.

'What on earth are you doing?' asked Lester Hembrow.

'Searching.'

'For what?'

'A hiding place.'

'Are you serious, George?'

'Very serious,' said Dillman, rising to his feet. 'When we worked for the Cunard Line, we sailed on the *Caronia* and were tipped off that someone was smuggling narcotics. We identified the man but we could find no trace of anything in his cabin even though we were certain that he had a consignment aboard.'

'What happened?'

'When the ship was about to sail again, a young woman came aboard to leave some flowers in the cabin that our suspect had vacated. She said they were for a friend.'

'But they weren't.'

'No, Lester. It was a ruse to get her into the cabin. She opened a secret compartment behind the wood panelling and took out a large amount of cocaine, all neatly bagged up. When I arrested her,' he said, 'I thanked her for showing us where the drugs were hidden.'

'But you haven't found any hollow panels here?'

'No. The cupboard is bare.'

They were in the empty cabin that Dillman had taken note of the previous day. Nothing suspicious had come to light. The bed was made, the bathroom clean, and the whole place ready for the next occupant. There was no sign that anyone had been in there recently.

'You must have been mistaken, George,' said the purser.

'There was a key in the lock. No mistake about that.'

'One of the stewards might have been cleaning it.'

'Then why lock it from the inside?' asked Dillman. 'In any case, the person responsible for this cabin is Sidney Browne and he hasn't been in here. I got the chief steward to ask him on my behalf.'

'The mystery thickens.'

'We can't exclude the possibility that this cabin is in some way linked to the crimes that took place in J. P. Morgan's stateroom.'

'Well, you'd better find that link very soon.'

'Why?'

'Mr Morgan is on the warpath. He cornered me last night. I felt as if I were being roasted on the spit. He wants to speak to you today.'

'I'll try to calm him down.'

'Better you than me. Right,' said Hembrow, 'we can lock the place up again. You go and face the firing squad known as J. P. Morgan and I'll hunt down your partner.'

'Why? Has there been another theft?'

'I'm afraid so.'

'During the night?'

'No, it was some time yesterday. Mrs Penn – she's the victim – only became aware of the theft when she was dressing for dinner and opened her jewellery box. It's so maddening, George.'

'What is?'

'At a time when you need Genevieve most, she's preoccupied with all these thefts. Yet she insisted that there was no connection.'

'Between what?'

'This spate of thefts and the two more serious crimes.'

Dillman pondered. 'I think that Genevieve may be wrong.'

'Her argument was that nobody with a haul like the one they had from Mr Morgan's stateroom would bother with smaller targets. If you catch a whale, do you go off in search of sardines?'

'Yes, if it serves your purpose. We're being distracted, Lester. Someone is deliberately hampering Genevieve so that she can't devote her time to the murder investigation. My belief is that all the crimes are connected,' said Dillman with conviction. 'Murder, theft, or anything else, they're the work of the same person or persons.'

'Pass that on to Genevieve.'

'I will. What was stolen this time?'

'A whole range of items,' said the purser, trying to recall them. 'A sapphire necklace, matching earrings, various brooches, diamond rings and – oh yes – a gold bracelet that cost a pretty penny.'

Dillman's ears pricked up. 'A gold bracelet?'

The gold bracelet was inside the envelope with the note when Genevieve Masefield thrust it back into his hands. Jonathan Killick was dismayed.

'Didn't you like it?' he asked.

'I liked it very much.'

'Then why don't you keep it?'

'Because I don't accept gifts from people I hardly know.'

'Come now, Miss Masefield,' he said suavely, 'you know me very well. We attended a party together and we've twice dined at the same table. We're practically bosom friends.'

'I don't feel that.'

'Then what do you feel?'

'That your antics are beginning to irritate me.'

'Heavens, we can't have that. I do apologise. I'm just sorry you can't receive a gift in the spirit in which it was offered. It cost rather more than a bunch of flowers, I can tell you.'

'That's what worried me.'

'The cost?'

'Expensive gifts involve obligations.'

'But you're not obliged to me in any way, Miss Masefield. I meant what I said in my note. It was a token of my esteem.' He offered her the envelope. 'Are you sure you wouldn't like to keep it for a day?'

'Absolutely sure.'

'Try it on. Look at yourself in a mirror. Gloat.'

'No,' said Genevieve, pushing the envelope away. 'I didn't deserve the gift so I couldn't possibly accept it. I'd be grateful if you refrain from sending me anything else or trying to arrange meetings with me by devious means.'

'You arranged this meeting,' he protested.

It was true. Genevieve had lurked outside the dining room until he came for his breakfast. Accosting him at the door, she was as firm and unequivocal as she could be. He snapped his fingers.

'Ah,' he declared, 'I think I understand now. Blanche has been talking to you. She issued a warning about the Big Bad Wolf named Jonathan Killick. I sent her some gifts at one time, and she liked them enough to keep them. I wanted to show her how I felt.'

'I hope that I've done the same to you.'

'You have. I'll need to try something else.'

'Don't try anything at all,' she cautioned. 'I don't care if you leave a dozen gold bracelets for me, you'll not worm your way into my affections. Let's meet as little as possible from now on.'

'Would you at least agree to communicate by letter?'

'No!'

'But the ship's stationery is so decorous.'

'Write to someone else.'

'How would you respond to a sonnet in your praise?'

'Coldly.'

'Just as well I never tried to write one for you, then.' He slipped the envelope into his pocket. 'If you have a change of heart, the gold bracelet has your name on it.'

'I'm wondering whose name was on it beforehand.'

'What do you mean?'

'Well, it's a strange thing for a man to have in his possession,' she pointed out. 'Did you bring it on board in the hope that you could use it to dazzle some gullible young lady?'

He grinned broadly. 'A conjurer never reveals his secrets.'

'How did you come by it?'

'Let's just say that it fell into my hands.'

'You must have paid a lot for it.'

'Money and fair words.'

'It was made in France. The maker's name was on it.'

'So you did at least take the trouble to examine it. All may not be lost. Did you try it on, Miss Masefield? How did it feel against your skin?'

'I don't know. It's not mine so I had no right to try it on.'

'You had every right. I gave it to you to show my admiration, and I hoped to see you wearing it in public. What do you have against it?'

'The price.'

'I didn't have to pay too much for it.'

'I'm talking about the price that *I'd* have to pay,' said Genevieve, looking him in the eye. 'Please don't do this again.'

'As you wish.'

'If you really want to endear yourself to me ...'

'Oh, I do, I do.'

'Then please keep out of my way from now on.'

'Your wish is my command.' A wicked smile stole across his face. 'Would it have made any difference if I'd sent you a pair of diamond earrings instead?'

Ethan and Rosalie Boyd were eating breakfast together when a third person sat down at their table without any invitation. Hilda Farrant was still aggrieved. Without even bothering to wish them good morning, she launched into her diatribe.

'It's intolerable,' she said, rapping the table with her knuckles. 'I'll never sail with this shipping line again. They've had plenty of time to find my stolen property yet they still have no idea who the thief might be. It's disgusting. As long as the man is at large, nobody in first class is safe. He's free to plunder elsewhere.'

'I thought you told us that it was a female thief,' recalled Boyd. 'A man would be unlikely to go into a ladies' cloakroom.'

'*Anything* can happen on this ship.'

'What does Miss Masefield say?'

'All she did was to trot out the usual excuses,' said Mrs Farrant. 'As I was coming out of the purser's office just now, Miss Masefield was about to go in. I gave her a piece of my mind.'

'It's unfair to blame her, Mrs Farrant,' said Rosalie. 'With respect, it was your fault, not Miss Masefield's, that the earrings were stolen.'

'How could it possibly be my fault?'

'According to you, the purse was left unguarded.'

'Yes, Mrs Boyd – but in a very private place.'

'Other ladies had access to it.'

'You're beginning to sound like Miss Masefield.'

'Our sympathies are entirely with you, Mrs Farrant,' said Boyd, trying to rescue his wife from an argument. 'All that Rosalie was doing was pointing out that, even on a ship like this, vigilance is necessary. We know that to our cost because my wife's purse went astray.'

'Yes,' said Mrs Farrant enviously, 'but she was more fortunate than I. Nothing had been taken from it.'

Rosalie smiled. 'It proves that the thief was not a reading man.'

'Or woman,' corrected Boyd.

'Also, it showed how honest the stewards are. As soon as it was found, it was taken straight to the purser. I was impressed.'

'That's more than I've been, Mrs Boyd,' said the older woman. 'I've been saddled with a stewardess who might well have been involved in the theft in some way. It's the reason I leave nothing of value in my cabin.'

'What's her name?'

'Hurst. Edith Hurst.'

'Have you mentioned her to Miss Masefield?'

'Of course – and to the purser. But they deny that the girl could be in any way implicated. They point to her excellent record but I have an instinct about people, and there's something shifty about Miss Hurst.' She flicked her gaze to Boyd. 'You're a banker,' she remembered. 'In a place where security is of the essence, you must have developed instincts as well.'

'Oh yes,' said Boyd.

'Did you ever have any employees you suspected of wrongdoing?'

'I did, actually – on two occasions. The first was a clerk who was overeager to help and was always pushing himself forward. We kept a careful watch on him and discovered that he was stealing money in small amounts from clients' accounts.'

'The other case was much more serious,' said Rosalie. 'A robbery at Ethan's bank in New York. Luckily, it went wrong.'

'I'd had my suspicions about one of my associates for some time,' explained Boyd. 'When the bank was robbed, it was clear to me that inside help was involved. The robber was caught because he injured himself when he jumped from a first-floor window. He refused to admit the name of his accomplice in the bank but I knew who it was.'

'Was the man convicted?'

'No, alas. When he realised that we were wise to him, he took to his heels and has never been heard of since.'

'What about the robber?'

'He was caught red-handed with seventy-eight thousand dollars.'

'I hope that he'll spend the rest of his life in prison.'

He sighed. 'The case never came to court, Mrs Farrant. The man tried to escape and was killed in police custody. I was enraged with him at the time,' confessed Boyd, 'but he did us a big favour, really.'

'Favour?'

'Yes, he showed us a glaring fault in our security arrangements. We were able to put that right.'

'Nobody was ever able to rob that bank again,' said Rosalie. 'In that sense, your own loss may have prevented any others.'

'I don't see how,' said Mrs Farrant.

'You haven't been back to that cloakroom, obviously.'

'I'll never make use of it again, Mrs Boyd.'

'There's a notice in there now,' said Rosalie. 'It warns people against leaving anything unguarded as they make use of the facilities.'

'What help is that to me?' complained Mrs Farrant. 'The notice should have been on display from the start. I'll make that point in my letter to the managing director. The White Star Line has responsibilities. I demand full recompense.'

Before she could continue, three people came into the room and looked around for a table. Her attention was diverted. Abednego Thomas was hand in hand with his wife while Dominique Cadine walked behind them. They sat down beside Florence and Vane Stiller.

'Look at them!' said Mrs Farrant, given a fresh cause for outrage. 'They shouldn't be allowed in first class. That artist dresses like a hobo and those women are no better than they ought to be. The younger one exposes her naked body to that disgusting old libertine.'

'Dominique is his model,' said Boyd, waving in acknowledgement to the trio. 'She's an interesting young lady.'

'You *know* her?'

'We dined with them last night, Mrs Farrant.'

'Nothing would make me share a table with such creatures.'

'I wasn't sure that we'd get on with them either,' said Boyd, 'but we had a very pleasant time. Once Mr Thomas had forgiven me for being in such a hateful profession, that is.'

'Yes,' said Rosalie, laughing, 'he wasn't very happy about having a meal with a banker. He regards them as his mortal enemies.'

'It was just as well that J. P. Morgan wasn't sitting with us. That would have been disastrous.'

Mrs Farrant sniffed. 'Mr Morgan would never lower himself.'

'Abednego Thomas is pursuing a vendetta against him. He calls him a monster. So I doubt very much if Mr Morgan will be buying any of his paintings for a while.' Boyd smiled to himself. 'Even if they do feature Dominique Cadine.'

George Dillman had an early indication of the vile mood that J. P. Morgan was in. As he approached the man's cabin, he saw a steward dart out through the door and shut it behind him with relief. Sidney Browne's face was pitted with anguish. Grabbing his trolley, he pushed it along to the next cabin.

'I take it that Mr Morgan is in there,' said Dillman.

'Yes, sir,' replied Browne. 'He had breakfast in his cabin.'

'Did it disagree with him?'

'I wasn't allowed in there long enough to ask him, sir.'

'Thank you for the warning.'

Dillman knocked hard and waited. J. P. Morgan eventually opened the door. He glowered at the detective as if he had never seen him before.

'George Dillman,' said the visitor. 'You wanted to see me.'

'I didn't *want* to, Mr Dillman. You are not a person with whom I would willingly choose to spend any time. But necessity gives us strange bedfellows. Although I don't want to do so, I *need* to see you.' He stood back. 'Come inside.'

'Yes, sir.'

Dillman stepped into a room that was very different from how it had been on his first visit. The collection of art treasures that Morgan had accumulated in Paris had all gone. So had the corpse of Howard Riedel. The place felt cold, empty and functional. Morgan resumed his seat at the table. In front of him was a set of documents he had been studying. He indicated that Dillman should sit down.

'Hembrow tells me that you have a list of suspects,' said Morgan.

'That's right, sir. It's in single figures now.'

'And these are all people who boarded the ship at Cherbourg?'

'Yes, sir.'

'In other words, you have no suspicions of anyone who embarked at Southampton.'

'With one exception, Mr Morgan.'

'And who's that?'

'I think it's better if I keep the name to myself until we've had time to make some inquiries about the man. The burden of proof is with us. He's innocent until proven guilty.'

'Will you disclose the names on your list?'

'No,' said Dillman. 'I see no reason for you to know at this stage. It will only create unnecessary suspicion in your mind of people who'll turn out to be wholly unconnected with the crimes.'

'At least, tell me if you have Abednego Thomas on your list.'

'His name is not included.'

'Then it should be.'

'Why do you say that, Mr Morgan?'

'Damnation!' roared Morgan. 'Do I have to do your job for you? Thomas is an obvious suspect. For reasons of his own, he's conceived a violent dislike of me and he'd stop at nothing to cause me pain or discomfort. Why, only yesterday, he caught up with me on the way to dinner and harangued me for buying all those paintings and antiques.'

'I would have thought that was a clear indication of innocence. If he was involved in the crimes, Mr Thomas would have the sense not to attract attention to himself.'

'He was goading me. Taunting me with my loss.'

'I've got to know him reasonably well, sir, and he doesn't strike me as a thief, still less as a man capable of murder. I accept that he leads a somewhat irregular life,' continued Dillman, recalling the night-time visit of Veronica Thomas, 'but I can't arrest a man for sexual license.'

'He will flaunt his debauchery.'

'Whatever his faults, he's an entertaining dinner companion.'

'Really, Dillman, I deplore your taste.'

'You're at liberty to do so,' replied the detective. 'The one thing on which we can agree is that Abednego Thomas has a wide knowledge of art and of its commercial value.'

'So?'

'Why would he steal three minor French paintings from this room when he could have taken others that were worth vastly more? Given his contacts with private collectors, he'd know how to sell them. Thieves look for maximum benefit, Mr Morgan.'

'I still think that you should search his cabin.'

'Not without good reason.'

'I've given it to you. The man loathes me and what I stand for.'

'He pours scorn on anyone who leads a conventional life,' said

Dillman, 'but that doesn't mean he's impelled to steal from us, still less commit murder. What does he stand to gain?'

'My humiliation.'

'I think you'll find that Mr Thomas has other things on his mind, sir, and they keep him more than occupied. As for searching his cabin, I've already been there. It's like any artist's studio, in a state of mild chaos. I've been invited to go back for the unveiling of his latest work,' recalled Dillman. 'If Abednego Thomas was hiding anything in there, he'd never dare to let any visitors in.'

'You're forgetting that model of his,' said Morgan.

'No man would forget a young lady like Dominique.'

'She tricked her way in here that night.'

'It was a challenge.'

'I'm wondering if she was sent.'

'By whom?'

'Thomas, of course. For the purpose of reconnaissance.'

'We've touched on this before, Mr Morgan, and I say the same again. I don't believe that Dominique Cadine is either a thief or a killer. Our chief priority is to find the stolen property. Once we locate that, we'll also have the man who murdered Howard Riedel.'

'How close are you to an arrest?'

'His name is somewhere on this list in my pocket.'

'Then find him soon, Dillman.'

'We will, sir,' said the detective. 'It won't be long before you are reunited with your art treasures. Even on a ship this large, they can't remain hidden for long.'

When the notion was first put to him, Lester Hembrow was not in favour of it. After considering the matter for a few seconds, he shook his head.

'I'm sorry, Genevieve,' he said. 'I'm not at all happy.'

'You will be if I find what I'm looking for.'

'And if you don't?'

'Then I admit that I was wrong and there's no harm done.'

'But there will have been. You'll have searched a passenger's cabin without his permission. That's trespass.'

'Justified trespass,' said Genevieve. 'We have strong grounds for believing that Jonathan Killick is a thief. He offered me a gold bracelet as a gift. When I interviewed Mrs Penn just now, she gave me a description of a similar item that was stolen from her cabin yesterday.'

'That doesn't mean that it *was* the same bracelet.'

'It's too big a coincidence.'

'No, Genevieve,' he argued. 'What fool would steal something from one passenger in order to give it to another, knowing that she might wear it in public? It would be a ridiculous risk to take.'

'I thought about that, Lester. A bracelet is less likely to attract attention than the sapphire necklace and matching earrings that were taken. Dozens of ladies have gold bracelets,' said Genevieve, 'and many look similar. He could have relied on my wearing it without being spotted by its former owner.'

'He'd still be taking a chance.'

'The Honourable Jonathan Killick lives by taking chances.'

'Not that kind.'

'Mrs Penn's bracelet was made in France, just like the one that I was given as a gift. It also had an unusual clasp that matched mine. She's an old lady with poor eyesight,' explained Genevieve. 'How could she possibly detect her bracelet on another woman in such a crowd? There are more than four hundred people in first class – safety in numbers.'

'I'm still not persuaded, Genevieve.'

'Then remember what Blanche Charlbury said about him. He's a thief. He was expelled from school and sent down from Oxford for stealing. Also,' she went on, 'there's the small matter of how he can afford such a stylish way of life when he has no apparent income.'

'People like that always get by somehow.'

'And I think I know how. Jonathan Killick is our man.'

'You believe that he stole from Miss Stiller as well?'

'Probably.'

'What about Oskar Halberg? Is Killick a pickpocket?'

'I certainly wouldn't put it past him.'

'Even you can't accuse him of taking Mrs Farrant's purse,' he said. 'However many chances he'd take, Killick would draw the line at going into a ladies' cloakroom.'

'All I'm concerned about at the moment is that gold bracelet. If that's hidden away in his cabin, then so are the rest of the things he took from Mrs Penn's jewellery box. Please,' she said, 'let me have the key.'

The purser sat back in his chair. Since they had sailed from Southampton, all kinds of problems had been brought to his office and he had been able to solve most of them without undue difficulty. That was not the case here. There were too many imponderables.

'I don't like it, Genevieve,' he told her.

'Why not?'

'Searching a cabin has to be a very last resort.'

'Lester, this is an opportunity for us to catch a thief. Let's take it.'

'What does George say?'

'He was as suspicious as I was when he saw that gold bracelet. Whatever is a man doing with such a thing? George said it would bear further investigation.'

'But he didn't actually urge you to go into Killick's cabin.'

'No,' she admitted.

'Then I'd like to discuss it with him first.'

'But we might miss our chance if we delay,' she said. 'Jonathan Killick is having coffee in the lounge with friends. This is a perfect time to act. I may not get an opportunity like this again. Terrible crimes have been committed aboard the *Oceanic* and George needs my help to solve them. I can't do that if I'm running around after a thief.' She leant over his desk. 'Let me catch him, Lester. Then you can have the pleasure of giving Mrs Penn's jewellery back to her – and even to the others.'

'Mrs Farrant is the real headache. Since Killick couldn't possibly have filched her diamond earrings, we're looking for two thieves.'

'He must have a female accomplice.'

'A very unusual one,' said Hembrow cynically. 'What woman would help him to steal jewellery in order for him to give some of it to another woman?' He chewed his lip in thought. 'Have you spoken to George since he and I went into that empty cabin?'

'Not yet.'

'He disagrees with you, Genevieve. He believes that the thefts are part of a deliberate plan to distract us from the murder investigation. In short, one person is behind all the crimes. Could you accept that?'

'It's a possibility.'

'Then you have to accept that Killick is both murderer and thief.'

'I think he's capable of anything.'

'We need to bring George into this discussion.'

'He has enough on his plate,' she urged. 'If George is correct and one man is responsible for the crimes, that's an even stronger argument for searching Jonathan Killick's cabin.'

'Even though he didn't join the ship at Cherbourg?'

'Even then.'

'No, Genevieve. It's too dangerous.'

'Give me the key,' she pleaded. 'It will take me less than a minute to see if I'm right. What do we have to lose, Lester?'

He began to waver. 'I shouldn't be authorizing this, you know.'

'Pretend that I took the master key when you weren't looking.'

'The captain would have me keel-hauled.'

'Not if we catch the killer.' She extended her hand. 'Well?' Hembrow capitulated. 'You'll need someone to watch your back in case he returns to his cabin,' he said, unlocking a drawer and taking out a key. 'I'll come with you.'

He handed the key to Genevieve. She thanked him then opened the door to find that three people were outside, waiting to see the purser. Hembrow invited the first one into his office.

'I'll be with you directly, Miss Masefield,' he said.

The look in his eye told her not to take any action without him but Genevieve was afraid that any delay would rob her of an opportunity to search the cabin. Leaving the purser with the passengers, she went first to the lounge. Jonathan Killick was still there, conversing with a group of people over coffee. It was all the prompting that she needed. Walking swiftly along the corridor, she went down a companionway and located the number of his cabin. Nobody was about. She tapped on the door to make sure that no steward was there. The cabin was empty. Genevieve was inside in a flash.

She felt a sudden rush of fear. When she had set out, she wanted to prove that Killick was a thief but it now transpired that he might be a killer as well. The enormity of the risk she was taking paralysed her for a couple of minutes. If she were caught, anything might happen. Genevieve had to force herself to do what she was there for, slowly opening drawers, searching the wardrobe, and checking all of the hiding places that thieves had used in the past to conceal their loot.

Jonathan Killick was a collector. When she opened a valise, she found a series of photographs, held together by a red ribbon. Genevieve flicked through them and saw that they were all pictures of beautiful young women, some of whom had written endearments to Killick on the backs of their photographs. Blanche Charlbury's face suddenly came into view and it shocked Genevieve. She wondered if her friend knew that she was part of Killick's private gallery.

Putting the photographs away, she felt inside the valise until her hand came into contact with a small silk bag. The moment her fingers closed around it, she knew that she had found jewellery and her heart began to pound. She took out the bag and emptied its contents into the palm of her hand. The gold bracelet was there and so were some brooches and a pair of diamond earrings. There was also a large bundle of notes, and she unfolded it to find British currency and American dollars, wrapped haphazardly together. The last item in the bag was even more conclusive. It was a business card bearing the italicised name of Oskar Halberg.

Genevieve was so thrilled with her discovery that she wanted to shout with joy. It was at that point that she heard a key in the lock.

ELEVEN

Genevieve was frozen to the spot. It flashed through her mind
that her only faint chance of escaping detection was to dive into
the bathroom with the valise and pray that nobody would come
in there, but she was quite unable to move. Overcome with guilt
and trepidation, she trembled as she put the jewellery back into
its bag. She cursed herself for being so impetuous. Searching a
cabin without a lookout to assist her was both foolish and reckless.
Genevieve had been caught in the act. Her one hope was that the
bedroom steward was about to come in.

She was out of luck. It was Jonathan Killick who entered
the cabin and who stared at her with a mixture of hostility and
amazement.

'What the devil are you doing in here?' he demanded.

'It's not how it looks,' she replied meekly.

'I'd say that it's exactly how it looks. Bless my soul! I knew that you were a cool customer, Miss Masefield, but I hadn't realised that you were a thief. How did you get in here? Never mind that,' he went on, stretching out a hand. 'Could I please have my property back?'

'If it really is your property, Mr Killick.'

'Well, it's certainly not yours. Of all the nerve! When I offered that gold bracelet as a gift, you refused it. Yet now you break in to my cabin and try to steal it.' His tone sharpened. 'Give it to me!'

'We need to discuss this first.'

'I won't ask again.'

Taking a step closer, he adopted a threatening pose. Genevieve was scared. She had fought her way out of awkward situations before but Killick was tall and powerful. Over dinner the night before, he had talked about his sporting achievements. Genevieve would be no match for him in a tussle and if, as she assumed, he might already have killed one victim, she did not wish to provoke him in any way. She handed over the bag and its contents. Putting them on the table, he stood there with his hands on his hips and appraised her.

'Now, then,' he said, 'what am I going to do with you?'

'Could we go elsewhere to talk about this, please?'

'Oh no – you're staying here.'

'You can't keep me.'

'Yes, I can, Miss Masefield.'

'That's not the behaviour of a gentleman.'

'Stealing from my cabin is hardly the correct behaviour of a lady,' he countered. 'In the circumstances, I think that we can abandon the finer points of etiquette, don't you? Sit down, please.'

'I don't want to.'

'Sit down!'

He accompanied the order with a firm push. When she felt his hand on her shoulder, she realised how powerful he was. She was shoved down onto a chair without ceremony. He stood over her, his arms folded, his legs almost touching hers. Genevieve was in a quandary. To admit that she was a ship's detective might give him a reason to silence her for good. If he were the person responsible for the crimes on board the ship, then he would certainly not give himself up. Somewhere in the cabin, he might have the knife that had killed Howard Riedel and the gun taken from the dead man. Genevieve did not want to give him an excuse to reach for either weapon.

She could scream for help but, with Killick so close, she knew that her cry would soon be stifled and that, in any case, there might be nobody near enough to hear. However loud she could yell, the insistent throb of the ship's engines and the constant swish of the waves would muffle her voice. All that she could do was to keep her captor talking until the purser arrived to save her. Lester Hembrow knew where she was and – once he had disposed of the passengers who had come to see him – would start to look for her. That, however, might take too much time. Genevieve hoped that she would still be alive when he finally got there.

Killick was still gazing at her with mingled lust and calculation. 'You only had to ask,' he said, reaching out to touch her cheek.

'Ask what?'

'To have the gold bracelet.'

'I didn't want it.'

'Then why did you try to steal it?' he asked. 'Or did you wish to see what else I had so that you could take your pick? Is that what this comes down to – a question of choice?' She remained silent.

'Out with it. Tell me the truth, Genevieve – I think I'm entitled to call you that, don't you? Now that we're on such intimate terms, that is.'

'I'd rather you didn't touch me,' she said, moving her head away from his hand.

'I'd rather you didn't sneak into my cabin, Genevieve, but you did and so I have to make the best of the situation. You've committed a crime and you have to be punished.'

'Report me to the purser,' she pleaded. 'Take me to him now.'

'That would let you off the hook, wouldn't it?'

'Would it?'

'Yes,' he said, leering at her. 'You'd be locked up and I'd be deprived of your company. Nothing was actually stolen from me, after all. My property is still intact. I'm prepared to be forgiving.'

'Thank you, Mr Killick.'

'My name is Johnny.'

'This has all been a horrendous mistake. I apologise profusely for coming in here. Let me go and I promise that I'll never do it again.'

'We haven't decided on your punishment yet.'

'You talked about forgiveness a moment ago.'

'Everything comes at a price, Genevieve.'

Her blood ran cold. 'I'd rather be turned over to the purser.'

'I'm sure that you would.'

'Mr Hembrow will know what to do with me.'

'But I have a much more appealing notion,' he said, holding her chin so that she was unable to move her head. 'Something from which we can both reap enjoyment. I'll strike a bargain with you.'

'Mr Killick—'

'Johnny,' he insisted. 'That's my first condition. From now on, you call me Johnny. Do you understand?'

'Yes, Johnny,' she said.

'That's better. I've so wanted to hear my name on those gorgeous lips of yours. Now, listen to my offer, Genevieve. I'm ready to forgive and forget this appalling intrusion into my privacy, if you let me have what I want.' He smiled. 'I can't be fairer than that, can I?'

Genevieve's heart constricted. Her mouth was so dry that she could not speak. She felt almost dizzy. Her eyes darted around the cabin but there was no means of escape. She was trapped.

'Well?' he prompted. 'What's your answer?'

George Dillman was determined to find out if his steward was implicated in any of the crimes that had occurred. Manny Ellway was as friendly as usual when they met but the detective was not deceived by his surface geniality. There was something about the man that did not ring true, and his interest in the empty cabin had left a number of unanswered questions hanging in the air. Having taken the trouble to find out what Ellway's routine was from the chief steward, Dillman knew that he had a mid-morning break when he was supposed to join his colleagues for light refreshment. He, therefore, positioned himself where he could watch Ellway's cabin at the appointed time. Four stewards came out and three of them, including Sidney Browne, headed off towards their canteen. Holding back from them, Manny Ellway set off in the opposite direction.

Dillman followed at a discreet distance, wondering why the man did not go with his friends. Instead, moving furtively, Ellway went along a corridor and down a companionway that led to the second-class decks. Demarcation on board was very strict. Like passengers, stewards were confined to their particular class and forbidden to wander at liberty around the vessel. Ellway had no legitimate reason for being where he was. Dillman had caught him out in a breach of the rules. Reaching the bottom of the steps, Ellway had to unhook a rope that barred access to the second-class area. After looking up and down the corridor, he replaced the rope behind him and scuttled off.

When the detective went down the companionway, he was just in time to see Ellway turning a corner at the end of the corridor. Dillman removed the rope barrier then hooked it up behind him. His long strides took him at speed along the thick carpet. Ellway was up to something and Dillman wanted to know what it was. But he was too late. Peering around the corner, he saw to his consternation that he had lost the steward. Somewhere in a long corridor, Manny Ellway had disappeared.

Genevieve Masefield did not know what to do. Her mind was racing but it offered her no easy solution. With her captor looming over her, a dash for the door would be pointless. She considered grabbing the valise so that she could use it to knock him aside but if that bid for freedom were to fail, she would be locked in a cabin with an enraged man. Another possibility was to fall back on deceit, pretending to faint in the hope that it would induce some sympathy. Genevieve quickly rejected that option. After one look at his face, she could see that he would take advantage of her defenselessness. Talking her way out of danger was the only thing that she could do. She ran a tongue over parched lips.

'I'm not waiting much longer,' he warned. 'Decide.'

'I prefer to be dealt with by the purser.'

'That's not a choice on offer, Genevieve.'

'Then what is?'

'An intelligent woman like you should be able to guess.'

'You want me to agree to your disgusting bargain.'

'Precisely.'

'Or?'

'I shall have to give you some encouragement.'

'Even you wouldn't force yourself on me, surely?'

'I'd see it as my right, Genevieve. You've only yourself to blame for coming in here. I'll tell you what,' he said, stroking her shoulder. 'Just to show how magnanimous I can be, you can select any piece of jewellery as a keepsake – afterward.'

'I don't want any of it.'

'Then why were you trying to take it?'

'I wondered why you had something like a gold bracelet in your possession,' said Genevieve. 'When I asked you about it, you were so evasive that I thought it might have been acquired by suspect means.'

'Is that why you refused to take it?'

'That was part of the reason, Johnny.'

'You believed that I'd *stolen* it?'

'Jewellery of that kind is not a normal thing to find in a man's cabin. You must admit that. And it's not only the gold bracelet. There were other expensive items in that bag.'

'I don't have to explain to you where they came from.'

'Is that because you're afraid to do so?'

'No, Genevieve.'

'Your conscience is clear?'

'I make no pretence at having one,' he said. 'Conscience is a device to stop people enjoying pleasure and nothing will do that

244

to me.' He offered his hand. 'Now, will you come willingly or do I have to give you some assistance?'

'Touch me,' she said, 'and you'll be charged with assault.'

'It will be your word against mine – the word of a common thief against that of the future Sir Jonathan Killick. Whom do you think they will believe?'

Genevieve was becoming desperate. 'Why do you keep those photographs?' she asked, changing tack. 'I saw them in the valise. Don't you think it's rather sad if a man carries around pictures of young ladies who have rejected him?'

'They didn't all reject me,' he bragged, fingers in the pockets of his waistcoat. 'A few of them succumbed with very little protest.'

'Blanche Charlbury was not one of them.'

'There's still time for Blanche.'

'Not now that she's engaged to Mark Bossingham.'

'Thanks to me, that relationship is already starting to leak water. By the end of the voyage, Blanche will be turning to me for comfort.'

'Don't bank on that.'

'Let's forget Blanche,' he said, suddenly lifting her to her feet. 'I'm only interested in Miss Genevieve Masefield at this juncture – the latest addition to my private collection of beautiful ladies.'

'Take your hands off me, Mr Killick.'

'Johnny. How many times do I have to tell you – it's Johnny.'

'Only to your friends.'

'And to my intimates – like you.'

'No,' said Genevieve, holding her ground as he tried to ease her across the cabin. 'This has gone far enough. I know that you stole those items of jewellery and took that money from Oskar Halberg's billfold.' He laughed in disbelief. 'Where have you hidden the art treasures you took from Mr Morgan's cabin?'

'I've no idea what you're talking about.'

'They're not in here so you must have stowed them elsewhere.'

'You're just trying to delay the inevitable, aren't you?' he said, moving her by force towards the bed. 'Feminine wiles won't work on me, Genevieve. You'll just have to resign yourself to your well-deserved fate.'

'Let go of me!'

'Enjoy it, why don't you? I know that I will.'

Genevieve struggled but his grip was too strong. When she tried to call out, he clapped his palm over her mouth. Tugging at her clothing with his other hand, he broke off a button from her dress. His breath was hot, his body was rubbing against hers. When his fingers touched her breast, he gave a long sigh of pleasure. She was just about to surrender to panic when there was a loud knock on the cabin door. Killick was motionless. He was obviously not going to respond to it. Genevieve had to take action or she was doomed. She did the only thing that she could think of. Removing a brooch from her dress, she used the pin to jab into the hand that covered her mouth. He withdrew the hand in pain.

'Help me!' cried Genevieve. 'I'm being held against my will.'

Stepping into an alcove, Dillman waited patiently for the steward to come back into sight. Ellway was only allowed a short break before going back on duty so he was bound to return to the first-class decks soon. The detective would be ready for him. When he finally appeared, Ellway ran along the corridor so that he could get back to his post in time. Dillman stepped out from the alcove to accost him.

'What are you doing here, Manny?' he asked.

Ellway gaped. 'I might ask the same of you, sir.'

'I'm employed as a detective on this ship and I'm investigating some serious crimes that have taken place. I've reason to believe that you may be involved in those crimes.'

'We're not really criminals, Mr Dillman,' said Ellway, horrified that he had been unmasked. 'It was the only way that we could meet.'

'We?'

'Edith, sir. Edith Hurst. She's one of the stewardesses.'

'And you came down here to meet her?'

'Yes. There's nowhere else during the day, you see. I found this empty storeroom in second class so we've used that. Edith herself will be along in a couple of minutes. We never leave together.'

'What's in the storeroom, Manny?'

'Nothing much, sir,' he replied. 'It's not the most romantic place to meet but it's better than nothing. At night, of course, it's a different matter. There's that vacant cabin in first class.'

'Ah,' said Dillman, beginning to understand. 'Were you in there last night around ten, by any chance?'

'Yes, sir. How did you know?'

'The door was locked from inside.'

'I know it's against the rules, sir, but the chance seemed heaven-sent. I wasn't supposed to be on the *Oceanic* at all, you see. When I was transferred to this ship, it meant that I could be with Edith.'

'That's highly irregular, Manny.'

'Please don't report us or our secret will come out at last.'

'Your secret?'

'Yes, Mr Dillman,' said the other, quaking visibly. 'Edith and I got married last Tuesday. This voyage is our honeymoon.'

* * *

It was Lester Hembrow who had knocked on the door of the cabin and, when he disclosed his identity to Killick, the man was forced to release Genevieve and let the purser in. She breathed a sigh of relief. Jonathan Killick tried to make light of the situation.

'Miss Masefield and I were just having a little game,' he said.

Hembrow was concerned. 'Really?'

'She dropped in for a talk, didn't you, Miss Masefield?'

'No, Mr Killick. You disturbed me when I was searching this room for evidence. There it is,' she said, pointing to the jewellery and the wad of money. 'We know who the thief is now.'

'Wait a minute,' protested Killick. 'You were stealing from me.'

'Calm down, sir,' soothed Hembrow.

'How can you dare to accuse me of theft?'

'Before we go any further, sir, I think you should know that Miss Masefield is employed by the White Star Line as a ship's detective. She gained entry to your cabin with the master key that I provided.'

Killick was flabbergasted. 'A detective?'

'Yes,' she said, enjoying his discomfort. 'Now you can see why I was more than happy to be handed over to the purser. I'm no thief. What I wanted was what I found in your valise.'

'Clear evidence of theft, by the look of it,' resumed Hembrow, picking through the items on the table. 'This gold bracelet matches the description of one that was stolen yesterday from an old lady named Mrs Penn. The diamond earrings were taken from Hilda Farrant.'

'Not by me.'

'Then perhaps you'll explain how these items came to be here, sir.'

'Certainly, Mr Hembrow. I won them.'

'What?'

'Everything you see on that table was won fairly and squarely at the card table. Baccarat, mostly. I had a lucky streak, you see.' He shot Genevieve a rueful glance. 'Unfortunately, it didn't continue with Miss Masefield. The gentleman who gave me that jewellery had run out of ready cash, you see, and wanted to raise the stakes. He wagered what was left of his wife's jewellery – the poor woman died last year in Monte Carlo. It's just a coincidence that the bracelet resembles one that was stolen.' He saw their looks of astonishment. 'If you won't accept my word, ask the gentleman himself. His name is Jameson – Leander Jameson of Oak Park, Illinois.'

Genevieve and Hembrow looked at each other. If Jonathan Killick was telling the truth – and he sounded very plausible – then they had made an embarrassing mistake. Genevieve picked up the business card.

'What about this?' she asked, thrusting it at him. 'A pickpocket relieved Mr Halberg of his billfold the other night. It contained a lot of money in British and American currency. This card of his could only have come from that billfold.'

'Turn it over, Miss Masefield.'

'Why?'

'Turn it over,' he urged. 'The amount of money written on the back is what Mr Halberg owes me. Forgive the squiggles. He was rather drunk when he tried to write down the numbers. You're quite right,' he went on. 'His billfold was stolen so he was unable to pay up. Fortunately, he keeps his business cards in his inside pocket so they were not taken.' He gave Genevieve a patronizing smile. 'What you're holding in your fair hand is an IOU.'

'We'll need to check that with Mr Halberg,' said the purser.

'I insist that you do. I want my name cleared.'

'I think that it already has been,' conceded Genevieve, returning the card to him. 'With regard to the thefts, anyway. I'm sorry that there's been a misunderstanding but we had definite grounds for suspicion.'

'What was all that about a theft from J. P. Morgan?' asked Killick. 'I sat next to him last night and he didn't breathe a word about it.'

'That was at our request,' said Hembrow.

'Art treasures stolen. Jewellery pinched. Billfolds taken from the pockets of their owners.' Killick looked from one to the other. 'Would one of you have the grace to tell me exactly what's going on?'

Manny Ellway sat beside Edith Hurst with a happy smile on his face. They were in Dillman's cabin and it was the first time that they were appearing as a married couple before anyone on board the ship. The detective had promised to divulge their secret to nobody and agreed to turn a blind eye to any marital arrangements that they contrived to make. Edith was tearfully grateful.

'I thought that Manny somehow borrowed a master key from his colleague,' Dillman told them. 'I couldn't see how else he could get into that empty cabin.'

'I had my own key,' explained Edith. 'I look after some of the cabins in that corridor, you see. I was able to let us in when nobody was about.'

Ellway squeezed her hand proudly. 'When you saw me peering through the keyhole, sir,' he explained, 'I was checking to see if Edith was inside. She'd have left the key in place. That was her signal.'

'Then Manny would knock three times. That was his signal.'

'In the day, it was the storeroom and all that we could do there was to talk. At night, we could be man and wife in a first-class cabin.'

'True love will always find a way,' said Dillman.

He admired their courage and was sympathetic to their situation. He and Genevieve were also forced to conceal their marriage and to resort to snatched moments of pleasure in a busy day. Unlike Dillman and his wife, Manny Ellway and his bride were unable to visit each other in their respective cabins. They had found the ideal solution.

'I'm not just being sentimental, mind you,' continued Dillman. 'If I keep silent about all this, I expect a quid pro quo.'

Ellway was alarmed. 'We can't afford to give you a quid, sir,' he said. 'A pound would make a real hole in our wages. I never thought you was the sort of man to blackmail us.'

'Rest easy,' said Dillman, amused. '"Quid pro quo" is a Latin phrase. It means something in return for something else. Because I'm helping you, I need you to help me.'

'What can *we* do, sir?' asked Edith.

'Quite a lot. The first thing is to say nothing whatsoever to anyone about the theft that occurred in Mr Morgan's cabin. That must remain a secret. I only told you about it so that I can enrol you as deputies.'

'I won't tell a soul, Mr Dillman,' she said.

'Nor me,' said Ellway. 'What surprises me is that Sid Browne hasn't caught wind of it. You did well to keep it from him.'

'That was essential. Now,' said Dillman, 'we must recover that property. It's hidden away on this vessel, almost certainly in first class.'

'And there was Mrs Farrant complaining like mad,' said Edith, nudging her husband. 'Mr Morgan loses things worth a fortune and says nothing. Mrs Farrant loses a pair of earrings and you'd think someone had taken the crown jewels from her cabin.'

'Worst of all,' said Ellway, 'she blamed you, love.'

'I think we can leave Mrs Farrant aside as a potential suspect,' said Dillman dryly. 'Look at the other passengers. Between the two of you, you must go into a lot of cabins in the course of a day. Have you noticed anything at all unusual, however slight it may be?'

'No, sir,' said Edith. 'What about you, Manny?'

'Well, there is that artist and his two ladies,' recalled Ellway. 'They're not only unusual, they're plain eccentric and I can't pretend that I approve of what they do. Marriage vows is marriage vows to me.'

'I'm familiar with their liberal attitudes,' said Dillman, thinking of the nocturnal visit from Veronica Thomas. 'Have you spotted anything else in their cabin that struck you as odd?'

'Everything in there is odd, Mr Dillman. But there was something,' he said, thinking hard, 'now you mention it. Maybe artists do this all the time so I'm probably showing my ignorance. It was funny, though.'

'What was?'

'Well, Abednego Thomas has got these paintings in there. To be honest, I was too ashamed to look at them, but I did peep at the ones by Mrs Thomas. They're very good. Very good indeed.' 'Yes,' said Dillman, 'I've seen them.'

'Before or afterward, sir?'

'I don't follow you, Manny.'

'When I first saw them paintings, they had lovely frames that Mrs Thomas had specially made.'

'Yes, I noticed them.'

'One of them has been turned upside down.'

'Upside down?'

'Yes,' said Ellway. 'The beading along the top is slightly different from the strip at the bottom. That caught my eye straightaway.'

'Manny has always been very observant,' said Edith.

'A couple of days ago, Mr Dillman, it changed. The beading was the other way round on one frame. It was almost as if she'd taken out the painting and turned it upside down before putting it back in its frame. Is that usual, sir?'

'No,' said Dillman thoughtfully. 'It's highly unusual.'

Genevieve Masefield was still jangled by her confrontation with Jonathan Killick. She blamed herself for being too eager to search his cabin. Her rash action had almost resulted in a personal nightmare. What made her humiliation worse was that Killick was completely innocent of the crimes that had occurred. He was guilty of assault and – had the purser not arrived when he did – of something far more serious, but Genevieve was not ready to reveal the details to Lester Hembrow. As they sat in his office, she was doing her best to rid her mind of the perilous situation into which she had unwisely put herself. Only her husband would hear the full truth.

'I did warn you,' said the purser harshly.

'I know.'

'We've been left with egg on our faces, Genevieve.'

'I'm sorry.'

'Why didn't you have the sense to wait for me? I had a bad feeling about this exercise from the start.'

'It was all my fault, Lester. I accept that. But you must admit that there was compelling evidence. When I saw what was hidden away in his valise,' she went on, 'I was convinced that we had our man.'

'Instead of which, we now have an angry passenger, berating us for searching his cabin behind his back. Everything he told us was quite correct. Mr Leander confirmed it and so did Mr Halberg. The bag you found contained nothing but his winnings at the card table.'

'That's how he funds his trips to New York – by gambling.'

'I'm not interested in Jonathan Killick anymore,' said the purser. 'He's not a genuine suspect. The only consolation is that he's not going to kick up a stink with the captain.'

Genevieve knew why. While he had legitimate cause for complaint, Killick also had a reason to keep quiet about what had occurred in his cabin. When she was at his mercy, his treatment of Genevieve had been disgraceful and verged on a heinous crime. It was in his interests to suppress details of what had happened. The word of a minor aristocrat might outweigh that of a common thief but not that of a ship's detective with a reputation for honesty and integrity. Killick had also promised not to reveal Genevieve's true identity. He had been shocked to learn what her role on board really was, and his overweening confidence had been dented. He would not admit to anyone that a woman had so easily deceived him. It was too galling.

'So where do we go from here?' asked the purser.

'We continue with our inquiries.'

'No more searches of passengers' cabins.'

'It's a weapon we must use, Lester,' she argued.

'Not when it can so easily be turned against us.'

'A search is the only way to get conclusive evidence.'

'I'll need a lot more persuading before I allow another one. This could all have been avoided if you hadn't been so hasty, Genevieve. I knew that we should have consulted George beforehand.'

'He would have advised the search.'

'But he'd also have insisted on a lookout.'

'Yes,' she conceded. 'I'll be more careful next time.'

'Those passengers are partly to blame,' he said. 'If they hadn't diverted me at the critical moment, I could have helped you.'

'I felt so excited when I discovered that jewellery,' said Genevieve. 'Those diamond earrings were exactly like the ones that Mrs Farrant described. In assuming that Jonathan Killick had taken them, I forgot that the thief had to have been a woman.'

'Who on earth can she be?'

'I don't know, Lester, but one thing is certain. She won't rest on her laurels. My guess is that she's waiting to steal from someone else.'

The woman only put her bag down for a minute. Bright sunshine had enticed her out on deck with hundreds of other first-class passengers. Wearing coat, hat, scarf, and gloves, she stood at the rail and gazed at the horizon. When she got something in her eye, she put her bag down so that she could use a handkerchief to extract a speck of dust. The woman reached for her bag a minute later but it was no longer there.

Veronica Thomas was alone in the cabin when George Dillman called. She was thrilled to see him. He was given a cordial welcome but she made no attempt to kiss or embrace him. He was glad that there was no sense of embarrassment between them after their last meeting.

'I hope that I'm not interrupting you,' he said.

'No, George. I was working on some designs for jewellery,' she said, moving to the table. 'I suddenly had an inspiration.' She turned some sheets of paper over so that he could not see them. 'I'm sure that you didn't come to look at my sketches.'

'I'm interested to see any of your work, Veronica.'

'Thank you.'

'Most of the time, you work in gold and silver, don't you?'

'That's right.'

'But you could work with base metal as well, presumably.'

'What are you suggesting?' she said with a laugh. 'That I make the pieces out of lead and simply cover them with paint? That would be cheating, George. I could never do that.'

'Making intricate jewellery must take immense skill.'

'It's something I've developed over the years.'

'So it would be child's play for you to make something simpler.'

'Such as?' she asked. 'Do you want to commission something?'

'That depends,' he said, keen to see her reaction. 'Could you, for instance, make a key to fit one of the cabins?'

Veronica went pale. 'A key?'

'A master key. It wouldn't be too difficult. All you'd need would be a wax impression of an existing key. But I'm sure that you know that.'

'I haven't a clue what you're talking about,' she said.

'Then let's start with the reason you wanted to hide these from me,' said Dillman, turning over the sheets of paper on the table. A series of elaborate dress designs were revealed. 'This is strange jewellery indeed! Are the gowns going to be encrusted with diamonds or something?'

'That's nothing to do with you, George,' she said, snatching up the designs from the table.

'I'm afraid that it is. The time has come to tell you that I'm working on the *Oceanic* as a detective, and I'm investigating a string of crimes that have been committed.'

Veronica stared at him. 'I thought you were our friend.'

'I don't befriend criminals. It's against my religion.'

'We've done nothing wrong.'

'I think you have, Veronica,' he said, indicating the drawings. 'These are not your designs at all. They have the initials O.H. on them. Unless I'm much mistaken, they stand for Oskar Halberg, the famous couturier. Instead of creating your own designs, you're blatantly copying someone else's.'

'That happens all the time in the fashion world,' she said airily. 'Each of us borrows from the other. There's no copyright on ideas. We pick them up wherever we find them.'

'And where did you find those particular ideas? I can't imagine that Mr Halberg gave you his exclusive designs out of the goodness of his heart. Could they have disappeared from his cabin somehow?'

'That's ridiculous!'

'Why don't we go and ask him right now?'

'No, no.' A hunted look came into her eyes. 'There's no need to do that. Mr Halberg will get his designs back. We only borrowed them.'

'*Borrowed?*'

'To be more exact, Dominique was given them on loan. She was going to return them to him today.'

'After you'd had plenty of time to plagiarise his ideas,' remarked Dillman. 'You say that Dominique was given them?'

'Oskar Halberg saw her at the party in Mr Morgan's stateroom. Ever since then, he's been trying to persuade her to work for him as a mannequin. He's a grotesque little fellow,' said Veronica, wrinkling her nose. 'If she got involved with him. Dominique would spend as much time taking dresses off as putting them on. In any case, she'd never agree to leave Abednego. She loves him.'

'So she'd rather pose naked for your husband than wear the latest creations of Oskar Halberg. I admire her dedication,' said Dillman, 'but I have to point out that the designs were obtained under false pretences.'

'Dominique had to endure being ogled by that lecher. She told him that she'd consider his offer if he'd let her study a selection of the dresses that she'd be wearing at fashion shows.' She put the sketches on the table. 'That's the truth, George.'

'Does Abednego know about this?'

'No, he'd be upset if he did. He can be very moral at times.'

'So can I, Veronica,' warned Dillman. 'Now that we've established that you and Dominique are involved in a deception, let's move on to the real reason that I'm here.'

'And what's that?'

'To find out if you still have that master key.'

'No!' she protested.

'You got rid of it, then?'

'There was nothing to get rid of, George.'

'Let me refresh your memory,' he said patiently. 'On the first night we dined together, a robbery took place in J. P. Morgan's stateroom, the very place where Dominique Cadine had earlier visited. We had a clear idea of what time the crime occurred so I remind you of two salient facts. After dinner, Dominique complained of a headache and went back to her cabin to get some tablets.'

'She often suffers from headaches.'

'It was more than a coincidence that this one came when it did. As soon as she went, Veronica, you left the table for a while as well. I put it to you,' he went on, watching her closely, 'that the pair of you went to Mr Morgan's stateroom and gained entry by means of a key that you had made earlier.' Her cheek muscles tightened involuntarily. 'I also suggest that some of the stolen items are concealed in this cabin.'

'Then see for yourself,' she challenged.

'I will.'

'You won't find a thing, George.'

There was a ring of certainty to her voice but Dillman was not deterred. A combination of his instinct and Manny Ellway's vigilance had convinced him that he was on the right track. He went straight to the paintings that were stacked against the wall and sorted out those belonging to her. Ellway was right. The frames had decorated beading on them that varied slightly in size at the top and bottom. The frames matched each other exactly with one exception. The smallest of the paintings had a marginally larger pattern at the top of the frame.

Dillman lifted up the painting. Veronica darted forward at once.

'Leave that alone,' she cried, trying to wrest it from him. 'That's my property, George.'

'You allowed me to conduct a search.'

'Yes, but I don't want my work damaged in any way.'

'I'll handle it with great care,' he promised, easing her fingers off the painting before turning it over. 'Ah,' he noted. 'It looks as if someone has had the back off this recently. This seal is fresh.'

'I took the painting out to add some brushwork.'

'I wonder. Let's find out, shall we?'

Veronica watched with growing anxiety as he produced a penknife from his pocket and slit the passe-partout that held the backing in place. Removing the piece of wood, Dillman took out the three paintings that had been hidden inside behind the one by Veronica Thomas. He looked down at the first of them with a smile of appreciation.

'Edgar Degas,' he observed. 'You're in good company, Veronica.'

It was Blanche Charlbury's turn to approach Jonathan Killick and she did so on the arm of Mark Bossingham. The two of them were strolling contentedly around the promenade deck when they caught sight of Jonathan, brooding alone at the rail as he smoked a Turkish cigarette. They closed in on him.

'Well,' said Blanche, teasing him, 'it's not often that we see you without a young lady beside you, Johnny. You must be slipping.'

'I wanted to be alone,' he said.

'We've got news for you.'

'Oh?'

'In spite of your crafty attempts at pushing us apart, Mark and I have been drawn even closer together. He's told me absolutely everything about Alicia Tremaine, so we need no more sly innuendoes from you.'

'Nor any more vile slander about my fiancée,' said Bossingham crisply. 'Blanche has explained exactly what happened during her unfortunate association with you. For a hundred good reasons, I prefer to trust her account rather than yours.'

'But you've never really heard my account,' said Killick.

'I don't wish to. From now on, we won't even talk to you.'

'We're cutting you dead, Johnny,' added Blanche. 'I should have done that years ago, as so many other people had the sense to do.'

Killick smirked. 'I'm to be treated as a leper, am I?'

'You *are* a leper,' said Bossingham, 'a man with a terrible disease that's a menace to civilised society.'

'I think that you're just jealous of my charm, Bossingham.'

'Charm? You have the appeal of a venomous snake.'

'Then beware of my fangs.'

'Crawl off and find a stone under which to hide.'

'My goodness!' said Killick, amused. 'He's starting to sound like a human being at last. What have you done to him, Blanche?'

'Reaffirmed my love and commitment to Mark,' she said.

'A fatal mistake. You'll soon learn.'

'Not from you.'

'I'm an excellent teacher.'

'Goodbye, Johnny. Please don't speak to us again.'

'No,' said Bossingham sharply, 'you don't deserve to be in decent company. You're a social outcast.'

'J. P. Morgan doesn't think so. I've dined with him twice.'

'Only because Mr Morgan isn't aware of your depravity.'

'I have connections. That's something you'll never have.'

'I have Blanche,' retorted Bossingham, slipping an arm around her. 'That's something you'll never have, whatever little plots you hatch.'

'And you won't be spending any more time with Genevieve either,' said Blanche. 'When I tell her of the cunning way you tried to break up our engagement, she won't want to be within a mile of you.'

'Miss Masefield is a fine woman. Keep away from her, Killick.'

'Do something honourable for once in your life.'

Killick was on the defensive. The events that had taken place in his cabin earlier on had taught him something that he did not know. He had a conscience, after all. When he recalled the way he had tried to take advantage of Genevieve, he felt deeply ashamed. After inhaling once again, he blew out a last cloud of smoke before dropping his cigarette and grinding it into the deck with his heel.

'There's one thing I can promise you,' he said ungraciously. 'Miss Masefield and I won't be seeing anything more of each other on this voyage. Goodbye.'

Touching the brim of his hat to them, he marched quickly away.

It was the first time that George Dillman had seen any sign of pleasure on his craggy face. When the three stolen paintings were returned to J. P. Morgan, he actually smiled. The smile did not remain in place for long.

'This is all you've recovered, Mr Dillman?' he asked.

'It's a start,' said Dillman.

'A very good start,' added Hembrow, glad that they finally had a way of appeasing their most important passenger. 'Mr Dillman has solved one crime and unmasked the ladies who committed it.'

They were in Morgan's stateroom and the paintings were laid out side by side on the table. Dillman explained how a remark by a sharp-eyed steward had helped him recover them, and to unmask Veronica Thomas and Dominique Cadine as thieves.

'When they realised that the game was up,' he said, 'they told me how they did it. The first task was to get hold of a key to this stateroom. They noticed that Sidney Browne, the steward, tended to leave his master key in the keyhole of each cabin he serviced. Dominique simply had to distract him for a short while so that Mrs Thomas could take a wax impression of the key. From that, she was able to fashion a replica. That enabled them to steal the paintings that night and hide them in the one place I'd never have dreamt of looking – behind another painting.'

'Manny Ellway deserves a medal for this,' said the purser. 'And I think that the steward has earned your thanks as well, Mr Morgan.'

'He'll get more than that,' promised Morgan, gazing at the three paintings. 'This calls for a reward.' He turned to Dillman. 'I did warn you that Dominique Cadine might be involved.'

'And you were right,' admitted the detective. 'I dismissed her as a possible suspect because I thought that the thief and the killer had to be the same person, and I could not accept that Mademoiselle Cadine would commit a murder. She and her accomplice stole the paintings before the murder had taken place.'

'Abednego Thomas is behind all this.'

'That's not true, sir.'

'He must be. The man hurled abuse at me for what he claims I've done to the world of art. He suborned his wife and his model to get his revenge against me.'

'Mr Thomas was completely ignorant of what happened,' said Dillman. 'He was not only shocked when I told him, he was extremely upset. The ladies were acting of their own volition.'

'What possible motive could they have had?'

'Patriotism, Mr Morgan. Of a rather perverted kind, perhaps, but that's how they accounted for what they did. They only stole your French paintings,' said Dillman, indicating them with a hand. 'Minor works by Degas, Monet, and Renoir that were still part of the French artistic tradition. Mademoiselle Cadine felt that they should remain in France and, since Mrs Thomas regards herself as a native of her adopted country, she was quick to agree. Monet is one of her favourite artists.'

'And mine,' said Morgan.

'Then you can enjoy this example of his genius,' said Hembrow.

'Where are the thieves now – locked up, I trust?'

'No, actually There seemed no point in handing them over to the master-at-arms. They're very contrite and it's not as if they can go anywhere. Why put them behind bars for the rest of the voyage?'

'Because it's where they belong.'

'They'll be handed over to the authorities in New York,' said Dillman, 'then it will be your decision as to whether or not you wish to prosecute them. The only things that they stole were the three paintings. We still have to find the major part of the haul.'

'Not to mention the man who killed Howard Riedel,' said Morgan.

'We'll get him,' affirmed Hembrow.

'And his female accomplice,' said Dillman. 'I'm absolutely convinced that we're looking for a man and a woman.'

Genevieve Masefield saw the passenger too late to dodge her. She was going up the main staircase when Hilda Farrant began to descend it. The older woman hurried down the steps towards her.

'Well,' she demanded, 'have you found my earrings yet?'

'Not yet, Mrs Farrant.'

'Why not? You've had days.'

'I appreciate that but we have to move with great stealth. That, inevitably, takes time.'

'This is hopeless, Miss Masefield. I don't believe that you'll ever find my property. You haven't made the slightest progress.'

'That's not true at all,' said Genevieve. 'You're right to feel upset but the theft of your earrings is only one of a number of crimes that have occurred on board, and that we believe are linked together. We're pitted against some very clever people, Mrs Farrant.'

'They're certainly much cleverer than you.'

'We can only do our best.'

'It's patently not good enough.'

'You're entitled to your opinion about me, but I'd be grateful if you didn't voice it to anyone else. May I remind you that you did agree not to discuss the theft with anybody?'

'And I kept my word,' said the other woman indignantly.

'Not according to Mr and Mrs Boyd. They told me that you even showed them a letter of complaint about the White Star Line.'

'Only because Mrs Boyd had had something stolen as well – or, at least, she thought she had. Her purse had been mislaid in the library.'

'How do you know that?'

'She told me.'

'Wait a moment,' said Genevieve, suddenly alert. 'Do you mean that she approached you? I'd always assumed that you'd sounded off in front of them and had thereby gone back on our agreement to keep quiet about the whole thing. Rosalie Boyd came to you?'

'Yes, Miss Masefield. What's so strange about that?'

'You'll find out in due course. Thank you, Mrs Farrant,' she said, pumping the other woman's hand. 'Thank you very much. You've no idea how much help you've just been.'

George Dillman had returned to his cabin to review the situation and decide on his next steps. He chided himself for believing that all the crimes were the work of the same people. It had never crossed his mind that two sets of thieves had visited J. P. Morgan's stateroom on the night in question. He was sorry that he had had to apprehend Veronica Thomas and Dominique Cadine, both of whom he liked immensely. They were not professional criminals but two ladies driven by a misguided belief that they were serving the interests of France by reclaiming the work of three of its most celebrated artists. Dillman was also sad that he had had to break the news to Abednego Thomas. The Welshman had been devastated to learn that, as a result of their crime, both his wife and his model might be sent to prison.

All thought of the trio had to be swept from Dillman's mind for the time being. Far more dangerous people were still at liberty and he had to concentrate on catching them. He was still wrestling with the problem when Genevieve arrived. As he let her into the cabin, he could see that she was in a state of high excitement.

'We've had some crucial help at last, George,' she said, 'and it came from the most unlikely person.'

'Who was that?'

'Hilda Farrant. She was befriended by Ethan and Rosalie Boyd so that they could keep track of how our investigation was going.'

'Why would they want to do that?'

'Why else? I thought that Mrs Farrant had simply blurted out her troubles to them but that was not the case at all. They sought her out, George, and they could only have done that if they knew that she was the victim of theft.'

'Quite,' said Dillman, realizing the importance of the clue. 'And if they knew about the crime, one of them must have committed it.'

'That was the wife. You remember she said her purse was stolen?'

'Yes, she left it by mistake in the library.'

'It was no mistake,' said Genevieve. 'I spoke to the steward who found that purse. He had tidied up in the library at midnight and there was no sign of any purse then. It only appeared the following morning.'

'Put there, no doubt, by Ethan Boyd.'

'It *has* to be them, George.'

He was cautious. 'Let's go over it all very slowly.'

They examined the evidence with meticulous care and decided that they had finally identified the true culprits. Dillman told her about the arrests that he had made, and how he was able to return at least part of the stolen property to J. P. Morgan. 'It's easy to gain entry to a cabin by making a replica key.'

'Do you think that that's what the Boyds did?' said Genevieve.

'I don't know.'

'Where could they have hidden everything?'

'Some of it may be in their cabin,' he said. 'It will have to be searched. Lester told me that you landed yourself in hot water when you went into Jonathan Killick's cabin, and he's loath to sanction another search. But it's imperative.' He saw the anguish in her eyes. 'What's the matter, darling?'

'There's something I didn't tell the purser,' she admitted.

'Why not?'

'Because I couldn't bear to.'

'Well, you can tell me,' he said, taking her in his arms to give her a reassuring hug. 'What exactly happened when he caught you in his cabin? Did he threaten you?'

'It was worse than that, George.'

Genevieve told him what had occurred and he pulsed with anger. She had to hold on to her husband to stop him from charging off to confront Killick. She had never seen Dillman so furious.

'It can wait, George,' she said. 'The Boyds come first.'

'You're right.'

'So what do we do?'

'Search their cabin, for a start. This time, we do it properly.'

'I'll act as your lookout.'

He kissed her. 'Then I'll close with that offer, Mrs Dillman.'

Ethan and Rosalie Boyd were circling the promenade deck when they encountered Hilda Farrant. At first, they didn't recognise her. The old lady wore a fur hat, pulled down over her forehead, and a fur stole that covered her chin. She greeted the couple with a nod.

'Are you enjoying the fresh air?' said Rosalie.

'No,' replied Mrs Farrant. 'I feel the cold.'

'The breeze has stiffened since we've been out here.'

'But it's much healthier to be out here than stuck inside,' said Boyd. 'I love the smell of the sea. It's invigorating.'

Hilda Farrant pulled a face. 'Not at my age.'

'There must be something you enjoy about this voyage.'

'I wish there were, Mr Boyd.'

'No news about the theft of your earrings?' asked Rosalie.

'None at all. I spoke to Miss Masefield earlier and she's still obviously in the dark. Though she was pleased at something I told her,' recalled Mrs Farrant. 'It was when we talked about you, as it happens.'

'Us?' Rosalie glanced nervously at her husband.

'What exactly did you say?' pressed Boyd.

'Only that you'd approached me to offer your sympathy about what had happened,' said Mrs Farrant. 'I thought it was very kind of you both to console me. Miss Masefield couldn't thank me enough for helping her but I still don't know why.'

'Excuse us, Mrs Farrant,' said Boyd, taking his wife by the arm. 'I've just remembered an urgent appointment.'

Moving brusquely away, he and Rosalie broke into a trot.

It had seemed like the perfect spot. Stationed near a comer, Genevieve could look down the long corridor that led to the main staircase. If either Ethan or Rosalie Boyd came down the steps, she simply had to hurry to the cabin that Dillman was searching and bang on the door. Both of them could then escape unseen down a nearby companionway. There was a flaw to the plan. It worked only if the Boyds were unaware of the fact that they were now under suspicion.

Instead of descending the steps at a leisurely pace, they came down it as fast as they could. Ethan Boyd then ran along the corridor with his wife behind him. Genevieve was dismayed. There was no time for her to warn Dillman and for the two of them to get safely away. She had to employ some diversionary tactics. Coming into view, she pretended to be seeing them for the first time. She held up a hand to stop them.

'I've just been to your cabin, looking for you,' she said.

'Why?' asked Boyd suspiciously.

'The purser sends his compliments and requests that you call at his office immediately. He wants to discuss something of importance with you both.'

'Something of importance?' repeated Rosalie.

'She's stalling us,' said Boyd.

He pushed Genevieve roughly aside and ran to the corner before rounding it. Unable to stop him, Genevieve could at least detain his wife. As Rosalie tried to get past, she was firmly grabbed.

'Let go of me, Miss Masefield!' she cried.

'Not until the purser has heard a few answers from you first.'

George Dillman had searched so many cabins during his time as a detective that he knew exactly where to look for hiding places. Swift and thorough, he took only a few minutes to complete his search. When he heard the key in the lock, he realised that one of its occupants was coming back to the cabin. He stood with his back against a wall.

'Mr Dillman!' cried Boyd, bursting in. 'What are you doing here?'

'Just looking around,' said Dillman, calmly.

'How did you get in?'

'The purser loaned me a master key. I'm sure you can guess why.'

Boyd blenched. 'You're a *detective*?'

'Miss Masefield and I work together. I was rather hoping that she might forewarn me of your arrival, but that was not possible, it seems. Since you're here, Mr Boyd,' he said, 'perhaps you could help me.'

'You still haven't told me what you're searching for.'

'Stolen property, sir.'

'Belonging to whom?'

'A number of people – Mr J. P. Morgan, principally.'

'And did you find any?'

'No,' said Dillman, 'but then I wasn't able to look inside that.' He pointed to the large cabin trunk in the comer. 'Perhaps you could oblige me by opening it?'

'Of course,' replied Boyd, reaching in his pocket for the key. 'I think you'll find that your visit has been a waste of time, Mr Dillman.' He unlocked the trunk and lifted the lid. 'Go ahead – look inside.'

The detective peered at a pile of clothing, neatly folded, then reached in to feel the bottom of the trunk. He stood back to appraise the piece of luggage from the side.

'You see,' said Boyd, coolly. 'Everything in there belongs to us.'

'Everything visible, perhaps. But there's the small matter of the false bottom to the trunk. That's why I felt inside. At a guess,' said Dillman, 'the secret compartment is six to eight inches deep. You could hide a lot of things in an area that big.'

'You're mistaken, Mr Dillman. There's no false bottom.'

'Prove it, sir.'

'With pleasure.'

He bent over the trunk as if about to tap the bottom of it. Instead, he released a catch that opened an aperture and grabbed something that was inside. When he stood upright, Boyd held a gun on Dillman. The detective seemed remarkably unperturbed.

'I presume that that once belonged to Howard Riedel,' he said. 'You took it from him after you'd cut his throat.'

'It was no more than he deserved.'

'Why?'

'The man was an animal. When he was a captain in the New York Police Department, he once clubbed a friend of mine to death with the butt of his gun. It was a case of overzealous questioning,' said Boyd with bitterness, 'but that's not how it was reported in the press. They said that the prisoner tried to escape and died resisting arrest.'

'So that's what this is all about,' said Dillman. 'Revenge.'

'I've waited a long time to exact it, Mr Dillman.'

'Even to the extent of trailing your enemy to Paris.'

'I'd have followed that man to the ends of the earth in order to make him pay,' said Boyd. 'It's what I do to people who upset me, Mr Dillman, and that's what you've just done.'

'Killing me won't help you to escape.'

'No, but it will give me intense satisfaction.'

'Then be my guest,' invited Dillman, unbuttoning his coat and holding it open. 'Choose your target. Before you do, however, let me make a small confession. I lied to you about the trunk.'

'What do you mean?'

'I opened it myself and found the false bottom. I also found these,' he went on, taking some bullets from his pockets. 'I think you'll find that a Smith and Wesson revolver works much better with them.'

Ethan Boyd pulled the trigger time and again but the chambers were all empty. He howled in frustration then held the gun by the barrel.

'This is the weapon that killed my friend,' he said. 'I'll show you exactly how it was done, Mr Dillman.'

He lunged at the detective but Dillman was ready for him, tossing the bullets into his face to confuse him before grabbing the wrist that held the gun. Boyd was frantic, grappling with Dillman, biting, kicking, and doing everything he could to get free. But he had neither strength nor skill enough. Pushing him against the door, Dillman banged the man's hand repeatedly against the timber until he was forced to drop the gun. Before he was able to defend himself, Boyd was hit with a fierce relay of punches then thrown bodily across the cabin, completely dazed when his head made sharp contact with the trunk.

Dillman recovered the gun and slipped a few bullets into it before holding it on his prisoner. With his other hand, he took out his penknife.

'Let me give you a piece of advice,' he said.

Boyd was still groggy. 'What's that?'

'You don't need a key to open that cabin trunk of yours, Mr Boyd. A penknife like this can do the job just as well.'

J. P. Morgan was so delighted to have his art treasures and Book of Hours returned, and to know that Howard Riedel's killer was finally behind bars, that he insisted on dining with George Dillman and Genevieve Masefield. The financier was in his stateroom with the purser when Genevieve arrived. Both men complimented her on her stylish evening gown of aquamarine blue velvet.

'Thank you, gentlemen,' she said. 'Oskar Halberg may have been right all along. Blue does become me.'

'Every colour becomes you, Miss Masefield,' said Morgan with gruff courtesy. 'But you've come at the ideal time. Mr Hembrow is just telling me how the killer got in to my stateroom that night.'

'The simplest way of all,' explained Hembrow. 'He was brought in here by the murder victim – not that Mr Riedel knew that he was marked to die, of course. Ethan Boyd got to know him as a result of the robbery at his bank in New York. In fact, he had set up the robbery himself and was incensed when it went wrong. He was even more incensed when his accomplice was beaten to death in police custody. They said that the prisoner tried to escape but how far can a man who broke his ankle during the robbery actually run?'

'Didn't the police realize that Boyd was involved?'

'No, Mr Morgan. They knew that inside help had been given but Boyd was clever enough to frame an associate of his. When the man fled, it seemed like a confession of guilt. No suspicion fell on Boyd himself.'

'He took me in completely,' said Genevieve.

'And me,' admitted the purser. 'The reason that Captain Riedel, as he then was, clubbed the prisoner to death was that he wouldn't name the employee who had fed him information about bank security. Since his accomplice had protected him to the last, Ethan Boyd wanted to avenge his death. It took him three years to achieve his aim.'

'And rob me in the process,' said Morgan.

'Almost everything he took was concealed in the false bottom of his cabin trunk,' said Genevieve. 'George found it there along with the items that he and his wife had stolen from other passengers.'

'They had such audacity,' said Hembrow with a dry laugh. 'What could not be hidden in their cabin trunk was put into a bag and given to me to lock in a safe. In that sense, Mr Morgan, I was a receiver of stolen goods. Where better to hide loot than in the ship's safe?'

'Ethan Boyd has such a convincing disguise,' observed Genevieve. 'If you're looking for a thief, who would suspect a successful banker?'

'I would,' said Morgan, stroking his moustache. 'But, then, I deal with bankers all the time. If they're that successful, I want to know how they contrived that success. It's not always by honest means.'

'Mr Riedel was not as perceptive as you, sir. When Boyd treated him as a friend, he didn't realize that he was, in fact, the man's worst enemy. Boyd courted him assiduously during the voyage to Europe on this ship,' said the purser. 'He got to know his habits, his likes and dislikes, his daily routine.'

'So, on that night, he came down here with Howard.'

'Yes, and he brought a bottle of whiskey with him – one that had been drugged beforehand. By the time that your bodyguard let him in here to show off your collection, Mr Riedel must already have been woozy.'

'Ethan Boyd seized his chance and cut his throat.'

'Then he took what could be easily carried,' said Genevieve. 'His wife, meanwhile, was standing outside as his lookout.'

The purser nodded. 'She's an accessory to murder, Genevieve.'

'The pair of them will be arrested,' boomed Morgan, 'and I'll not shed any tears over that. But I owe you an apology, Miss Masefield. I take back all I said about you and your partner. The pair of you handled this investigation with exemplary skill.'

'Not quite,' she said, recalling her botched search of a particular cabin. 'We just have to be grateful that Rosalie Boyd stole those diamond earrings. It was Mrs Farrant who provided a vital clue.'

'Yes, but you knew how to interpret it properly. You deserve my heartiest congratulations.'

'Thank you, Mr Morgan.'

'So does Mr Dillman.' He took out his fob watch and consulted it. 'By the way, where is he? I said that we'd meet in here before dinner.'

'Yes,' asked Hembrow. 'He's very late. Where can George be?'

Genevieve smiled. 'I think that he has some unfinished business.'

The Honourable Jonathan Killick had lost something of his customary swagger, but he was determined to cut a dash in the dining room once more. Adjusting his bow tie in the mirror, he flicked out the tails of his coat and opened the cabin door. Before he could step outside, however, Killick was pushed firmly backward. George Dillman went into the cabin after him and shut the door.

'What the blazes do you thinking you're doing?' cried Killick.

'We need to have a conversation, sir.'

'I don't know you from Adam. Who are you?'

'A friend of Miss Genevieve Masefield. I believe that you and she are acquainted. Indeed,' said Dillman, squaring up to him, 'I have it on impeccable authority that you tried to become more closely acquainted than Miss Masefield desired. Is that true?'

'Get out of here!'

'Did you try to force yourself on her?'

'I'm not talking to you,' said Killick defiantly.

'Then I'll take silence as consent,' announced Dillman.

'Miss Masefield sneaked in here behind my back.'

'Is that any reason to molest her?'

'The bitch is lying. I hardly touched her.'

Dillman's fist shot out and caught him in the eye, sending him sprawling to the floor. Killick was enraged and scrambled to his feet but a second punch caught him in the stomach and he doubled up in pain. Dillman delivered a fierce uppercut that sent him to the floor again.

'Get up,' taunted Dillman. 'I hardly touched you.'

While preserving their anonymity as detectives, J. P. Morgan exuded gratitude towards them the whole evening. He was seated at the head of his table with Dillman and Genevieve on either side of him. The room was full but there were some notable absentees. Ethan and Rosalie Boyd had been locked up in separate cells by the master-at-arms. Abednego Thomas was too distraught to dine in public so he shared a meal in his cabin with his wife and his model. It seemed that Jonathan Killick, too, felt unable to put in an appearance.

'Incidentally,' said Morgan, taking out his billfold, 'what was the name of that steward who was so helpful to you, Mr Dillman?'

'Ellway, sir. Manny Ellway.'

'Perhaps you'd be good enough to give him this.' He took a note from his billfold and handed it over. 'Thank him on my behalf.'

'Fifty pounds,' said Genevieve, recognizing the denomination. 'That's a huge amount for a steward.'

'Yes,' agreed Dillman. 'Manny will think he's on his honeymoon.'

A delicious meal was served and the detectives were able to relish it much more than on previous evenings. They had solved a brutal murder, returned stolen items to their owners, and arrested those involved. From now on, sailing on the Oceanic would be an unalloyed pleasure. It was only at the end of the meal, as they got up from the table, that Genevieve was able to whisper something to her husband.

'I didn't want to draw attention to it, George,' she said, 'but you have blood on your right cuff.'

'Don't worry,' he told her. 'It's not mine.'

POSTSCRIPT

The *Oceanic* remained in service until the outbreak of the First World War in 1914, when it was taken up as an armed merchant cruiser, a role she had been designed to fill at need. She was wrecked in the Shetlands just a week later, a sad end for such a luxurious and popular vessel.

Edward Marston has written over a hundred books across many series. They range from the era of the Domesday Book to the Home Front during WWI, via Elizabethan theatre and the Regency period. He is best known for the hugely successful *Railway Detective* series set during Queen Victoria's reign.

edwardmarston.com

If you enjoyed *Murder on the Oceanic*,
look out for more books by Edward Marston . . .

To discover more great fiction and to place an order
visit our website
www.allisonandbusby.com
or call us on
020 3950 7834

EDWARD
MARSTON

BESTSELLING AUTHOR OF THE RAILWAY DETECTIVE SERIES

MURDER ON THE
LUSITANIA

EDWARD
MARSTON

BESTSELLING AUTHOR OF THE RAILWAY DETECTIVE SERIES

MURDER ON THE
MAURETANIA

EDWARD MARSTON

BESTSELLING AUTHOR OF THE RAILWAY DETECTIVE SERIES

MURDER ON THE
MINNESOTA